DON'T LOOK NOW

DON'T
LOOK
NOW

MICHELLE GAGNON

HARPER

An Imprint of HarperCollins*Publishers*

ISBN 978-0-06-210293-5

Typography by Tom Daly

13 14 15 16 17   CG/RRDH   10 9 8 7 6 5 4 3 2 1

❖

First Edition

For Kirk

Be to her, Persephone,
All the things I might not be:
Take her head upon your knee.
She that was so proud and wild,
Flippant, arrogant and free,
She that had no need of me,
Is a little lonely child
Lost in Hell,—Persephone,
Take her head upon your knee:
Say to her, "My dear, my dear,
It is not so dreadful here."

—Edna St. Vincent Millay,
"Prayer to Persephone"

PART ONE
RETALIATION

CHAPTER ONE

"I thought California was supposed to be warm," Zeke grumbled, rubbing his arms.

Noa stayed focused on the tiny radio in her hand. It was new equipment they were trying out, top-of-the-line military-grade communicators. They hadn't been cheap, but hopefully they'd be worth it—during their last raid the radios had died, with nearly disastrous consequences.

Noa pursed her lips. The rest of her team was supposed to call in five minutes ago, and they were rarely late. "It's February," she said without lifting her gaze. "Everywhere is cold in February."

"For once, I wish they'd set up a lab in Hawaii," Zeke mumbled. "We could be having fruity drinks, instead of—"

The radio suddenly crackled to life in Noa's hands, and

she waved for him to shut up. Drawing it to her lips, she said, "Report."

"Lost him." Janiqua's voice crackled, distorted by static.

"What? How?"

"He went into one of the BART stations and got on a train."

Noa chewed her lip, irritated. They'd been tracking one of Project Persephone's mercenary squads for three days, watching and waiting to see what they were after. The two guys were cut from the same cloth, both obviously ex-military. Her team had been following them ever since they landed at SFO. But this morning the duo had unexpectedly split up, heading in opposite directions after leaving their hotel. She and Zeke were keeping an eye on one of the men, who was currently sitting in front of a café enjoying a cup of coffee. The news that the other team had lost track of their target was unsettling.

"What do you want us to do?" Janiqua asked.

Zeke was watching Noa expectantly. Sometimes serving as the de facto leader of a group of kids still threw her; they always assumed that she had all the answers. And right now, she felt as clueless as the rest of them. "Get on the next train and try to find him," she finally said. "We'll stay on his partner."

"Got it."

As the radio fell silent, Noa repressed a shiver. They'd been standing out in the cold for over an hour, hunkered against the side of a building. They couldn't stay in this position much longer—the owner of the bodega across the street kept throwing suspicious glances their way.

As if on cue, Zeke said, "Looks like he's going for the phone again. Time to put on another show."

Noa sighed and rolled her eyes. "I swear this is your favorite part."

"Definitely." Zeke smiled as he backed her against the wall, then lowered his face down to hers. They held the pose, just inches apart. His breath tickled her eyelashes, and with every inhale her nostrils filled with his distinctive scent: soap and shaving cream mixed with a sweet underlying musk. Past his shoulder, Noa saw the bodega owner watching them. After a moment's hesitation, he set the phone back down.

"We're good," she murmured.

"Maybe we should give it another minute, just to be sure," Zeke responded, resting his forehead against hers.

This was supposed to be for show, but his lips hovered a fraction of an inch away. Noa could see the gold flecks that dotted his brown eyes, like spokes of pure sunlight. She felt a shudder down her spine that had nothing to do with the cold. Trying to regain her composure, she noted wryly, "Try not to get us arrested for public indecency."

"I'm willing to risk it," Zeke murmured, leaning in so that his whole body pressed against her.

Noa was suddenly finding it hard to breathe. He was just messing with her, right? They were friends, partners. So why was her whole body careening into overdrive? She gently nudged his shoulder, easing him away as she sternly said, "Focus. We're supposed to be keeping an eye on our target, remember?"

"You really know how to suck all the fun out of a stakeout." Zeke smirked, stepping away.

Noa didn't answer. This wasn't the first time they'd pretended to be a teen couple making out; the last thing they needed was a beat cop nosing around, asking why they'd been standing on the same street corner for more than an hour. But this had felt different, like maybe it hadn't all been for show. She surreptitiously studied Zeke, who was peering around the corner toward the café. After all these months together, his face was almost as familiar as her own—slim and angular, sharp cheekbones, tan despite the climate. The first time Noa met him, she'd been flustered by how attractive he was; but since then he'd become more like a brother. Although she was pretty sure that what she'd just felt wasn't sisterly love.

Noa frowned—*now who is distracted?* She forced herself back to the task at hand, asking, "He's still there, right?"

"Yup. Still just reading the paper."

"Maybe we're wrong about this," Noa said. "Maybe they're not here on a job at all."

"Sure." Zeke nodded. "I hear that San Francisco is where all the bad guys come on vacation. They just can't get enough of the chowder bowls and trolley rides."

Noa ignored him, leaning forward to catch a glimpse of the café. Their target was sitting at an outside table despite the cold, sipping from a large mug as he scanned a newspaper. He was a bulky guy with close-cropped hair, dressed in dark jeans, a peacoat, and combat boots. If she didn't know better, she'd think he was just a soldier on leave, enjoying some down time.

But she did know better.

"Be ready to move," she warned Zeke, stretching her legs to get the kinks out.

He snorted. "I'm always ready."

"Sure you are." She grinned. "Like in San Diego, when you almost got left in the lab after the radios crashed."

"Hey, that wasn't my fault," Zeke protested, lightly

4

punching her shoulder. "I figured the kids might be in another part of the building."

They both fell silent at the memory. The raid had gone smoothly—except that by the time they got inside, there wasn't anyone left to save. Zeke cleared his throat, then said more soberly, "So you think these two are here to scout another lab?"

"I don't know," Noa admitted. "But something is going down." The two commandos hadn't gone anywhere near the warehouse district, though, which was unusual. She was having a hard time getting a handle on what they were after; they'd spent the entirety of the past two days walking through the Mission District.

"He's on the move," Zeke announced.

Noa's head snapped up—the guy was halfway down the block, headed toward Valencia Street. "Remember to stay half a block behind me," she said in a low voice. "If I have to pass him, you take over."

"Got it," Zeke said.

Noa pulled her watch cap lower, ducked her head, and trotted across the street in pursuit.

Teo Castillo was tired and hungry. He'd spent the day pan-handling on BART, shuffling from one subway car to the next, begging spare change from commuters who studiously avoided eye contact.

He was halfway back to the encampment where he'd been living the past few months when he realized someone was following him. A lanky, rough-looking street kid. No one he recognized, though, and by now he knew all the home-less teens on this side of town. Teo had first noticed him studying the subway map near the turnstile at the Twenty-Fourth Street BART station. And now here he was again, walking down Mission Street fifty feet behind him.

Teo stopped abruptly and bent to retie his filthy Vans. Covertly, he glanced back. The kid was standing in front of a dollar store, examining their inventory with the same intense interest he'd given the subway map. He was tall and gangly, with knobby elbows jutting out of an oversized white T-shirt and jeans belted halfway down his thighs.

Teo tried to brush aside his paranoia. The kid was probably just headed in the same direction as him.

Five blocks later, he was seriously doubting it. The hair on the back of his neck prickled; he'd been jumped before, and wasn't eager to go through it again. Last time he'd suffered three broken ribs and a concussion.

Plus, over the past year he'd heard plenty of horror stories; some kids even claimed that a group was snatching runaways off the streets to experiment on. Teo wasn't sure he believed that; it sounded too far-fetched. But he knew bad things happened to kids like him if they were out here long enough.

And he had no intention of becoming a cautionary tale. He'd make a break for the underpass where he'd been crashing; hopefully some of the others would already be there. As he turned the corner onto Cesar Chavez Street, Teo broke into a trot. Within seconds, his lungs throbbed and he felt sick. He'd barely eaten all day, so even slight physical exertion made him dizzy. Pathetic. Not so long ago, he'd been the star sprinter at his high school. Might even have had a shot at a college scholarship if everything hadn't gone sideways.

After seven blocks, he hazarded a glance back over his shoulder. The kid was not only still there, he'd been joined by two others—a black girl and guy. They weren't even pretending not to follow him anymore—they were flat out chasing him.

Crap, Teo thought. Three against one—he'd end up in the ER again for sure. He tried to run faster, but his legs were shaking too hard to maintain the pace.

To throw them off course, he abruptly darted left down Hampshire Street, then took a sharp right through the empty soccer field at the rec center. Dodging left again, he lurched onto a footpath that led through overgrown bushes. It was hard to spot unless you were right on top of it; with any luck, they hadn't seen him make the turn.

Seconds later he emerged in the camp, a bare patch of earth beneath a busy section of highway. It was hemmed in on all sides by soundproofing walls, a chain-link fence, and large bushy hedges. The clearing was cluttered with makeshift shelters: big boxes with tarps for roofs, a couple of muddy tents. The ground was dotted with soiled food wrappers, empty bottles, and syringes.

Teo's heart sank: There was no one else there. He was on his own.

Suddenly, a hand grabbed his arm. He winced reflexively, bracing for a blow. . . .

It never came. Teo opened his eyes and did a double take when he saw not the ragged trio of teens, but a good-looking guy in his thirties, well-dressed in jeans and a dark jacket. He was huge, easily six inches taller than Teo, and built like a tank.

"Teo Castillo, right?" the guy said with a smile.

Teo jerked his arm free and took a shaky step back. "Who are you?" His chest was still heaving, and his legs felt rubbery.

The guy held up both hands. "Hey, man, take it easy. Just wanted to make sure you were okay."

The guy looked normal, but something felt off. Teo eased back a few more inches. "How do you know my name?"

The guy squinted and cocked his head to the side. "You don't remember me?"

Teo shook his head slowly. The guy didn't look familiar, but the way he was acting . . . maybe one of his former social workers? Or a teacher? But what was he doing here?

"That's okay, it was a long time ago." The guy was still grinning, although the smile hadn't made it all the way to his eyes. "I'm here to help you, Teo."

"I don't need any help," Teo said quickly. "Thanks anyway, though."

"Oh, I think you do. What about those kids back there?" The guy jerked his head toward the bushes. "Looked like you were in trouble." He stepped forward. "And living in this dump? Not good."

"I'm fine," Teo snapped. He was sick of adults thinking they knew what was best for him. He turned and marched deliberately toward the other side of camp, where a narrow path led out to Potrero Avenue.

Before he reached it, though, another big guy emerged from the bushes, blocking his way. He was dressed in jeans and a fleece jacket, with a ball cap pulled down over his ears. Teo halted, confused.

"We're here to take you somewhere safe," the first guy said from behind him. "Trust me."

Teo's mind raced. The two guys were blocking the exits: The only other option was the chain-link fence on his left. If he could get over it, there were cars a block away—plenty of witnesses.

He bolted toward the nearest section of fence. Panic sent adrenaline coursing through his veins, spurring him faster than he'd ever run before.

He was halfway over the fence when a hand clamped down on his leg. Teo yelped in pain as he was yanked back and slammed to the ground. Both guys loomed over him; one of them was holding a syringe.

"Hey, listen . . . I don't do drugs," Teo said, panicked. "Seriously, I'll do whatever you want. Just don't stick me with that thing."

"Got a clean one here, Jimmy, you hear that?" the first guy said.

Ball Cap nodded. "That's why they want him. Nice, clean subject."

"A clean . . . what?" Those experiments he'd heard about, Teo realized suddenly. *They were real. . . .*

The guy with the needle leaned over and tugged at his jacket collar. Teo struggled, but the other guy pinned his arms and pulled his head to the side, exposing his neck.

Teo squeezed his eyes shut and prayed it would be over soon. He waited for the needle to pierce his skin.

And waited.

Suddenly, there was a strange chattering noise close by. Teo opened his eyes: The guy with the needle was standing bolt upright, his whole body twitching uncontrollably. His mouth gaped open, exposing gleaming rows of white teeth.

Simultaneously, Ball Cap's legs buckled. He landed on the ground looking perplexed, and oddly frozen.

Teo lurched to his feet, grasping the fence for balance. His first thought was, *What the hell just happened?* Followed immediately by, *Who cares—get out of here, now!*

As he turned to run, Teo nearly crashed into a girl who'd

materialized right behind him. He'd never seen her before: She was stunning, with close-cropped dark hair and bright-green eyes. She was dressed all in black like the other guys, and held something that looked like an oversized TV remote.

"Relax," the girl said without taking her eyes off the guys on the ground. "We got this."

A group of teenagers swarmed out from behind her. They were all dressed differently: a few Goths, some skate rats, a couple of stoner types. All straggly and unkempt looking, like most street kids. But Teo had never seen any of them before.

He'd heard of them, though. This had to be the other thing everyone murmured about, late at night as they huddled in the dark. The group that was trying to protect street kids: Persefone's Army. He hadn't believed in them, either—a bunch of teenagers acting like some modern-day version of Robin Hood? He'd assumed it was just another urban myth.

But here they were. His eyes swept around the group—the three kids who'd been chasing him were standing guard over the guys on the ground. And the girl with them, who was clearly the leader . . .

"You're Persefone," Teo said, his voice filled with awe.

The girl gave him a funny look. "Actually, my name's Noa. You all right?"

"Yeah, sure."

The kid who had been following him earlier came up and sneered, "You were lucky. Why the hell did you run?"

"I thought—"

"He thought you were chasing him, Turk," Noa snapped. "You were supposed to stay on your target. What happened?"

Turk hunched his shoulders and mumbled, "Janiqua lost him."

"Oh, yeah, it's my fault." The black girl rolled her eyes. "*You* were supposed to keep up with the target on the train. The hell'd you go, anyway?"

"I didn't see him get off." Turk kept his eyes glued to the ground. "'Sides, I knew that dickwad was after the kid, he couldn't stop staring at him. Even followed him through a few cars."

"So you lost the guy, but not the kid?" Janiqua snorted. "That doesn't make sense."

"That's what happened," Turk snarled back, jutting his chin out as he stepped menacingly toward her. Janiqua didn't give an inch, though—she closed the space between them while reaching into her pocket for something—

Noa quickly intervened, stepping between them. "Enough. We'll sort it out later. Now get moving, these guys'll be coming around soon."

After another long, hard stare, the two of them separated, heading to opposite ends of the camp. Janiqua pulled a plastic cord out of her pocket as she bent over one of the guys, then used it to tie his wrists behind his back. Two other kids helped her.

Teo's head was spinning—this was all too surreal. There were eight kids total, and they each moved with purpose. On the concrete buttress next to where he kept his sleeping bag, a scrawny black kid was spray painting a logo in red: the letters *P* and *A*, intertwined. The rest of the group hunkered down around the two guys who'd assaulted him, securing their ankles and wrists with impressive alacrity.

Teo suddenly saw the encampment through their eyes— small, cramped, dingy—and felt a twinge of embarrassment.

"Sure you're all right?" Noa asked, examining him. "You look a little shaky."

"I'm fine," he said, fighting to keep the squeak from his voice.

"What's your name, anyway?"

"T-Teo," he stammered. "Teo Castillo."

"Nice to meet you, Teo," Noa said distractedly, her eyes scanning the clearing. She raised her voice and announced, "We'll take the blonde."

Teo realized she was talking about the guy who had first spoken to him. He watched a girl in a black pleather mini-skirt and torn fishnet stockings matter-of-factly place a strip of duct tape over the blonde's mouth. "What did you do to them, anyway?"

"Taser," Noa explained, holding the remote up. "We don't like guns."

"Okay." He wasn't a big fan of guns, either. "So are these the guys who have been experimenting on kids?"

She scrutinized him. "You heard about that?"

Teo shrugged. "Yeah. Everyone has."

"Well, it's true. Don't go anywhere alone from here on out. They might still be after you."

A cold ball of fear formed in Teo's gut. He glanced back over his shoulder, half expecting to see more huge guys huddled in the bushes. He wondered where everyone else was—had the other kids known, somehow, that these guys were lurking around? And if so, why hadn't anyone warned him? Suddenly, he felt more alone than ever. "Where are you taking him?"

"Better if you don't know." More loudly, Noa added, "Don't forget the tarp."

Obediently, a few of them wrapped the first guy up like a burrito in a large blue plastic tarp. Once they had him inside, they lifted him off the ground, spreading his weight between them. Teo watched them march toward the bushes. They were like an army, he realized. Organized, following commands . . . despite their ragged appearance, he was impressed.

A minute later, he found himself alone with Turk, Noa, and the girl in fishnets. She was cute, despite her wild shock of blue hair. She caught him looking at her and raised an eyebrow. Teo flushed and shifted his gaze, examining the ground at his feet.

"The usual with the other one?" Turk asked.

Noa eyed the guy in the ball cap. "Yeah."

"You want to mess him up first?" Turk asked solicitously, directing the question to Teo.

"What? Uh, no. I'm good." Teo stared at the man on the ground; Jimmy, the other guy had called him. Jimmy was coming around, his eyes darting frantically from side to side.

"We'll leave him for your friends, then. I'll bet they'll have some fun with you, huh, jerk-off?"

The guy flinched as Turk dealt him a hard kick to the ribs.

"Turk," Noa warned sharply.

Turk threw her a sneer, then seemed to catch himself. He knelt down to tighten the zip ties another notch. The guy on the ground winced as the narrow bands dug into his wrists. "Just wait," Turk muttered in a cold, flat voice. "World of hurt coming for you, buddy."

Teo watched Turk haul Jimmy to his feet and frog-march him to the nearest pillar. Turk held him in place while Fishnets wound duct tape around him, pinning him to the concrete support beam like a trapped moth.

"All right, let's get out of here." Noa lifted a small radio to her mouth and said, "Back at the van in five."

"Copy that," a voice crackled in response.

And without another word, the three of them headed for the footpath.

Teo stared after them. In less than five minutes, it felt like his whole world had been turned upside down. And now what was he supposed to do? Go Dumpster diving for dinner, then grab a little shut-eye? "Wait!" he called out.

Noa stopped and turned to face him. "What?"

"Take me with you," he said, surprising himself.

She shook her head. "That's not how this works, Teo. Sorry."

"Please," Teo pleaded. "I can help. Seriously."

She looked him over skeptically. "You do drugs?"

"No." He shook his head ferociously. "Never. I don't drink, either."

Turk grumbled something, but Noa threw him a look and he shut up. She stared at Teo for a long moment, then nodded brusquely. "Fine. But any trouble and you're out."

"Yeah, sure," Teo said, hurrying to catch up. As he followed Noa through the maze of brush that led to San Bruno Street, he felt something he hadn't experienced in a long time: hope.

Peter Gregory pulled down the brim of his Red Sox cap as they passed yet another security camera. He stuck close to the office assistant escorting him; the staccato tap of her high heels punctuated the steady chatter she maintained. Fortunately, she didn't seem to expect a response, aside from an occasional nod and sympathetic grunt. Terri was a moderately attractive woman in her midthirties with brightly hennaed hair, a form-fitting dress, and a gemstone manicure that flashed every time she waved her fingers to illustrate a point. Traces of a repressed Boston accent bubbled out during her diatribe against the gremlins bedeviling their mainframe. "It's the third time this week the servers have gone down," she said with another exasperated hand flourish. "Can you believe that? Do you know how embarrassing it is to explain to people that we can't even send email?"

Peter nodded, trying to look shocked while surreptitiously examining his surroundings. Knowing about the atrocities Pike & Dolan perpetrated, he'd expected their corporate headquarters to look more evil lair-ish. But instead of a shark tank, the lobby sported glossy floor-to-ceiling posters of cheerful people enjoying the company's many fine products, which ranged from vitamins and shampoo to pharmaceuticals.

The interior offices were even more of a letdown. Clearly Terri took her unofficial role as tour guide seriously; she was especially enthusiastic about a roof garden that offset carbon emissions, and the sustainably harvested bamboo floors. Listening to her prattle on, Peter was tempted to enlighten her about her employer's off-site facilities, where kidnapped street kids were treated like lab rats. He was willing to bet that none of them featured low VOC paint and solar hot water panels.

"For what we're paying them," Terri complained again, "you'd think our in-house IT guys could fix this mess." Holding a sparkling hand beside her mouth, she lowered her voice and said, "They'll probably all be fired over this."

Peter murmured something noncommittal. In spite of everything, he felt a twinge of sympathy for Pike & Dolan's beleaguered IT department. It wasn't their fault that the servers had crashed repeatedly after being bricked four months ago. Not only had Peter been the one to brick them, he'd made it his mission to continually develop bigger and better bugs to confound their firewalls.

Then last week, he came up with a way to take things a step further. His goal was to install a sort of Trojan horse known as a "packet sniffer" in Pike & Dolan's data center; basically, a wire-tap device that eavesdropped on network traffic. But instead of listening in on people's conversations, this "sniffing" program intercepted passwords and emails, and acquired all the data transmitted throughout the company.

With any luck, that data could finally give Noa and the rest of Persefone's Army an advantage over the conglomerate.

To gain access to the servers, he was posing as Ted Latham: freelance tech genius for top computer security firm Rocket Science. Ted was also the fictional foster dad that Noa had created to escape the foster care system and earn enough money to support herself.

Peter had been nervous about assuming the identity, especially since he hadn't cleared it with Noa first. But he was hoping that if things panned out, she'd be happy he took the initiative. At least, that's what he kept telling himself.

Based on what little Noa had told him, Peter knew that no one at Rocket Science had ever met Ted Latham; all of their business was transacted virtually. The CEO hadn't even blinked at "Ted's" rambling email about spending the past several months offline while doing a walkabout. Moreover, when "Ted" offered to step in and handle their most troublesome client, Pike & Dolan, the CEO was beside himself with gratitude.

Peter felt a little badly about the subterfuge, but Rocket Science had enough high-profile clients to weather one failure. And if his plan succeeded, and he gained a window into the inner workings of Pike & Dolan, it would all be worth it.

Hopefully Noa would think so, too. He had the feeling that if she saw him right now, strolling down the corridors of Pike & Dolan in geek business casual, she'd have some choice words for him.

But she's not here, he reminded himself, feeling a flare of resentment. In fact, he hadn't seen her for months; their only contact now was limited to brief online chats.

"Here we are!" Terri announced, waving her key card in front of a wall-mounted panel. The light turned green, and she pushed the door open.

Any halfway decent company recognized the importance of this room: These server towers were the modern-day equivalent of a treasure vault. The air inside was noticeably cooler than the outer hallway; temperature, humidity, and particle filtration were all precisely controlled. Also true to form, it was located in the center of the building, far from exterior walls, elevator banks, and any other sources of potential electrical interference or water damage.

The servers themselves were housed in tight lines of tall gray metal cabinets that resembled the lockers in Peter's high school. In between the cabinets, metal shelves held rows of what looked like strung-together car batteries, which wasn't far from the truth; those modules kept the precious servers humming along as they delivered everything from emails to shipping manifests.

Peter's palms started to sweat. This was way too easy. He'd expected to encounter resistance; heck, he could hardly believe he'd made it past the lobby. And now that he was here, the enormity of the crime he was about to commit hit him hard.

"So?" He turned to find Terri staring at him expectantly. "How do you fix it?"

"Um, I just need to access the servers, to . . . check some things," he mumbled.

Terri released a world-weary sigh and said, "Obviously. But do you need *me* to do anything?"

"Not really," he said. "Unless you want to help with the secure socket layers."

Terri rolled her eyes. "Well, they said to keep an eye on you, but you look harmless enough." Her eyes trailed over him, apparently confirming her assessment because she chirped, "Anyhoo, I was going to grab a latte. How much time do you need?"

"Not long," Peter mumbled. "Probably ten minutes."

Terri smirked. "Fix this in ten minutes and my boss will probably propose to you."

Peter shrugged, keeping his eyes down.

"All righty then." Terri sighed, clearly disappointed that her little joke had been wasted on him. "Back in a bit."

He waited until the door clicked behind her, then went to work. He wasn't an expert on data centers, but any server should suit his purposes. And for what he intended to do, two minutes would have been more than enough time.

Peter dug into his messenger bag and pulled out a small device. Hurrying deeper into the room, he ducked down the first aisle and quickly counted off rows. He didn't want to install the device anywhere too obvious, or on a server that was checked routinely. If the IT department was really stressed about their jobs, there was a good chance they spent a lot of time in here trying to resolve the problem. Fortunately for him, the powers that be at Pike & Dolan had assigned Terri to supervise him, rather than one of them. They probably didn't want the techs to know that there was a bull's-eye centered on their backs.

Which worked to his advantage. Peter was still blown away by how easy it had been to simply stroll inside. Over the past four months, he'd devoted hundreds of hours to scaling the extensive firewalls that protected Pike & Dolan's data.

Turns out all he had to do was knock at the front door. Peter shook his head in wonder. Humans were so much less reliable than computers.

Choosing a server on the next-to-last bank, he opened the front panel and knelt down. He carefully installed the device into a port about six inches off the ground. It wasn't the sort of thing you'd notice unless you were looking for it. And if he was lucky, no one would find it until he'd gotten what he needed.

The sound of a door opening and closing set his heart hammering. Peter quickly straightened and closed the cabinet, trying to still his trembling hands. He scurried along the row, almost crashing into Terri as he emerged in the main aisle. She raised a sparkling hand to her chest in alarm and said, "Christ, you nearly gave me a coronary," her Boston accent twice as thick as it had been minutes earlier.

"Sorry," he mumbled.

"Whatcha doing back there?" she asked, eyeing him suspiciously.

Keeping his eyes down, he muttered a string of incoherent sentences peppered liberally with every techie term he could come up with on the fly. Terri impatiently waved for him to shut up. "Whatever," she said. "You fixed it?"

"Yeah, I think so," he muttered.

"Really? What was wrong?" She scanned the room behind him curiously, clearly trying to figure out where he'd just been. "My boss gave me hell, by the way. Said I wasn't supposed to let you out of my sight." She glared at him, as if it was his fault that she hadn't been able to sneak out for a latte.

"Sorry," he said again.

"You apologize too much, you know that?"

"Sorry."

Terri laughed sharply. "Okay, well. If you're sure it's fixed." She smoothed her dress and said, "I'll walk you out."

Peter was careful to keep his head down as she led him briskly back to the lobby.

Minutes later, Peter was trotting to the nearest T station. From there, he'd switch trains a few times before returning to his car. Paranoid, maybe, but he wanted to make sure no one had followed him.

The thought of what his little device might already be intercepting added a bounce to his step. If the plan succeeded, he and Noa might finally get enough information to deal a fatal blow to Pike & Dolan, burying them. Peter practically felt like bursting into song.

CHAPTER TWO

The garage door opened and Zeke drove the van inside. Noa sat in the passenger seat, quiet and pensive.

"You all right?"

She turned to find Zeke looking at her with concern. "Yeah, I'm fine." She paused. "That was a good one today, right?"

"Definitely." He turned off the ignition. "If Peter hadn't found out that P&D was sending a squad here, Teo would be lying on a table right now getting his chest sliced open."

"Yeah, I know. Lucky he intercepted that email." Noa rubbed her wrist. For nearly her entire life she'd worn a jade bracelet, one of the last gifts her parents had given her. She'd awoken on an operating table four months ago to find it gone, the final vestige of her past life stolen. She missed the bracelet more than everything else combined. Whenever she felt stressed, she'd still catch herself reflexively touching the skin it had once rested against.

"Something's still bothering you," Zeke noted.

"I just feel like we're not doing enough," she admitted. "We saved one kid today, but they might have gotten a dozen more, and we'll never even know for sure."

"That's why we took one of their guys, right? Maybe he'll tell us."

"Maybe," Noa said, although she privately doubted he'd say anything. Much as she hated Pike & Dolan, she had to admit they knew their stuff when it came to hiring shadowy mercenary types.

"So what do we do with him after?" Zeke asked.

"I haven't decided yet," Noa admitted, lowering her voice so that the group in the back of the van couldn't hear. She'd discovered that a big part of leadership involved acting like you always knew what you were doing. Zeke was the only person she shared her doubts with. "I guess we just drop him somewhere when we're pulling out."

"We'll figure it out," he said comfortingly. "We always do."

Noa didn't answer. The van door slid open behind them, kids chattering as they piled out. She sometimes felt like she was trapped in a play, in a role she was ill suited for. These teens expected her to have answers for everything, down to what they'd be eating for dinner. It was a lot more exhausting than she'd ever have imagined, especially since six months ago she basically had been a hermit living alone in a studio apartment.

But it wasn't like she had a choice in the matter. No one else was doing anything to save these kids.

"C'mon," Zeke said, nudging her arm. "Let's get inside. I'm starving."

"Hey, Noa. What do you want us to do with this guy?"

Noa turned to find Janiqua standing at her window. She swiveled in her seat and looked into the rear of the van. The guy was still rolled up in the tarp, bound and gagged, with a black pillowcase over his head.

"Leave him for now," she said, forcing some authority into her voice. "We'll deal with him after dinner."

Janiqua nodded briskly and went inside the house. Noa took a second to gather herself—the kids were probably already going over every minute detail about the raid. After that there would be questions: What would they do with the prisoner, where were they going next . . . She felt a wave of fatigue coming on, and tried to fight it back. Ever since Pike & Dolan had experimented on her, Noa suffered from weird physical side effects: She slept less, but exhaustion would overcome her unexpectedly. She only needed to eat every few days, but when she did, she'd consume mass amounts of food in a single sitting. And she healed much faster than normal; sometimes a deep cut vanished after just a day.

She'd learned to manage; deep-breathing exercises usually helped with the fatigue, and she was careful not to gorge when the others were around. They seemed to sense that there was something different about her, though. That was probably part of the reason they followed her.

Unconsciously, Noa's hand drifted to her chest. A little over four months ago, P&D had transplanted an extra thymus in her chest, which partly explained why she'd undergone all these strange changes. But she was no closer to finding out exactly what that meant. All she knew for certain was that their experiments were continuing. And that the same people who had used her as a guinea pig were still determined to find her.

There was a muffled noise from the backseat. Noa watched in the rearview mirror as the guy struggled, trying to shift up to sitting. Her eyes narrowed; better make sure he was still tightly secured—the last thing she needed was for him to escape. She slipped into the back and checked the zip ties on his wrists and ankles. Out of curiosity, she lifted a corner of the pillowcase to get a look at him.

She immediately shied back in horror. Noa knew this guy; he'd chased her through Brookline high school last fall. Nearly caught her, too.

His eyes also widened in recognition, then narrowed to slits. He tried to say something, but the duct tape on his mouth muffled it.

She collected herself, trying to repress the sudden flash of panic. *He's tied up*, she reminded herself. He couldn't hurt her now. "Nice to see you again, too," Noa said. "You're not getting out of here, so you might as well chill."

The guy glared at her. Noa dropped the pillowcase and said, "Behave yourself, and we might even feed you. Chili tonight. Should be pretty good."

She climbed out of the van. In front of her, a plain wooden door led into the kitchen. They were hunkered down in a foreclosed house in Oakland. It was in a seriously sketchy neighborhood, on a street where half the residents had been forced out when they couldn't pay their mortgages. So far, no one appeared to have noticed the group of scraggly kids squatting there. But it had been a few days, and staying in the same place for too long increased the chances that they'd be discovered by the cops, or worse. They'd need to move on soon.

But first things first. Noa squared her shoulders, girding herself. Time to face the troops.

★ ★ ★

Can't talk 4 long.

Yeah I know, Peter typed. *U ok?*

Having a blast, got a new gold ring u'd like. Plus a silver one.

Peter Gregory frowned at his laptop screen. "Crap," he muttered.

"What is it?" Amanda asked, coming to peer over his shoulder.

Peter resisted the urge to close the laptop so she couldn't see. He'd been surprised to find Amanda hanging out in his room when he got home; surprised, and a little frustrated, since it meant he'd have wait to see if his device was working. She'd been acting weird and edgy, though, so he hadn't had the heart to turn her away.

But then Noa had logged onto The Quad to chat about her latest operation. The Quad was a virtual message board that only the best hackers in the world were privy to. Theoretically, only he and Noa had access to the private chat rooms they established there with password-authenticated key codes. Still, they were careful to converse in cipher.

And now his ex-girlfriend was squinting over his shoulder while he tried to find out how everything had gone. Peter shifted slightly to block her view.

"Is anything wrong?" Amanda asked.

"Not really." Peter debated how much to tell her. Amanda knew a bit about what Noa was doing on the West Coast, but he stopped short of sharing details. Not that he didn't trust her, but it would have felt like a betrayal of Noa's confidence. "They stopped another abduction. But they took a prisoner."

"That was stupid," Amanda said disapprovingly. "One of the commandos?"

"I think so. Noa said she might, but I thought I'd talked her out of it."

More words flooded on-screen: *Deciding where 2 go next, you still vote 4 the canyon?*

Peter got a flash of Noa hunched over a keyboard, choppy black hair swinging forward to curtain her face. It had been four months since he'd seen her, but he still thought about her almost constantly. Although it was getting harder and harder to remember the exact shade of green her eyes were, or how her voice sounded. . . .

"What's the canyon?" Amanda asked, shaking him out of his reverie.

"What? Nothing," he muttered. "Listen, can you give me a minute?"

"Oh, sure," Amanda said, clearly miffed. "Wouldn't want to get in your way."

"You're not," Peter said defensively. "I just hate people reading over my shoulder."

"You never used to," Amanda grumbled as she flopped back down on his bed.

Peter rubbed his eyes with a thumb and forefinger. Even though they'd broken up months ago, Amanda still had a knack for making him feel like a bad boyfriend. He bit back a retort and focused on his keyboard.

Still there? Noa typed.

Yeah, Peter wrote back hurriedly. *Sorry. Canyon is a go.*

Gr8, thx. 2 days?

2 days. He hesitated, then added, *b safe.*

But she'd already logged off.

Repressing an inexplicable sense of loss, Peter closed the laptop. It felt like more than a virtual link had been severed. Even though they never stayed online for more than a few minutes, it helped him feel connected to her and what they were doing. Which was important, because sometimes Peter felt like he was watching a kid who looked and sounded like him living his life on the other side of a pane of glass.

He'd first met Noa in person four months ago. Before that, she'd been an occasional participant in the hacktivist group /ALLIANCE/ that he'd established to punish internet bullies, child and animal abusers, and anyone else who took advantage of the weak and powerless.

Through a fluke of fate, the two of them had stumbled across P&D's secret research project, Project Persephone. The goal was to find a cure for PEMA, a disease that afflicted tens of thousands of teenagers. Peter's own brother had died from it; it was always fatal. And sure, a cure would be great—but kidnapping former foster kids and treating them like lab rats wasn't the way to go about finding one. Noa had been one of P&D's test subjects, until she escaped. Luckily, they hadn't infected her with PEMA. But she hadn't emerged unscathed, either.

And even though the two of them had managed to lure the FBI to a lab filled with victims of those experiments—in pieces—none of it had come to light. Which meant that someone powerful enough to call off the FBI was involved.

And that scared the hell out of him.

"So she has a hostage now," Amanda commented. Peter turned to find her flipping through a back issue of *World Soccer Magazine*.

"I wouldn't call it that," Peter said with a frown.

"No? What would you call it, then?" she challenged, eyeing him.

Peter shrugged. "She just wants to get some information. The last few labs they raided, the kids inside were already dead. She wants to know why."

"And she thinks this guy will actually tell her?" Amanda

snorted. "What's Noa going to do, torture him?"

"Of course not," Peter said, although privately he wondered. While he'd been going through the motions of being a normal high school senior, Noa had been living on the streets again, facing off against armed thugs in raids on top-secret labs. Maybe nonviolent retaliation just wasn't viable for her anymore.

Peter couldn't repress the sense that his life was unbearably dull in comparison.

Which was why he'd risked infiltrating that server room. Hopefully it was already funneling mass amounts of information to him via a remote server in Hungary.

Somewhere in there he was hoping to find concrete proof of what Pike & Dolan was up to, including locations of all their secret labs, names of kids they were targeting, and what their experiments actually entailed. Maybe he'd even discover why Noa had developed such weird symptoms after they gave her an extra thymus.

He should have told her about the packet sniffer. If she'd known he was close to accessing all that information, she might not have taken a prisoner.

The fact that she'd put her group in more danger, especially when it could have been avoided, just added to his discomfort.

"Well, I think she's wasting her time," Amanda declared.

Peter shifted uncomfortably. If Amanda hadn't been the one to initiate their breakup, he would have suspected that she was jealous. Even though Amanda had made it pretty clear that she only wanted to be friends, her mouth always got tight whenever he talked about Noa.

"So what's the canyon?" she asked again.

Peter cracked his knuckles, trying to figure out a way to

say that it was none of her business without setting her off. "Nothing, really."

"Phoenix." Amanda tossed a wave of honey-blond hair over her shoulder as she continued, "That's where she's headed next, right? You found another lab there?"

Peter tried not to react—sometimes Amanda was too damn smart for her own good. "I'm not supposed to say."

Amanda rolled her eyes and flipped onto her back, scooping up the magazine again as she said, "Right. The canyon. Brilliant code you two came up with. You should tell her to just let the guy go."

Peter chose not to respond. Noa was going to do whatever she wanted, no matter what he said.

It was frustrating, just sitting here waiting for news all the time. And he never got to hear much about the raids, thanks to their security protocols. All Noa usually sent were coded numbers of saved kids (gold rings) along with veiled questions about future targets. Amanda was right: Phoenix was next; the last time he'd hopped P&D's firewall, he'd found indicators of a major lab there. With any luck, his sniffer would provide specifics, and he wouldn't have to waste any more valuable time circumnavigating the increasingly sophisticated firewalls.

And this time, maybe there would still be kids left to save.

Peter sighed. All this cloak and dagger stuff was exhausting.

"You want to go to a movie tonight?" Amanda asked abruptly.

"What?" he said, startled.

Amanda frowned at him. The gesture created a little crinkle between her brows that he'd always secretly loved. "A movie. You know, where you get popcorn and watch things on a giant screen."

"I've kind of got a lot to do here," he said, gesturing to the computer.

"Fine." Amanda got to her feet and started pulling on her jacket. "I just thought maybe we could both use a little fun."

Peter watched her, perplexed. "Fun?"

"Yeah, something besides school and huge corporate conspiracies." Angrily, she tugged a scarf around her neck. "Forget it."

Now that she mentioned it, it had been a long time since he'd done anything that qualified as fun. It wasn't a terrible idea. "We could go tomorrow," he offered.

Amanda paused at the threshold, her hand on the doorknob. "Yeah?"

"Sure," he said. "But I'm not reading subtitles."

"I figured." She beamed at him. "Okay, then. It's a date."

"Let's rip out his fingernails," Turk snarled.

"No one is ripping out any fingernails," Noa said forcefully. She eyed the guy who was tied to a chair in the middle of the garage; he stared back at her balefully. The room was soundproofed—the previous owner had probably had a kid in a band, so they'd caught a lucky break there. The van had been moved to the driveway to make room for the interrogation. The rest of her group sat or stood in a circle around him.

There was a strange energy in the room—keyed-up excitement combined with bloodlust. If she allowed it, they'd probably rip this guy to shreds. Hell, they might do it anyway. He represented all the bad things that had ever happened to them, and despite their different backgrounds, the one thing they had in common was a consuming need for retribution and revenge.

Observing that now, Noa was forced to admit that taking

a hostage might've been a mistake. Peter had basically said as much, but by then, it had been too late. Not for the first time, she wished he was here. Sometimes Noa felt like she was fumbling through the dark on her own, struggling to find her way without a compass. Peter had been that for her, briefly; she hadn't realized how much she'd come to rely on him until he was abruptly gone.

But this was how things were now, she reminded herself. And she had Zeke.

He caught her eye from across the room and cocked an eyebrow. She could tell that he was worried, too.

"So, what? We just stand here and stare at him?" Turk spat. "This is bullshit."

Before Noa could answer, Zeke spoke up. "We've got the Tasers, right? We could use those."

Noa shifted uncomfortably. It was the middle of the night, and she still hadn't slept. The fatigue was starting to become overwhelming, to the point where she felt like she might keel over midsentence. But she'd decided that it would be better to deal with their captive sooner rather than later. They needed to get as much out of him as possible; keeping him any longer than necessary was too dangerous.

"What are we waiting for?" Crystal said impatiently. "Make him talk!"

The rest of the group murmured in assent.

Noa was tempted to call the whole thing off, but nine kids were staring at her expectantly. If she backed down now, she'd lose their respect. And the minute that happened, they'd turn on her.

She felt a hand on her elbow. In a low voice, Zeke said, "Whatever you want to do, I'll back you."

Noa nodded briskly, feeling a wave of gratitude. Zeke was

the one person she could always count on. Knowing that gave her the strength to say, "Take off the duct tape."

The charge in the room kicked up another notch as Turk ripped away the tape covering the guy's mouth.

The commando glared at Noa. "Stupid little bitch," he growled. "You've made a big mistake."

"Says the guy tied to the chair," Zeke muttered.

Noa bent over to look him in the eye. "Where were you taking Teo?"

"To the ballpark," the guy said with a snort. "Looked like the kid could use a hot dog."

"We left your buddy Jimmy for the others to find," Zeke chimed in. "Bet he's not laughing right now."

"He's not my buddy," the guy muttered, but his eyes shifted to the floor.

"They probably killed him, right, Noa?" Zeke added. "That's what happened to the last one."

There hadn't been a last one, actually; but maybe the guy wouldn't know that. She had no idea whether or not P&D's mercenaries communicated with one another. That was just one of the things it would be helpful to find out. "We could always take you back there," she said, watching him closely. "See if they might want to have some fun with you, too."

The guy didn't appear concerned, or maybe he was just good at hiding it. "You're going to kill me anyway," he snorted. "You have to."

"No," Noa said. "I don't. I can leave you at the ballpark, if you want. All you have to do is answer a few questions."

The guy tilted his head back and laughed. "You don't get it, do you? If you don't kill me, they will. They'll know I told you something. Hell, they'll kill me anyway, just for screwing up."

"So you're already dead," Noa pointed out. "Then why not talk?"

"Why should I?" The guy tried to shrug, but his arms were bound too tightly to the chair.

"They're killing kids," Noa said, fighting back a sudden swell of rage—she could practically feel the cold metal table beneath her again. "That doesn't bother you?"

"I never killed anyone," the guy protested. "My job was just to grab 'em. They were mostly trash, anyway."

At that, a few of the kids shifted. Noa could sense their anger growing, and she didn't blame them. They'd all probably been called trash at one point or another. And whether or not they acknowledged it, it always hurt.

"You're a dead man," Turk said, shoving his way into the circle.

"Turk, step off," Noa ordered.

"Screw that." He punched the guy in the chest hard, and the chair tipped back and slammed into the ground. Turk planted a Timberland boot squarely on the guy's throat.

Noa snapped, "Off him, Turk!"

Turk glowered at her. She met his gaze, chin raised. She'd been afraid of this moment from the beginning, knew that at some point one of them would challenge her. The fact that it was Turk was hardly surprising. She wasn't suited for this, had never been good with people to start with. The house of cards she'd constructed by forming her little "army" had always felt like it was on the verge of collapsing. A bead of sweat trickled down her spine as she stared into Turk's eyes. They were light blue, and too pretty for a boy, she thought nonsensically; funny she'd never noticed before.

After a beat, Turk stepped back. Without a word, Zeke

DON'T LOOK NOW

righted the chair; the front legs landed back on the concrete floor with a thump.

"Give me a Taser," Noa said.

Zeke met her eyes questioningly. Then he stepped forward and handed her one.

"How'd you like this today?" Noa asked, waving it in a slow circle. "Did it hurt?"

The guy shrugged, though for the first time she caught a glimmer of fear in his eyes. "It tickled."

"Yeah? Guess I should crank up the power, then." As she turned the knob, he swallowed hard. Noa continued, "You don't have a heart condition, do you? Because there was a warning on the box. . . . What did it say again?"

"Maximum of five milliamps on people," Zeke chimed in. "We had it set for three today. I think you're only supposed to go above that for large animals."

"He is pretty big," Noa said thoughtfully.

"Sure," Zeke said. "I bet he'll be fine."

Noa held it in front of his face and said, "Last chance."

The guy tried to rear away from the tip of the Taser. Noa pressed it up against his chest and cocked her head to the side.

"Ready?" she asked. "One . . . two . . ."

"We were driving him to south San Francisco." The words tumbled out in a rush. "There was a truck waiting for him."

"Just Teo?" Noa asked. "Or were you supposed to get others?"

"Three more," he said. "Two in Oakland and another in San Francisco. But he was first on the list."

"What are the other names?"

"I'll give you them, I swear," the guy said. "I'll tell you anything. But you gotta promise me something."

"What?" Noa asked, narrowing her eyes.

34

"Let me go somewhere outside the city. Just give me a little cash, enough to disappear for a while."

Turk snorted. "Yeah, I bet you'd like that. So you can run back and tell them all about us."

The guy shook his head and scoffed. "Smarten up, you little punk. They already know all about you. Mark Toledo, street name Turk. Mom was a junkie hooker, Dad was a pimp. Landed in foster care when you were two because she hadn't fed you for a week and the neighbors complained that you and your sister wouldn't stop screaming."

Turk looked like he'd been struck. Seeing it, the guy recovered some of his bravado and eyed the rest of them. "Crystal Moore. Trailer trash from Modesto. Mommy's boyfriend got a little too friendly one night, so you ran away. And there's little Danny Cepeda. Those cigarette burns healed up yet?"

The circle widened as kids backed away.

"Stop it," Noa said in a low voice.

"And you." The guy turned to her with a sneer. "The golden goose. Oh, they know all about you and your little 'army.' You really think you can beat them? You can barely take care of yourselves. You're just a bunch of whiny little brats that the rest of the world could give a shit about. In the end, you're all going to end up back on their tables. Just wait and—"

He suddenly went spastic, eyes wide, spittle flying from his mouth. Noa jumped back as sparks flew off the end of the Taser. But her hands were empty; Zeke had taken the stun gun and activated it.

"And you were worried he wouldn't talk," Zeke said, avoiding her eyes. "Turns out he won't shut up."

The guy had slumped over in the chair, unconscious. His chest rose and fell, so he wasn't dead. Noa clenched her hands into fists to hide the fact that they were shaking.

"How did he know all that?" Turk asked, a tremor in his voice. "How do they know who we are?"

"Some of you were rescued," Noa reminded him.

"Not me," Danny said in a low voice. "I found you online, remember?"

Noa chewed her lip. He was right. Some of these kids had already been part of the organization when she joined up; others like Teo had been rescued. Yet this guy claimed to know personal details about all of them.

"Someone's been talking." Turk marched back over to the chair. "I bet he knows who, too."

"Leave him," Noa said. "I'll deal with him myself."

"How?" Turk snorted. "You didn't seem to scare him much."

"I know," Noa said thoughtfully. "But I've got another idea."

"Fingernails?" Turk asked hopefully.

"No," Noa said. "PEMA."

Peter frowned at the monitor. After Amanda left, he'd started sifting through the initial data spewed out by his sniffer. Unfortunately, he quickly became overwhelmed. Thousands of emails, research reports, interoffice memos . . . It would probably take a team of people weeks to go through it all, and this was only a single day's worth of data. He'd have to come up with specific search parameters to narrow the field, maybe zero in on PEMA, Project Persephone, and other likely code words. If he skipped his afternoon classes, he could have the program ready by tomorrow night.

Still, there'd probably be a ton of stuff to go through. He mulled it over. There were a few other hackers he trusted, all of whom had been part of the /ALLIANCE/ when it was up and running. One in particular, Loki, was as good as Noa when it came to hacking skills. But he'd also made it pretty clear that Peter had pushed his luck last time by bricking the servers. He might not be willing to step up again.

Peter sighed. Better to tackle this on his own. He'd take his usual route over the firewall tonight, pushing the sniffer data to the back burner.

It was late, nearly two a.m. He had to be up for school in a few hours, but this was the only time of day he could be totally certain that he wasn't being monitored. Not that he'd seen any sign that the Project Persephone bastards were still following him, but better safe than sorry. So Peter was parked in the driveway of a house a block away from his own. The owners were a retired couple who wintered in Turks and Caicos. The driveway was long and sweeping, and didn't have a gate. It had been his spot of choice for the past month: not visible from the street, and far enough from his house that no one could tap into his computer activity.

It was hardly comfortable, though. He didn't dare run the engine for fear of attracting attention, which meant the interior of the car was freezing. Snow was forecasted for tomorrow, and he offered a silent prayer that the meteorologists would be right for a change. A snow day would give him a chance to catch up on sleep.

Suppressing a yawn, Peter sifted through recent emails. He'd homed in on a few accounts that seemed directly affiliated with Project Persephone. The messages were encoded, but pretty easy to figure out: lots of references to "new R&D products" being moved to the Phoenix facility. He'd spent the evening tracking the company's shipping manifests. Pike & Dolan had warehouses worldwide, most of which stored their legitimate products: shampoo, pharmaceuticals, even pet toys. But he'd become adept at figuring out which locations were being used as ad hoc operating facilities: primarily buildings where trucks drove shipments in, but rarely drove anything back out.

And there was one near the Phoenix airport.

He pulled up a satellite image of the property; it fit the profile of the other secret labs. Relatively isolated, and surrounded by half-finished buildings; probably all casualties of the economic crash. The warehouse itself looked unremarkable, a huge building the size of an airplane hangar.

Peter cracked his knuckles as he examined it. Not an easy place to sneak up on—surrounded by desert, with no cover visible in any direction. Only one road in and out, and the nearest highway on-ramp was two miles away.

He yawned again, then shook his head to try and wake up. The clock on his dashboard read 2:15. Crap, he had to get some sleep. Peter eyed the building again. Tomorrow he'd dig up blueprints for Noa to study; they were probably on file with the Phoenix building management office. Thankfully, municipal networks were notoriously easy to hack into. And they had some time. According to the emails, shipments were still arriving; the next was scheduled for the day after tomorrow. Noa wouldn't be able to get to the area before then anyway.

Peter powered down his laptop and turned off the satellite uplink. Starting the car, he eased down the driveway. When he reached the street, he peered in both directions: deserted. He drove down the block to his parents' house and pulled in, already fantasizing about lying down on his pillow.

Which is why he didn't notice the black SUV that rolled past a minute later, slowing to watch his Prius enter the garage.

CHAPTER THREE

"That was easily the worst movie I've seen all year," Amanda announced the next afternoon as they walked out of the theater. "Seriously, the worst."

"I thought it was awesome," Peter replied.

"You didn't," she said, exasperated. "I mean, really? The aliens turned out to be friendly all along?"

"That's what I liked about it. Total shocker at the end."

"Oh my God, that was terrible," she groaned. "And even worse was the part where the guy went after them with a paint gun—"

Peter smiled as he watched her talk. Amanda's face was animated, the color high in her cheeks as she gestured wildly with her hands. This was sort of a tradition they had after seeing a movie together; he'd enjoy it at face value, while she analyzed it to death. Few films stood up to her scrutiny. But this was what she liked best about going to the movies—tearing them apart afterward.

And he'd always gotten a kick out of seeing her riled up.

"Are you even listening?" Amanda demanded.

"Yeah, of course," he said defensively. "You're going on about how the diner scene didn't make any sense."

"Well, it didn't." She snorted. "I mean, that part practically belonged in a different movie."

"Like I said." Peter grinned. "Totally awesome."

"You're impossible." She smacked his arm.

"You gotta admit, though. Kind of the perfect movie for a snow day."

"Yeah," she said. "You're right."

They smiled at each other. It had been kind of a perfect day all around, Peter thought. The snow had started falling right before dawn, making it impossible for plows to clear the roads in time for school. So he'd gotten his wish, and slept until nearly noon. Then, on a whim, he'd called Amanda to ask if she wanted to check out a matinee. She'd said yes, and to his surprise, even offered to come to him, rather than meeting near Tufts. Stranger still, she'd agreed to go to a cheesy Hollywood blockbuster, instead of insisting on a documentary or something with subtitles.

Maybe she'd changed, too, he thought as they walked through the parking lot. The snow had already started to melt, leaving the pavement glistening. It was balmy enough to leave his jacket unzipped. The sun shone down brightly, reflecting off the gold in her hair.

She looked stunning. Peter had a flash of how she used to taste, strawberry and mint mixed together. Her lips were bright red, shiny from the beeswax lip balm she always used.

He had a sudden and overwhelming urge to kiss her.

And then, just as quickly, an image of Noa interceded. They were so different: Amanda with her bright wavy hair and small, compact frame; Noa, dark and willowy. Both passionate and intense, but that was where the similarities ended.

Peter cleared his throat. "Want to grab something to eat?"

Amanda didn't answer. She'd stopped dead in the middle of the parking lot and was staring past him.

"What is it?" he asked.

She started walking again, but her stride was different and strange, kind of a slow shuffle. "Amanda?" Peter watched with a growing sense of dread as she drifted right, then circled around him. He turned, following her with his eyes. Amanda's face had gone completely blank, her eyes unfocused. Her jaw hung slightly agape, lips loose. Like she'd suddenly turned into a zombie.

He grabbed her hand. "Amanda, stop."

Obediently she fell still, but didn't meet his eyes. Her hand felt icy cold, yet clammy. Her chest rose and fell faster than normal under her winter coat, her breath coming in short pants like she'd been running.

"No," he said softly.

"What?" Abruptly, Amanda blinked and looked at him, then down at their clasped fingers. "Why are you holding my hand?"

"You were . . ." Peter trailed off. Self-consciously, he dropped her hand.

"I was what?" she demanded when he didn't finish.

"Nothing." The sun vanished behind a cloud, and the sudden chill made him shiver. He closed his jacket and mumbled, "I was just asking if you were hungry."

"I should head back," Amanda said, obviously disconcerted. "I've got a test tomorrow."

"Yeah, sure," he said. "Let me drive you."

"I'll take the T," she replied, avoiding his eyes. The air
between them was suddenly thick with tension and discomfort. "Can you drop me at the Brookline Village station?"

"Sure, but I don't mind driving to your dorm. I don't
have—"

"I'll be fine."

"We could grab something to eat along the way," Peter
pressed as he climbed behind the wheel. "Someplace quick."

"I haven't been very hungry lately," Amanda said, buck-
ling herself in. "Stress, probably. I'm pretty swamped with
midterms coming up."

"Right," Peter said faintly. Now that she mentioned it,
she'd clearly lost weight. Her cheekbones had hollowed out,
and her clothes hung more loosely. Peter searched for something to say that would break the pall, and came up empty.

"Thanks," Amanda said when they finally pulled up to
the station. She turned to get out, then spun and leaned
across the seat to give him a quick peck on the cheek. "Let's
do it again soon, okay?"

"Okay," Peter agreed.

He watched, hands clutching the steering wheel, as she
hurried through the door to the T station. A car honked
behind him; the light had turned green. Peter drove a block,
then pulled over to the side of the road and parked. Dropping
his head down, he fought the hot tears pressing against his
closed eyelids.

"I'll kill him," he whispered under his breath. "I'll kill
him for doing this to her."

* * *

"So what now?" Zeke asked. "Do we go after the other three targets he mentioned?"

"Too risky." Noa shook her head. "Could be a trap."

"Yeah, I was thinking the same thing," he agreed, keeping his voice low.

They were sitting together in the living room. Everyone else was upstairs, still asleep after the long night. Their hostage had become a lot more forthcoming once Noa produced a vial of blood that was loaded with the PEMA virus, courtesy of their "little army's" raids. Apparently the fact that there hadn't been a single PEMA case in anyone over the age of twenty-five didn't matter; his eyes had widened with terror, and he'd proceeded to tell them everything, including the locations of three other lab facilities.

Not bad, considering that in actuality the vial had been filled with water tinted red with food coloring. None of the labs he'd listed had been in Phoenix, however, which was puzzling. She'd asked specifically about Arizona, and he claimed to have no idea what was going on there. So either Pike & Dolan only shared some information with their mercenaries, or he was still holding out.

Or Peter was wrong about the Phoenix lab. Although if he was, it would be a first.

Noa still didn't know the guy's name, and frankly preferred it that way. Maybe Peter was right, and taking him had been a really bad idea. But she'd become increasingly frustrated. Peter was able to provide some information, but it came slowly, which left her group with a lot of time to sit around doing nothing. And these kids weren't easy to handle unless they were occupied by a mission.

Zeke yawned. Noticing, Noa said, "Why don't you get some more sleep?"

"In a bit. You already crashed?"

Noa nodded. She'd gone down hard around five a.m. and had slept like the dead for twelve hours. That was pretty much all the rest she needed; now she'd be up and alert for days. Which was weird, but helpful given the circumstances.

"Hungry?"

"Not today." She'd gorged herself the day before last, eating several thousand calories in one sitting. That usually held her for a few days, too; in between what she'd started to think of as "feedings," Noa could only tolerate liquids. "Anyway," she continued, ignoring the small twinge she got whenever her physical quirks were being discussed, "I still think we should head to Phoenix."

"Right. Did Peter send any more details?"

"He's sending the blueprints today. If we start driving tonight, we could get there by the day after tomorrow."

"It's fourteen hours away, right?" Zeke rubbed his forehead. "We could make that in a day."

"But then we'd be tired when we arrived. This way we'll have time to set up a base."

"That should be easy. Lots of foreclosures in Arizona."

"Yeah, but more nosy neighbors, too, I'm guessing." Through a slit in the curtains, Noa could see a young boy on a BMX bike winding slow circles on the street in front of the house. He was the only person she'd seen on the block all day.

"Anything from the other groups?" Zeke asked.

"All quiet," Noa said.

"Feels like it's been a little too quiet lately, huh?"

Noa met his eyes. They were dark brown, like his hair. She was pretty sure he was Latino, but during all these months together, he'd never talked about who he was or where he came from. She knew only that he'd been trapped in the Boston foster care system, same as her, and that he'd escaped from one of the labs before they experimented on him.

Right after she'd gone on the run with Zeke, she'd sent out a kind of call to arms on wikigroups and memes. The response had been overwhelming. Chapters of "Persefone's Army" started cropping up across the country, faster than they could keep up with them. Unfortunately, most turned out to be kids looking for an excuse to raise hell: a coffee shop chain was vandalized, their *PA* logo spray painted across the windows; a car dealership was set on fire. Throughout the media there were scattered reports about this new, terrifying "teen army."

It all calmed down pretty quickly, though; the vandals either lost interest or were caught and arrested. Meanwhile, Noa and Zeke had assembled their own core group, filled with kids they trusted. Some were teens that Zeke had been working with before he met Noa; others were kids they'd set free together.

Now the official Persefone's Army was composed of four units, each based in a different quadrant of the country: the Northeast, Southeast, Northwest, and their own, the Southwest contingent. Each group was tasked with tracking the activities of Project Persephone in their area, trying to save targeted teens, and infiltrating facilities whenever possible. There was minimal contact between the units; Noa preferred to have them operate as individual cells, each with its own leader.

That way, if one group was captured, they wouldn't be able to bring the entire network down. It was kind of like the protections Noa used to set up for company networks, a real-world firewall.

But those precautionary measures meant that she never knew much about what the other units were up to. Peter was in charge of monitoring them, and he'd been in touch less and less frequently of late.

Which made Noa wonder if he was regretting the decision to stay involved. He was probably back with his old girlfriend, enjoying his old life. Helping her out might have become a burden.

No, she told herself. Peter cared about this as much as she did. After all, these monsters had killed his best friend.

"You sure Peter's right about Phoenix?" Zeke pressed.

Noa shrugged. "He hasn't been wrong yet."

He frowned. "Sucks that we can't just hack in ourselves."

"Too risky. If they tracked us and figured out where we were . . ."

"Yeah, I know," he grumbled. "Doesn't mean I have to like it, though."

Ever since going on the run, they'd stopped hacking into networks directly; P&D had proven too adept at finding infiltrators quickly. So Peter handled their online work and research, and Zeke clearly resented him for it. Hacker pride, which Noa understood—sometimes her fingers itched for a keyboard; she hated having to steer clear of the one place she'd always felt most comfortable. But they couldn't risk endangering their unit.

"He's right about Phoenix," Noa repeated firmly.

"If you say so." Zeke stood and stretched, exposing his lean lower belly. "I'm going to crash. Wake me for dinner."

"Sure," Noa said, forcing herself to look away.

"And Noa?"

She turned to find him framed in the doorway. "Yeah?"

"You're doing great. I mean it."

"It doesn't feel like it," she muttered, remembering the way Turk had challenged her last night. Sometimes it seemed like if she made one wrong move, the kids would pounce.

"Hey." Zeke hunkered down in front of her, wrapping his arms around his knees. "You okay?"

"Not really," she said, biting her lip.

He reached out and stroked her hair with one hand, smoothing it back from her face. In a low voice he said, "I think you're amazing."

Noa blinked, surprised. Suddenly she was having a hard time swallowing. Zeke was looking at her with a serious expression, his eyes warm and full. He started to lean toward her, and her breath caught.

"Um, hi?"

They both looked up, startled. Teo was standing awkwardly in the doorway. "Daisy wanted me to tell you the guy is awake again."

Zeke quickly straightened up. "I'll deal with it. You get enough sleep, Teo?"

"Sure, yeah. Slept great." Teo looked back and forth between them. "I just wanted to thank you again, for, y'know, letting me join you."

"No problem." Zeke clapped him on the shoulder. "We gotta work on your timing, though." He threw Noa a crooked grin, then turned and left the room. Teo hovered in the doorway an instant longer, then slunk back down the hall.

Noa tucked her chin on her knees and stared out the window. She was having a hard time sorting out how she felt about Zeke. If Teo hadn't interrupted, would she have let him kiss her? She rubbed her wrist with her thumb and sighed. As if life wasn't complicated enough right now, she suddenly had boy trouble. In spite of everything, Noa smiled. A year ago, that would have been pretty much inconceivable.

The kid on the bike was still outside, even though the shadows were lengthening and it was probably getting cold. He spun in slow, lonely loops, his head down. She wondered if a family waited for him, or if he was another lost kid, like her; like all of them. As night fell, she kept watching until he was just a shadow drifting in and out of the circle cast by a streetlamp overhead.

Peter hit Send, mailing the blueprints of the Phoenix warehouse to Noa's secret account. It was nearly ten o'clock, and he had to get home soon. He'd told his parents that he was studying at a friend's house. Taking time off to see a movie that afternoon probably hadn't been the best idea, especially since encoding the blueprints had taken longer than expected. Now he'd have to wait until tomorrow to program his data sniffing filters.

He glanced around. He was parked in his neighbor's driveway again, along the curve leading up to the house so that he was hidden from both the street and the front door. It was risky using the same spot to log on every time, even with all the precautions he took to cover his tracks. But he'd grown weary of driving to remote parking lots and shivering in the cold, then packing up and moving every time a random car drove by. This was an acceptable risk, he told himself. And it would take a hacker on the level of him and Noa to access his laptop, even if they were parked right beside him.

Peter sighed. This was starting to feel like a real job. On top of everything else, there were three other PA cells out there, and he was supposed to keep track of all of them. He logged on to The Quad, and entered their official PERSEF0NE

ARMY forum. There wasn't much posted. The Northeast chapter reported that no kids had disappeared in a few weeks. Same with the Southeast. The Northwest was working on outreach, making sure street kids knew what to watch for. But none of the other chapters had a real operation on the horizon.

All quiet, in other words—which made Peter uneasy. Over the past four months, Project Persephone activity appeared to have decreased markedly. He liked to think that they'd forced the company to curtail the experiments, but he suspected they'd just succeeded in driving them further underground. Which was exactly why he had to get that sniffer program up and running.

Tomorrow, he told himself. Tonight, he had other things to worry about.

He hopped the P&D firewall and started digging through personnel files. He was searching for one in particular, a man he knew only as Mason. They'd had several run-ins months ago when he first stumbled across Project Persephone. Mason and his operatives had chased Noa and Peter through Boston for days. He'd threatened Peter's parents. And Peter suspected he'd arranged the fire that killed his best friend, Cody, too.

Plus he'd kidnapped Amanda, leaving her drugged on a park bench with a message scrawled across her back in black Sharpie: *TELL PETER HE WAS WARNED.*

At first, Peter had assumed that was just another threat: Mason boasting that he could get to anyone Peter cared about.

But maybe it had been a declaration, not a threat. Mason could have infected Amanda with PEMA during the abduction.

Peter's vision blurred with rage as he recalled Amanda shambling around the parking lot. Stage Two of the disease frequently involved repetitive patterns: walking in circles, avoiding other people, lapsing into sleep midsentence. And there were only four stages.

Peter breathed out hard, trying to calm down. He could be wrong—what he'd seen wasn't definitive. He was tempted to talk to her about it, but Amanda had been so touchy and defensive lately, she probably wouldn't handle it well.

Better to wait until he was sure. If something else happened, then he'd say something.

Regardless, it couldn't hurt to check in on Mason; knowing about his recent activities would be valuable for PA, if nothing else. But previous searches of P&D's database had been fruitless.

Peter cracked his knuckles, fleetingly wishing that Noa was with him. She was good at coming up with different angles on a problem. How would she go about finding Mason?

He tilted his head back and closed his eyes. There was always a money trail, right? After all, Mason wouldn't work for free. So how was P&D paying him?

He sucked in a breath sharply. Of course Mason wouldn't be an official employee; he must be working as an independent contractor. Which meant that certain forms would have to be filed for taxes.

It took him all of five minutes to access the IRS database. Peter searched for every 1099 form filed by Pike & Dolan. His heart sank when the computer returned more than 5,000 records. He narrowed the search to anyone making over six figures from the company; Mason liked nice suits, after all, and he couldn't afford those on chicken feed.

That cut it down to a few hundred names. Peter scanned them quickly; he could eliminate the women immediately, along with anyone too old or too young. He just had to write a program that would filter the results down to a manageable number.

Feeling fried, he closed his laptop and turned the key in the ignition. He could write the program at home in the comfort of his bedroom, then run the results through the filter tomorrow. If he got lucky, he'd find Mason hidden somewhere in there, along with all his personal information: real name, address, social security number. Everything Peter needed to destroy him.

Satisfied, Peter checked his watch; he wanted to call Amanda before it got too late. He slowly drove up to the house; with the new snowfall, there wasn't enough room in the driveway to easily turn the car around.

As he circled in front of his neighbors' garage bays, he noticed a light on in a downstairs window. *They must be on timers*, he told himself.

Still, it was hard to shake the sense that the light hadn't been on the night before. Peter slowed as he passed the front door, but there was no sign of movement inside the house.

Just paranoia, he thought, running a hand through his hair. If this kept up, he was going to give himself an ulcer.

Noa sat in the shadows, watching their prisoner. He was sleeping well, considering the circumstances. His mouth gaped open, and for such a large man, he was issuing surprisingly delicate snores.

She, on the other hand, was wide awake. After dinner Zeke and the others had crashed, still exhausted after yesterday. Noa had taken advantage of the silence to go over the blueprints Peter had emailed. It would be another couple of days before she'd need sleep again; she'd have to time the Phoenix raid so that it didn't conflict with that.

Now it was three a.m. The only illumination came from a few camping candles scattered around the living room. They'd hacked into the local utility company to provide the house with light and heat for a few days, but Noa's eyes had always been extraordinarily light sensitive, and seemed to be getting even worse since the operation. She preferred candle-light.

They'd moved the guy in here after dinner. There was no heat in the garage, so keeping him there made it hard on whoever was designated to keep watch. Which, since she didn't need sleep, mainly meant her.

So far, the guy hadn't given them any trouble. In fact, she hadn't even had to bring out the needle again. He'd willingly provided more information than she'd ever hoped for: the names of other mercenaries, the way they received their orders, how often they were paid and how much. That sum had staggered her—these commandos made twice what she'd pulled in as a top computer security consultant.

In fact, Noa worried that he'd been a little too obliging with the information. It seemed odd that he was so rattled by the threat of a virus that might not even affect him. The P&D mercenaries should be experts on PEMA, after all.

She'd discussed it with Zeke after dinner. In his opinion, this was the lucky break they'd finally been waiting for. *Relax, Noa*, he'd said, awkwardly rubbing her shoulder. *It's normal for us to think things are messed up when they work out. But that doesn't mean they are.*

Maybe he was right. Still, she wanted to know more about

what the guy had meant, calling her the "golden goose"; this was the second time she'd heard that expression, and she wasn't entirely sure what it meant. Why was she so important, among all of these kids? Zeke had a theory that she was their only successful experiment, and through her they'd stumbled across a cure for PEMA. She wasn't so sure. And that, she admitted to herself, was really why she'd wanted to capture one of them: to find out once and for all what had been done to her, and if it could be reversed.

So far, though, all the guy had revealed was a nasty line of drool.

"You're staring at me."

Noa blinked. He was eyeing her, wide-awake. "I'm on watch."

"Yeah, I got that." He stretched his bound hands back and yawned. "Christ, this floor is uncomfortable. Gonna ruin my back."

"We leave tomorrow," Noa said. "Your back will be fine."

"Pulling out, huh?" He grunted. "Smart. Don't want to stay in one place too long, get comfortable. Gonna visit another lab?"

"No," Noa said flatly, her heart in her throat. Had he overheard them?

He grinned and shook his head. "Man, I almost feel sorry for you kids."

"Yeah? Why's that?"

"Because you're a bunch of amateurs," he said dismissively.

"We got you," she pointed out.

He rolled up to sitting, pushing off the floor with his bound hands. The zip ties were starting to dig into his wrists; there was dried blood where they'd chafed. Noa bit her lip, wondering if taking them off would be a bad idea. Noticing, he chuckled and said, "See?"

"See what?"

"Softhearted. You were just thinking about cutting my zip ties." He winked at her. "And sweetheart, I don't recommend it."

"I've got the Taser," Noa said, holding it up.

"Ooh, scary." He rolled his head from side to side, then said conversationally, "You'll never get away from them, you know."

"Yeah? Why not?"

"Because they want you too badly. They've got money, resources, guys like me. . . ." His smile reminded Noa of a hyena—it looked like someone had jammed extra teeth in his mouth.

"I still don't know why they want me," she mumbled, examining her hands.

"Sure you do," he scoffed. "They changed you. Don't try to deny it."

"What do you know about it?"

He shrugged. "I heard things."

"Yeah? Like what?"

"Like you're worth your weight in gold. Like when they find you, they'll develop the best drug the world's ever seen. I hear they might even be able to cure cancer with it." He regarded her narrowly. "Funny, you don't look so special. Kind of cute, but other than that you're just like all the other trash we've been picking up."

"Go to hell," Noa growled.

"Oh, so you don't want to hear everything after all? Like what's going to happen when they find you?"

"They won't find me," she said obstinately.

"Sure they will. Hell, you're making it easy for them. You could've just disappeared, changed your name. Gone to Canada or Mexico, maybe." He eyed her. "But you got together this pitiful group of misfits and went after them. That was stupid."

"Someone had to stop them," Noa said.

"That's what you're not getting," he said, leaning forward. Noa had to resist the urge to shy back. "You can't stop them. You're playing right into their hands. Making them look like the victims. And in the end, all of you are going to die because of it."

"Noa?"

She turned to find Zeke framed in the doorway. Noa pushed to her feet, ignoring her stiff muscles, and went over to him.

"That's right, little birdie. Fly away," the guy muttered.

"What's going on?" Zeke asked with concern, looking past her shoulder.

"Nothing," Noa said without meeting his eyes. She hated to admit it, but the guy had gotten under her skin. The way he'd talked about all of them dying, like it was inevitable . . . She tried to shake it off. "I took over the watch, since I can't sleep anyway."

"You all right?" He put a hand under her chin and tilted her head up.

Noa stepped back, and his hand fell away. "I'm fine."

"All right," he said skeptically, his eyes still searching hers. "Why don't you let me take over?"

"You need sleep," she protested.

Despite the dark circles under his eyes, he smirked. "Please. Out of this whole group, I'm the only one who doesn't need beauty sleep."

Noa hesitated. "He might talk some more."

"That's what I'm worried about," Zeke said in a low voice. "And I'm better at ignoring him. So go work on the Phoenix plan. I'll handle this."

"All right," Noa said with a wave of relief. In truth, she didn't want to spend another minute with the creep. "If you need a break, just come get me."

"Sure." Zeke made a move as if to hug her, and she stiffened. He looked wounded, but all he said was, "Night."

"Night," Noa said awkwardly, crossing her arms in front of her chest as she walked away. She wasn't sure why she'd reacted so strongly—it wasn't that she didn't want him to touch her. More that she was afraid of what might happen next. And worse yet, how they'd act around each other tomorrow.

She didn't have time for romance, anyway—she had work to do. Zeke of all people should understand that.

The blueprints for the Phoenix warehouse were stacked on the kitchen table, alongside a map of the Southwest. She planned on dumping the guy somewhere near Bakersfield with fifty dollars; more than they could spare, really, but they couldn't just leave him with nothing. Hopefully he wouldn't go running back to his cronies at Pike & Dolan.

But was Bakersfield too obvious? Noa traced her finger along the map. It made more sense to leave him outside Stockton, before they turned south. He might already suspect they were headed to Phoenix, no need to make it obvious.

Although she was starting to think the Phoenix raid was a bad idea. Peter's messages were always coded, but with everything he'd sent in relation to Phoenix, he'd added *take care*. Noa bit her lip, wishing she could just call him.

Noa brushed the thought away, along with the strange yearning that accompanied it. He probably just shared her belief that the longer this went on, the more dangerous everything became. Plus he had things to lose that she didn't have: parents, friends, a future. *And his normal girlfriend*, Noa reminded herself.

She pulled a chair out and sat, then started sifting through the documents. As always, Peter had come through in spades; not only were there blueprints, but he'd included outside shots of the warehouse, and a manifest from the security firm that installed the surveillance cameras. She felt a flash of appreciation for him. With all this information, getting inside would be easy. Now she just had to come up with a plan.

Amanda shook her head, trying to concentrate. These all-nighters were killing her. She should've stayed in yesterday to finish this paper, but Peter had wanted to go to the movies.

It was funny. Last fall, Amanda had felt saddled with Peter, like he was a final vestige of high school that she couldn't shake. Now, he sometimes seemed older than she was. What made it even worse was that he clearly didn't feel the same way about her anymore. So she found herself resenting a girl she'd never even met, this Noa person he was so fixated on. A girl, ironically, just like the ones she volunteered her time to help at the shelter.

Only Noa didn't sound like the kind of kid who would have taken advantage of the Runaway Coalition. She was running around the country fighting a powerful corporation, while Amanda was stuck in an office filing papers. It made her feel like all the protests she'd gone to over the years, the petitions she'd marched from door to door, everything she'd done in the name of making the world a better place was pitiful in comparison.

Amanda shook off the ruminations and tried to concentrate on the blank computer screen in front of her. This paper on the repression of Victorian women was due tomorrow, and she'd barely done any work on it. Which was unlike her; she never procrastinated, in fact she usually turned work in early. But lately, she'd found it hard to focus.

With effort, she typed a sentence, then another. *Good*, she thought with relief. The coffee was working. Now if she could just write the final few pages, she'd be able to get some sleep. . . .

"Amanda? Are you okay?"

Amanda blinked. She was still sitting at the computer, her hands on the keyboard. Her roommate, Diem, was looking down at her with concern while she towel-dried her long dark hair.

"Yeah, I'm fine. Must've just drifted off for a minute," Amanda mumbled, rubbing her eyes with the back of her hand. "What time is it?"

"Nearly nine o'clock," Diem said.

Amanda jolted upright and checked the clock in the corner of her computer screen. "What?" Her heart leapt into her throat. Class started in five minutes, and she hadn't finished the paper. Frantically, she scrolled through the Word doc, and frowned.

"What's wrong?" Diem asked. She was a tiny Vietnamese-American girl whose enormous eyes always reminded Amanda of an anime character. She bent over to study the screen. "Wow, what's that?"

"I don't know," Amanda said, her panic increasing. There

were words on the screen, but they were a nonsensical jumble: bird, hat, tree, car . . . on and on, a string of basic words that made no sense.

"Your professor is going to love that." Diem laughed, but not unkindly. "Maybe you should just skip class."

"I can't," Amanda mumbled. "I've already missed too many this semester."

"Well, just tell her your computer crashed. That got me an extension on my poli-sci midterm."

"Right," Amanda said faintly, still staring at the words. They went on for page after page, ten of them total. Yet she had no memory of writing them. Maybe she'd done it in her sleep? Was that even possible?

"Hey." Diem laid a comforting hand on her shoulder. "It's not the end of the world. It's just a paper."

"I know, it's just . . ." Amanda unexpectedly burst into tears, astonishing herself. What was happening to her?

Diem pulled her into a hug. Amanda leaned against her and wept while Diem stroked her hair. They weren't particularly close roommates; they were friendly enough, but Diem spent a lot of time at her boyfriend's dorm, and they basically just shared the space. After a minute Amanda drew back, feeling awkward. "Thanks," she muttered, wiping away tears.

"Listen, maybe you should go to the infirmary."

"Why? I'm not sick." Amanda looked up. Diem was eyeing her with concern.

"Well, you just seem . . . different lately," Diem said hesitantly. "Out of it. Maybe they can help."

"I'm fine," Amanda snapped. "I better get to class."

"Me too—I've got an inorganic chem midterm today, and I barely studied." As she walked over to her dresser, Diem called over her shoulder, "Good luck!"

Amanda pushed the chair back and stood, trying to organize her thoughts. No time to change; she'd just wear the same outfit to class. She tugged on her jacket and grabbed her keys, stuffing them into her pocket as she tore out of the room.

As the door closed behind her, she heard her roommate say, "She is definitely not okay."

CHAPTER FOUR

Peter blew on his fingers to warm them, wishing he'd thought to bring a pair of gloves. It was a cold morning—despite staying up late the night before, he'd forced himself out of bed right after dawn so that he could beat the rush hour traffic into Boston.

He was quickly developing an appreciation for cops on stakeouts. On TV they complained a lot, but usually seemed to be having a pretty good time hanging out and snacking.

So far, he'd found it to be a miserable experience. He was parked in front of an apartment building on Newbury Street, in one of the toniest neighborhoods in Boston. Finding a parking space close to the entrance had been a challenge; he'd circled the block for nearly an hour before someone finally pulled out a dozen feet away from the door on the opposite side of the street. After hurriedly parking, Peter shut off the engine and waited.

The real hassle was that because he was sitting in the driver's seat, people kept assuming he was on the verge of vacating the spot. He'd hear an angry honk and find a car pulled up behind him with its blinkers on, waiting for the space. After that happened a couple of times, he slid into the passenger seat, hoping that would stop them. But every so often a driver would still pull up, motion for him to roll down his window, and ask if he and his buddy were leaving soon.

They never show that sort of thing on TV, Peter thought ruefully. He got why they brought snacks now, too. He was starving, but terrified that if he left the car he'd miss something. And of course he also really had to pee, since the only thing he'd had the foresight to bring was water. *This would be a terrible cop show*, he thought.

The irony was that when he'd found this address last night, Peter had been pretty proud of his detective work. He'd filtered through the initial IRS results for Pike & Dolan's independent contractors and found fifty likely candidates. Skimming that list, he quickly realized that he hadn't needed an algorithm after all; a single corporation received a huge amount of money from P&D every year, millions of dollars marked simply as "consultant's fees."

And the name of the corporation clinched it: Maurer Consulting. Maurer, according to a quick Google search, was the German word for Mason.

The address for the company was a PO Box; he felt a pang when he saw that, thinking of Noa, and how she'd used a similar address to get paid for her IT work.

Peter dug deeper, finding out everything he could about

Maurer Consulting. And while sifting through property tax records, he'd stumbled across this address. The penthouse apartment wasn't an office, though; the building was zoned residential.

And he had a pretty good idea who lived there. Peter glanced at his watch: It was nearly noon. He'd been parked here for over four hours, and so far the only people to leave the building had been a nanny with a stroller and an elderly man walking a basset hound. Of course, there was a chance that he'd missed Mason entirely while looking for a parking space. Which would really suck, because even though he could get away with skipping school today, if it happened two days in a row his parents would freak. His prep school had a strict policy about missing school in the spring term; they'd already threatened to alert the colleges he'd applied to if he kept playing hooky.

All of which would draw unwanted attention. And Peter knew that his parents were still monitoring him. Returning to his room after school, he'd discover things shifted around slightly, like someone had been riffling through his stuff. As a safeguard, Peter kept his computer with him at all times and scanned it periodically for spyware.

On the face of it, he and his parents were getting along better than they had in years. But in truth it was like living in a really friendly prison, where during dinner everyone chatted while covertly sharpening knives under the table.

Peter sighed and cracked his knuckles. He couldn't wait any longer—the pressure on his bladder was starting to get serious. There was a Starbucks on the far corner. He could be in and out in less than five minutes.

Deciding, he got out of the car.

And froze with his hand on the door handle. Mason was

strolling out of the building. He wore a dove gray wool coat and a Burberry scarf. At the sight of him, Peter's insides turned to ice. He looked exactly the same: slightly taller than average, with cropped black hair, a square jaw, and thin lips. Nothing about him would really stick out in a crowd, unless he looked at you. Mason had shark eyes, unusually large black pupils surrounded by pale irises. Peter found them creepy as hell.

Fortunately, Mason didn't appear to have spotted Peter. He turned right out the door and started up the block.

Peter locked his Prius and hurried to stay half a block back, keeping as many people as possible between them. He needn't have bothered. Mason maintained a brisk pace, clearly intent on a specific destination. He brushed past slower pedestrians, lengthening his stride to catch lights before they turned.

Peter nearly had to break into a trot to keep up. He prayed that Mason wouldn't stop suddenly, or turn around. He was suddenly hyperaware of the fact that he was an amateur at this, going up against a trained professional. He felt terribly exposed, despite the people between them.

For a second, he lost sight of the gray coat and nearly panicked. Peter hustled forward, then stopped dead. Mason had paused at a newsstand to buy a newspaper. Tucking it under his arm, he turned and hurried down the steps into the Copley T station.

Without pausing to consider, Peter followed him. Funny, Mason hadn't struck him as a public transportation type.

Luckily, he still had credits on his CharlieCard. He slid it through the turnstile and rushed toward the stopped train, getting on one car down from Mason. *Something else you rarely see in cop shows*, he thought as the doors slid closed.

He couldn't see into the next car, and would have to get out at every stop to see if Mason dismounted, which seriously increased the likelihood of being recognized.

Peter did that for three stations; each time his heart throttled his rib cage as he stepped off the train. At the fourth stop, Mason got off and headed for the exit. Peter tugged his baseball cap down farther and followed.

They emerged at the Park Street station, in the thick of downtown. Peter kept an eye on Mason's back as he wove confidently through the crowd. Leaving the station, he turned right and strode into a large building. Peter continued past the entrance, then crossed the street to survey it. It was a glass and steel skyscraper. He noted the address, then returned to the front doors. By now, Mason should have left the lobby.

Entering, he saw a security guard stationed behind a large, imposing white desk. No building directory in sight. Peter hesitated, glancing toward the security camera mounted by the elevators.

"Help you?" the guard called.

Deciding, Peter replied, "Sorry, wrong building," and rushed out. Last thing he wanted was to have to present photo ID to a rent-a-cop. He could search who the tenants were online, and might even be able to puzzle out which office Mason had visited.

Besides, Peter realized, he had all the information he really needed. Now he knew for certain where Mason lived.

Adrenaline still coursed through his veins, making him feel lighter as he practically skipped down the stairs to the T.

Teo rubbed the sleep from his eyes. It had been a while since he'd slept in a house, and it was a refreshing change. Unlike camping on the streets, here he didn't have to sleep with one eye open, jolted awake every few hours by noise or the fear that someone was sneaking up on him. He'd slept better in the past two days than he had in years.

The rest of the room was filled with kids who were still zonked out. His heart swelled at the sight of them. At his last camp, he'd felt tolerated. He'd never really counted any of the other runaways as friends; they stuck together out of necessity, knowing they were easy prey on the streets.

Here, though, pretty much everyone seemed to genuinely like him. Especially Daisy. Teo watched her sleep. She looked tough when she was awake, with her spiked blue hair and piercings. But asleep, you could really see how pretty she was. They'd hung out yesterday, talking about the stuff she'd been doing with Noa and Zeke since they picked her up outside Vegas. It all sounded amazing, but the whole time, Teo found it difficult to focus; all he could think was that her hair was dyed nearly the same shade as her eyes.

Carefully, Teo picked his way across the room, trying not to step on anyone. Despite the fact that they were all sleeping on the floor, no one had complained. He guessed they all felt that having a roof over their heads made up for it. And they were an army, after all, he thought with a swell of pride.

It was still light outside—Daisy had explained that they usually slept days, since their work required them to be up all night sometimes. He wondered what time it was—morning? Midafternoon? It was hard to tell without clocks.

He was starving, though—he hadn't eaten anything since dinner the night before. *Maybe there's still some leftover chili*, he thought, shuffling into the kitchen and opening the fridge.

"Hey."

Teo whirled reflexively, all his instincts immediately

snapping into flight mode. But it was just Turk, staring at him from a dark corner by the sliding glass door. He looked rough, like he hadn't slept; his eyes were red rimmed, and he had a weird expression on his face.

"Hey," Teo said, fighting to sound like his heart hadn't just leapt into his throat. "Just looking for something to eat."

Turk grunted, "Chili's gone."

"Oh." Crestfallen, Teo closed the fridge. Turk was still watching him, hands jammed into his pockets as he bounced on the balls of his feet. Belatedly, Teo took in his pupils—they were huge, much larger than normal. *He's high*, he realized.

"Noa ran out for some food," Turk said, speaking fast. "And Zeke crashed. He was up keeping watch on the asshole last night."

"Okay." Teo eyed the door, mentally willing someone else to come in.

"Hey, you want to see something cool?" Turk said, lowering his voice.

Teo shrugged noncommittally. Turk jerked his head toward the living room. "In here."

Despite the bad vibe he was getting, Teo followed, mainly because Turk hadn't made it sound like a choice. The guy who'd tried to kidnap him was still lying on the ground. Even though his hands and feet were bound, Teo experienced a surge of fear. If Noa hadn't shown up . . . Daisy had told him stories last night about kids being sliced open, kept alive while people poked around inside them. At the thought, Teo repressed a shudder.

"Don't worry," Turk said, noticing. "He can't hurt you." He issued a low chuckle and added, "Hell, he won't be hurting anyone anymore. Check it out." Turk nudged the guy with his toe. He rolled forward an inch, then back.

Teo stepped closer. Weird, that the guy wasn't reacting at all. Had he passed out again?

"Watch," Turk ordered, a manic gleam in his eyes as he drew his foot all the way back. Teo let out an involuntary yelp as Turk's foot snapped forward, connecting hard with the guy's back.

The guy didn't make a sound.

"You want to mess with him?" Turk hissed.

"No, I'm . . . Is he . . ."

They were interrupted by the sound of the garage door opening and closing. Turk's head snapped up and the gleam in his eyes faded, replaced instantly by a look of concern. "Listen," he said urgently. "I need you to back me on something."

"I don't . . . What?"

"Say he came after us." Turk's words tumbled out in a rush. "Say we didn't have a choice, all right?" His eyes darted around the room, like he was looking for a way out.

He killed him, Teo realized with horror.

Noa stepped into the living room and paused warily at the sight of them. Again, Teo was reminded of a cat. She carried herself with a sort of grace that was rare in someone their age, especially a street kid. She also gave off a sense of authority, like you wouldn't want to mess with her. "What's going on?" she demanded.

Turk cast a desperate look at Teo, and stuttered out, "Uh, he was going after the kid, so I—"

"Why isn't he moving?" Noa interrupted, crossing the room in a few long strides. She crouched down beside the still figure on the floor and rolled him onto his back, then cursed. Looking up, her eyes narrowed as she asked, "What happened?"

"It was the kid," Turk said.

Teo realized with horror that Turk was pointing at him. "What? Wait, no, I never—"

"Bullshit," Noa snapped, straightening up and backing Turk against the wall. Even though he outweighed her by at least fifty pounds, he cowered. "What the hell did you do, Turk?"

"What's going on?" Zeke appeared in the doorway.

"Turk killed the guy," Noa said, without taking her eyes off Turk.

"Oh, crap," Zeke said. His eyes flicked to the still form on the floor. "You're sure?"

"Yeah. And he's high."

"Great." Zeke scowled. "What the hell, Turk?"

Turk's eyes darted back and forth between them. "Sorry, man. I just . . . The guy wouldn't shut up, you know? He was saying all this crap about my sister, and I just . . ." His head dropped down.

"I told you to wake me if you couldn't handle it," Zeke said pointedly.

"We couldn't have let him go anyway." Turk was still staring at the floor, but there was a set to his jaw now. "He would've told them everything about us."

Noa and Zeke exchanged a glance. Teo sensed some sort of silent communication taking place between them. Zeke crossed the room in a few strides until he was right in front of Turk. Getting in his face, he snarled, "Where'd you score?"

"What?" Turk seemed puzzled by the question.

"Where. Did. You. Score?" Zeke repeated slowly.

Turk shrugged. "I dunno, man. Just . . . when we were out following him . . ."

"You know the rules," Noa said, a thick undercurrent of

rage beneath her voice. It was hard to say how much was because Turk had murdered a guy, and how much was due to the fact that he'd gotten high. "No drugs."

"It was just a taste," Turk said sullenly.

"What now?" Zeke asked, directing the question to Noa.

She regarded the body on the floor, brow furrowed. "We find a place to dump him on the way."

"All right. I'll get everyone up." Zeke stifled a yawn with his hand. "We should get on the road soon."

"What about me?" Turk interjected.

Zeke raised an eyebrow at Noa. She regarded Turk coolly. "You're not coming."

"What?" he protested. "But—"

"I said, you're done. Get out."

Turk turned a pleading face toward Zeke, but he just shrugged. "You heard her."

"This is some freakin' bullshit!" Turk spat. He stalked out of the room; a second later, the front door slammed.

They all stood in silence for a minute.

"He might call the cops on us, if he's pissed enough," Zeke noted. Teo couldn't believe how calm they both were. He, on the other hand, felt like puking, passing out, or both. He tried to avoid looking at the body on the floor—*the body*—but no matter where he focused, he couldn't stop seeing it.

"He won't." Noa squared her shoulders. "Turk'll score again, then sleep it off."

"Still, we should get out of here."

"Yeah." As if noticing him for the first time, Noa turned to Teo. "You all right?"

"I, um . . ." Teo swallowed hard, feeling like he had no saliva in his mouth. His mind was reeling, trying to process everything that had happened in the past five minutes.

"Teo." Noa stepped forward and laid a hand on his arm. "This never should have happened. But it'll be okay. I promise."

"All right," he said, fighting the urge to tug his arm free. "I'm good."

"You sure?"

"Yeah, I'm sure. I just gotta . . . I'll be right back."

Spinning on his heel, Teo raced to the bathroom, making it inside just in time. He heaved for a few minutes until there was nothing left, then sat back. He'd seen some crazy stuff the past few years, but a dead guy in the living room . . .

Teo ran his hands through his hair, fighting down panic. After everything he'd heard about Persefone's Army, he'd assumed it would be awesome, they'd be heroes. But armies killed people, he realized. And the way they'd been so cool about it, like this sort of thing happened all the time . . . he didn't have what it took to do that.

They'd been discussing Arizona last night. He'd never been, but it should be warm there. Probably a good place to sleep outside. Once they got there, he'd just tell Noa that he'd been wrong, he wasn't cut out for this. He didn't want to see anyone else die.

"Almost done," Mrs. Latimar said with a sigh. "Would you mind finishing up the last of them?"

"Sure," Amanda said. She was feeling better. After class that morning she'd taken a long nap, and woke up feeling refreshed. She'd glanced back at the string of babble on her computer screen, deleted it with a sigh, and rattled off a copy of the paper she'd meant to write. Tomorrow she'd hand it in to her women's studies professor. It was no big deal, really; her own fault for pushing too hard, staying up late to finish the paper when she was clearly exhausted.

But now she felt fine. It was nearly the end of her volunteer shift at the Runaway Coalition, a small nonprofit that offered outreach services to teens who were living on the streets.

It was an organization that Amanda felt passionately about, since her brother, Marcus, had run away when he was fifteen years old. He was found dead on an icy park bench less than a year later. She couldn't help but think that if he'd been helped by the Coalition, he might still be alive today. . . .

She brushed away the memory and tried to focus on the stack of folders in front of her. The waiting room was empty, so she was helping Mrs. Latimar sort through the files of all the kids who had visited today. In a small way, she was helping these kids—just like Noa. Amanda wondered if that's how Peter saw it. *Probably not*, she thought darkly. As far as he was concerned, Noa was practically a superhero.

"I'm going to make some tea," Mrs. Latimar announced, pushing back from her desk and standing. Absentmindedly, she tugged at her long gray ponytail. "Would you like some, dear?"

"No thanks," Amanda said.

She kept her eyes down as Mrs. Latimar eased her considerable bulk out the narrow doorway and headed toward the break room in the back. Amanda mentally counted to ten, listening as the footsteps receded down the hall, then dug a small key out of her pocket and opened the locked file drawer in the bottom cabinet. Hurriedly, she shuffled through the files, checking to see if any new ones had been added.

This had become her pet project, her secret. Right around the time she'd been kidnapped, Mason, the man Peter claimed was spearheading illegal experiments on runaways, had appeared at the Coalition during one of her shifts. And Mrs. Latimar had handed over some of their files, information that was supposed to be private.

Amanda hadn't made the connection right away. She'd never seen Mason again, and Mrs. Latimar had never mentioned it. But she'd started noticing that after certain kids came in to see the doctor for a free physical, Mrs. Latimar set their files aside. They were never in the stack she was assigned to file. And there was that locked drawer, the one Amanda had always assumed held the Coalition's financial records. . . .

On a hunch, Amanda had lifted the key from Mrs. Latimar's desk one day when she was out for lunch. She'd copied it and replaced the original before her boss noticed it was gone. Then, late one night when she'd been manning the phone lines, she'd looked inside the drawer and found the missing files: ten of them. All of the kids were between the ages of fourteen and sixteen, and they were relatively healthy for street kids. Amanda had to repress a twinge of guilt as she scanned their records: The doctor who did pro bono work for them kept meticulous notes, and alongside stats like their blood pressure and general health were all sorts of other information. Terrible stories about abuse and incest; the worst pain adults could inflict on children. Amanda was forced to blink back tears as she read them. Afterward, she'd carefully set the files back and relocked the drawer.

When she checked a week later, the files were gone. And those particular kids never returned to the Coalition. Which made Amanda wonder.

She started asking around, trying to be casual about it so she wouldn't raise suspicions. Most of the kids brushed her off, but one girl had listened. She went by the street name Mouse, probably because she was a tiny, sharp-featured girl with drab brown hair. Amanda had seen her before—Mouse came in once a month or so, always looking for a missing friend named Tony. Amanda took her out for coffee. In between devouring all the food Amanda bought her, Mouse had complained about other kids disappearing. Whispering urgently across the cracked laminate tabletop, she'd shared rumors about well-trained men who snatched them off the streets.

Which jibed with everything Peter had told her. Suddenly, it clicked into place. This was the same Mason, the same rogue group abducting kids.

And Mrs. Latimar, the woman who up until that moment had been her personal hero, was *helping* them.

At first she'd wanted to confront Mrs. Latimar, then call the cops and the media and anyone who would listen. But Peter had argued that the group they were up against was too powerful; they couldn't be beaten that way. So Amanda did the next best thing, by keeping an eye on that locked drawer. She copied names off the files, then ferreted them to Mouse, who warned the targeted kids to watch their backs.

So far, it seemed to be working. According to Mouse, no kids had gone missing in Boston for the past two months. And Mrs. Latimar had no idea that her dirty secret had been discovered.

It was hard for Amanda to be in the same room with her now, never mind trying to act normal. It took all her self-discipline to follow Peter's advice, but she kept her mouth shut, figuring this at least gave her the chance to do *something*.

There were three new folders in the cabinet today. Amanda skimmed them quickly, keeping her ears pricked for Mrs. Latimar. She was supposed to meet Mouse later, on her way back to campus. She always took the girl to the same diner, mainly to make sure she ate at least one decent meal a week. Mouse was skinnier every time they met, and the past few times the girl had had a worrisome deep, throaty cough.

Amanda suddenly heard Mrs. Latimar's heavy tread coming back down the hall. Hurriedly, she slid the file door shut and locked it with shaking hands, then tucked the list of names in her skirt pocket.

"Everything okay?"

Amanda turned to find Mrs. Latimar standing in the doorway, looking down at her with concern.

"Fine," Amanda said, forcing a weak smile. "I'm just tired. I pulled an all-nighter last night."

"I thought you seemed a little off today." Mrs. Latimar bustled over to her desk, set down a steaming mug of tea, and settled heavily in the chair. "Why don't you leave early, Amanda? I can manage the rest of the filing."

I'll bet you can, Amanda thought sourly. Reluctantly, she handed over the remaining files. "That would be great. Thanks."

"Thank *you*. I honestly don't know what I'd do without you, dear." Mrs. Latimar smiled warmly at her. "You're the best help I've ever had."

"I'll see you on Thursday, then?" Amanda said weakly.

"Yes, of course. See you then." Mrs. Latimar was already turning back to her work. She flipped through the files; her eyes seemed to devour them hungrily.

The sight made Amanda's stomach turn. She threw on her jacket, wrapped her scarf around her throat, and pushed through the double doors.

★ ★ ★

Noa splashed some water on her face. Her skin felt unnaturally hot, and her breath was coming in short gasps. Remembering the dead guy in the living room, a wave of nausea washed over her again and she gripped the sides of the sink with both hands.

She'd managed to hold it together in front of Teo, Turk, and Zeke, but now that she was alone, tears fought their way past her eyelids. She could hear a low murmur outside the door as the others packed up their stuff, getting ready to head out. Ten minutes earlier she'd gathered everyone in the kitchen and explained what had happened. There had been a lot of shuffling feet and sidelong glances, but no one had really said anything. Which in a way made things even worse. She knew that these kids had seen some terrible things in their short lives—hell, she had, too. But murder . . .

She could still picture the cold, dead look in Turk's eyes. She'd had a bad feeling about him from the beginning, but he'd already been part of the group Zeke was working with. Turk was one of the first kids rescued from a facility, and one of the few who hadn't been exposed to PEMA. The Project Persephone doctors hadn't operated on him, either, just dosed him with an experimental medication that apparently either hadn't worked or had no ill effects.

Unless they had. Maybe it wasn't the street drugs that had made Turk kill the guy. Maybe those earlier medications had made him psycho or something.

It doesn't really matter, Noa reminded herself. Turk was gone, and they had to get out of here. And somehow, they had to deal with a dead body.

When Noa told the group what happened, she could feel them scrutinizing her for signs of weakness, but no one had said a word. Part of her had almost wanted someone to speak up. To yell at Zeke for leaving Turk alone with the guy, or at her for insisting they take him in the first place.

Not that he'd been a good person. He'd called them trash, sneered at what they were trying to do. She could still hear his voice in her head. She tried to silence it, but everything he'd said played in her mind on an endless reel, including his last words: *That's right, little birdie. Fly away.*

Noa closed her eyes and fought her breathing back to normal by sheer force of will. She had to keep it together. Now more than ever, they were looking to her for leadership. She wished for the thousandth time that Peter was there. He'd crack a dumb joke, then come up with a decent plan.

But he was three thousand miles away, and she was here. And the rest of her "army" was waiting. Noa examined herself in the mirror, brushing her hair out of her eyes. She was pale as ever. To her surprise, at least on the face of it she appeared calm.

You can do this, she whispered to her reflection. *They need you.*

Drawing up to her full height, she walked out of the bathroom.

CHAPTER FIVE

Peter stared at the entrance, willing someone to show up. He'd bailed on class right after lunch, figuring he could afford to skip history without eliciting the wrath of his parents. Now it was a little after one p.m., and he was standing a few doors down from Mason's building with his school backpack slung across his shoulders. The door locked automatically, and there was a security camera at the entrance that ID'd anyone who rang a tenant's buzzer. No guard in the lobby, though. And as far as he could tell, the camera wasn't recording; it only displayed the faces of visitors for tenants to identify before buzzing them up.

So to get inside, all he needed was for a tenant to show up; then he'd stroll in behind them. It was a large building with thirty-two apartments. Which made it unlikely that the people who lived here knew all their neighbors.

At least, that's what he was counting on.

A young Asian woman approached the door pushing a stroller. She struggled with a set of keys, rooting through her pocketbook with both hands while she leaned the stroller against her legs. It was cold outside, a few degrees above freezing, and she didn't appear to be enjoying the weather any more than he was.

Peter hurried up behind her. She glanced up as he approached, and he threw her what he hoped was a reassuring smile.

She frowned. Peter rushed through the story he'd spent the past hour concocting. "Hey, I forgot my keys. So glad you showed, I can't get my folks on the phone. . . ."

The woman's frown deepened as the baby started wailing. She bent over, retrieved a toy, and shook it furiously in the child's face, which only served to make it scream harder.

"Want a hand?" Peter offered.

The woman grunted and produced a key ring, then handed it to Peter. There were at least ten keys on it. He sifted through them, trying to keep his hands from shaking.

"Gold one," she directed.

"Right. Mine looks just like it," he said with relief, finding a gold key on the ring. He inserted it into the lock, then held the door as she shoved the stroller through. The woman stopped inside the doorway and turned to stare at him.

"Yes?" he asked, terrified that she'd guessed something was off.

"Keys?" she said pointedly.

"Oh, yeah." He handed them over. She dumped them unceremoniously back in her purse and marched to the elevator, jabbing the up button. As the doors slid open, he bent to tie his shoe. "Don't hold it," he called out. "I'll just catch the next one."

The doors slid shut. Peter quickly got to his feet. He'd scanned the directory closely, and was pretty sure Mason lived in the top floor unit, which was listed under the initials "M.C." That had to be Maurer Consulting. He waited until the elevator light stopped at the fifth floor. After counting to ten in his head, he hit the recall button. As the elevator descended, he fidgeted. What he was about to do was highly illegal, and really, really dangerous. What if Mason didn't live alone? Or if he had some sort of super high-tech security system installed?

He'd just have to risk it. Getting inside that apartment was his only shot at finding out more about Mason and his goons. He pictured Amanda circling him in the parking lot, which hardened his resolve.

Peter got on the elevator and pushed the button for the top floor. It seemed to take forever for the car to ascend, ticking past each floor so slowly that by the time the doors finally slid open, Peter was shaky from adrenaline.

He stepped off the elevator into a fancy hallway, like something in a hotel. There was a door at either end. In between them sat an elaborate marble table with an enormous orchid perched on top. Peter cracked his knuckles nervously as he checked the corners: no cameras in sight. Score one for him.

He made his way to the door on the right, where a brass *32* hung. His pulse quickened as he bent to examine the lock. A basic dead bolt, just what he'd been hoping to find. Peter dumped his backpack on the floor and dug a tool out of the outer pocket.

Boston's finest spy store was only a few blocks away from Mason's apartment. Peter had been there before to check out all the cool gadgets. Today marked the first time he'd bought anything, though. He'd pretty much emptied his bank account purchasing a variety of different items. Including a master key that promised to open "any and all dead bolts, regardless of brand."

He hadn't wanted to use it on the building's front door, though; if it hadn't worked, it could've attracted unwanted attention. So this was the moment of truth.

Saying a small prayer, Peter inserted the key into the lock and turned it.

A *click* as the bolt gave.

Peter exhaled, and paused. This was it. Now he was officially crossing the line into breaking and entering.

Feeling like he was stepping off a cliff into a void, Peter opened the door and entered the apartment . . .

. . . and blinked in surprise. He was standing on the edge of a large living space. Light streamed through the floor-to-ceiling windows at the far end of the room; they showcased an incredible view of downtown. All that, he'd pretty much expected.

What took him by surprise was how plush everything was. Rather than a sterile environment heavy on chrome and steel, the floor was covered by thick Oriental rugs. Furniture his mom would kill for, lots of Louis XVI chairs and velvet divans. Brocade curtains draped in heavy folds along the windows.

It looked like something out of a museum; not at all the decor he'd envisioned for Mason. Which made it seem much more likely that he lived with someone.

Peter strained his ears as he stepped into the room. He counted out a full minute, then took another step. And another, until he was next to the large couch in the center of the room, facing the window. From this vantage point he could see a kitchen, separated from the living room by a raised island lined with wooden barstools. To his right, a door led into a dining room. Through it he saw an enormous mahogany table that appeared to be cowering beneath a massive chandelier.

"Damn," he whispered. The rooms could have been lifted directly from the lifeless pages of an interior design magazine. There were no framed photos around, not even the random stacks of papers found in meticulously upkept houses.

He went quickly into the dining room. In addition to the massive table, there was a matching sideboard and glass cabinet packed with silver serving dishes and china. Peter shook his head, trying to imagine Mason at the head of the table carving a roast. He just couldn't get a handle on this guy.

The door at the far end of the dining room opened into a foyer. Three doors led off it. Opening the first, Peter discovered a master suite with an enormous bed that Napoleon would have felt right at home in. He repressed a snort and checked the next room: *bingo*. A library, not unlike his father's; lots of leather-bound volumes lined the shelves. Peter scanned the titles: Dickens, Chaucer, Shakespeare. All the classics, along with histories of wars he'd never heard of.

A laptop sat on the desk at the far end of the room. Peter hustled over to it and cracked the case: a password box illuminated as the screen flared to life.

Which shouldn't matter, unless Mason had taken more care with his computer than he had with his apartment.

Peter rummaged through his pack again and drew out a flash drive, then inserted it into a USB port. The computer hummed as the program loaded. It was a deceptively basic spyware program; with it, Peter would be able to open a mirror image of Mason's computer on his own, shadowing all his activity. Peter had fine-tuned it to make sure that unless Mason spent a few days digging through code, he would never know it was there.

A *ping* signaled that the program had finished loading. Peter tucked the drive back into his bag and checked the time. He'd been inside for five minutes; staying much longer would be pushing it. He'd have to come back another time to install the other toys in his arsenal. Although if he was lucky, the spyware program would provide enough information that he'd never have to risk this again.

A minute later, Peter was charging down the stairs. He was about to tear into the lobby when some instinct caused him to pause. He opened the door a slit and peeked through.

His heart nearly stopped. Mason was standing five feet away. Thankfully he was looking up, focused on the elevator display. At the sight of his familiar profile, the sharp nose and prominent chin, Peter felt himself quail.

As quietly as possible, he eased the door shut and stepped to the side of it, closing his eyes. The elevator chimed, followed by the sound of doors sliding open. Footsteps, then they closed again. He waited another full minute before checking again.

The lobby was empty.

Saying a silent prayer of gratitude under his breath, Peter trotted through the door and back onto the sidewalk.

He was so relieved at having gone undiscovered, he didn't notice the black SUV idling at the curb behind him.

Noa sat in the passenger seat of the van. The clock on the dashboard read seven p.m.; they'd left the Oakland house during rush hour, and spent forty-five minutes in stop-and-go traffic.

The silence inside was oppressive; no one had said a word yet, which was strange. There was usually a lot of banter and story swapping.

Unable to help herself, Noa glanced again at the mound of garbage bags lining the back of the van. The kids were all hunched well away from it, even though that forced them to squeeze together uncomfortably. But clearly no one wanted to come in contact with the dead guy.

"Nearly there," Zeke said in a low voice.

"Good." Noa sat back in the seat and closed her eyes. They'd decided to leave the body in Modesto. Crystal was originally from there, and she knew about a deserted farm outside town with its own access road. She claimed that no one ever went there, so the body probably wouldn't be found for a while. And by then, there would be nothing to tie them to it.

We're dumping him out like garbage, Noa thought to herself. Exactly what he'd called them, trash. It wasn't comforting. The whole thing felt dirty and wrong. When she'd joined Zeke a few months ago, and they'd expanded his operation into Persefone's Army, she'd felt like she was starting something positive, helping kids like her who'd been horribly mistreated.

Now she worried that they were becoming just as bad as the people they were fighting. Her mind flashed back to the crab pots at the Rhode Island lab, one of P&D's more gruesome methods for disposing of their victims. Bile rose up in her throat; Noa swallowed hard to choke it back.

"You all right?" Zeke glanced at her with concern

"No. Not really."

"Yeah, me either." He kept his voice low as he said, "I still can't believe Turk did this."

"I can," Noa said darkly.

"You know," he continued, "they messed him up badly when they had him."

"They did bad stuff to all of us," she retorted.

Zeke shook his head. "Not like that. He was part of the project early on, when they were just mucking around, seeing what they could do."

"They didn't infect him, though."

"No. They infected his twin sister instead."

"What?"

Zeke kept his eyes on the road as he continued, "The two of them got snatched off the street at the same time. I guess the Project hadn't managed to get many kids who were related, never mind twins, so they took their time with Turk and his sister. They wanted to see how the treatments would affect kids who were genetically similar. So they tested her and used him as a control."

"A control?"

"They did everything they could think of to her, but he was more or less left alone. If we hadn't gotten him out, they probably would have started in on him next."

"What happened to her?"

"She was too sick to save." Zeke's fingers had gone white against the steering wheel. "Turk didn't want to leave without her, but we made him. I don't think he's ever gotten over that."

"She had PEMA?" Noa asked.

"Yeah. And they tried a bunch of stuff with her, drugs, surgery . . . she was a wreck." Zeke frowned as he continued softly, "It was one of the worst things I've ever seen."

Noa had read Project Persephone's files, and knew all about the terrible experiments they'd been conducting. She couldn't even begin to imagine how Turk must've felt, leaving his sister in the hands of those monsters, knowing that in the end they'd kill her. "Still," she said in a low voice. "I can't stop thinking that this makes us as bad as them."

"No," Zeke said firmly. "Not even close. For one thing, this wasn't you or me."

"Yeah, but we're still responsible." Noa stared out the window. They were passing through farm country, but at this time of year the fields were barren, the grass brown and dead. "I never should have suggested capturing one of them."

"Look, we knew going into this that it wasn't going to be easy," Zeke said. "And that we were probably going to make mistakes."

"I didn't know that," Noa mumbled.

Zeke laughed. "Hell, I can't believe it's been going as well as it has. We've saved how many kids so far?"

Noa shrugged. "I don't know."

"Forty-two, and that's not counting how many know to be careful because you put the word out on the web. That's not nothing, Noa."

Noa wanted to tell him that it wasn't enough, and didn't even begin to make up for things like Turk's sister. Instead, she said, "Thanks. That helps."

"Yeah? Good." He grinned, then added ruefully, "I'm glad it's not just Peter who can make you feel better."

Noa fidgeted, wondering if he'd guessed that she'd just been thinking about Peter. "What do you mean?"

"I don't know. It just seems like you're pretty hung up on him." Zeke looked uncomfortable.

"We're just friends," Noa protested.

"You always say that." He glanced at her, then back at the road as he asked lightly, "So nothing ever happened?"

Noa flashed back to lying on a futon bed in Cody's cold apartment. Peter on the floor beside her, his voice low and sleepy as they talked. A lock of hair kept falling in his eyes, and she had to resist the urge to brush it back for him. The next morning, he'd made her laugh over burnt toast and eggs. . . . "No. Nothing."

"Huh," Zeke said quietly. "That's good."

"Why is that good?" she asked, puzzled.

"We're almost there," Crystal announced, suddenly poking her head between them. "The turnoff is about a mile ahead on the right."

"Great," Zeke said, a little too brightly. "Stay close so we don't miss it."

"Sure." Crystal glanced into the backseat and shuddered. "I can't wait to get rid of . . . it. It's starting to stink back there."

"You're sure this place is abandoned?" Noa asked, grateful for the change of subject.

"Yeah, I'm sure. It's been empty since I was a kid."

Noa resisted the urge to point out that Crystal was still a kid, barely sixteen years old.

"There's the turn," Crystal announced.

Zeke eased the van onto a long dirt driveway that wound off into a stand of trees. In the distance Noa could see the remains of a farmhouse, gray and slumped like some sort of dying elephant. A barn in even worse condition hunched a few hundred yards away.

"So you grew up here?" Zeke asked.

"Yeah, a few miles away. We used to come here to party."

"I thought you said people never came here." The words came out more sharply then she'd intended, Noa realized, as a wounded look crossed Crystal's face.

"They won't find anything," Crystal mumbled. "There's a well, or at least there used to be one. We can leave him in there."

"Good idea," Zeke said. "Nice job, Crystal."

"Yeah, great," Noa said, but she couldn't bring herself to meet the girl's eyes. *We're going to dump the guy down a well?* This was turning into something out of a horror movie.

The other kids started to chatter, palpably relieved that the worst part of the journey was almost over. Their voices grated on Noa, and she had to bite her tongue to keep from snapping at them. Suddenly all she wanted was to get away. The guy had been right. She should have run when she had the chance, and taken care of herself. She could have reestablished herself under a fake name in Canada somewhere, and gotten more freelance work for IT companies. Instead, she was the den mother for a group of kids who could kill someone and dump him down a well without blinking.

"Noa." Zeke had stopped the van. He looked at her across the seat, his brow furrowed with concern. "It's going to be okay."

"You know what?" she said under her breath as she climbed out. "It's not. There's nothing okay about any of this."

Mouse was late as usual. Amanda sipped her tea, trying to repress a swell of aggravation. Of course, it wasn't as if the kid had a watch. Still, she'd been waiting in the diner for over an hour, and all the caffeine she'd consumed had heightened the edginess she'd felt at the Coalition.

She'd read the same page in the textbook that lay open in front of her at least ten times, and still had no idea what it said. Which was worrisome. She'd always been an excellent student, and practically had a photographic memory. But recently, Amanda was having a hard time remembering the most basic words. Last week she'd spent five minutes trying to describe something to Diem, who finally looked at her as if she were insane and said, "Are you talking about a parking meter?"

Her grades were slipping, to the point where she was seriously concerned about passing all of her classes this semester. And her parents would kill her if she failed.

Too much stress, Amanda thought, running a hand through her hair. She wasn't sleeping well and had no appetite. Diem had recommended that she go to the medical center, brightly adding that she'd heard Ritalin was a wonder drug for studying. But Amanda hated the thought of taking any medication. Her brother had been a drug addict, and ended up dead because of it. She had no intention of following in his footsteps.

"Hey."

Amanda looked up to find Mouse staring down at her. She had on the same ratty jeans she'd been wearing last week, more holes than denim. Over them she wore one of Amanda's old sweaters and a thick down jacket that Amanda had bought for her at REI—it was only a few weeks old, but already looked like it had been through a war.

"Hi." Amanda handed over a plastic bag and said, "I was going through my stuff to get rid of some things, and thought you could use them."

Mouse took the bag but didn't answer. Internally, Amanda sighed. She'd given practically half her wardrobe to the girl, and had yet to get so much as a thank you. *Of course, that isn't why I do it,* she admonished herself. Passing along old clothes was the least she could do.

"You hungry?" she asked as Mouse slid into the booth across from her.

Mouse nodded and tugged at her sleeves, a nervous habit that Amanda recognized. So Mouse was using again. *None of my business,* she reminded herself. It wasn't her job to get the girl clean. They were working together to help save other kids. Although at some point, if Mouse seemed amenable, maybe she could gently refer her to a treatment program. . . .

A waitress approached the table, looking less than delighted to see Mouse sitting there. They'd become regulars, meeting at the same diner once a week. Amanda always tipped well, but it didn't seem to make a difference. Mouse usually smelled terrible, which provided the added bonus of keeping the tables around them clear so they couldn't be overheard.

Mouse muttered her usual order: a heaping stack of pancakes with extra whipped cream. Amanda bit her tongue. Once she'd made the mistake of suggesting that Mouse try some protein instead, maybe eggs or a sandwich, and the girl had just glared at her. Sighing, she asked, "So, how is everything?"

"Fine."

By now, Amanda was acclimated to their monosyllabic, largely one-way discussions. She pressed, "I mean, did you manage to talk to any of the kids on the list?"

Mouse shrugged. "A few. Everyone pretty much knows now, anyway."

"About the . . . guys?" Amanda scanned the diner quickly,

keeping her voice low. No one seemed to be paying attention to them.

Mouse nodded. She pulled a piece of hair into her mouth and started sucking on it, a habit that always turned Amanda's stomach.

She cleared her throat and said, "And no one has gone missing recently?"

"No."

"Has anyone seen anything suspicious?"

"No." Mouse pulled the hair out of her mouth, studied the wet tips, and reinserted it before adding, "We think they're gone."

"They're not gone," Amanda said impatiently. "They're still collecting names. They wouldn't do that if they were stopping."

Mouse shrugged as if it was a moot point.

"Anyway, I've got some more for you." Amanda drew the slip of paper out of her pocket and slid it across the table, feeling as if every eye in the room had suddenly homed in on her. *Which is silly*, she told herself. Paranoia. There was no reason for anyone to suspect her of anything.

Mouse picked the paper up and tucked it into her jacket pocket. Watching, Amanda asked, "Aren't you going to read it?"

"Later." The waitress came back and placed a round plate stacked high with four pancakes and an alarming tower of whipped cream in front of Mouse. The plate had barely touched the table before Mouse dug in with her fork, shoveling a huge bite into her mouth.

"You're not eating," Mouse observed, chewing with her mouth open. Her eyes narrowed as she examined Amanda. "You look sick."

"I'm not sick," Amanda grumbled. *Why was everyone saying that lately?* "I'm fine."

"Well, you look like crap," Mouse said matter-of-factly as she piled more food on the fork. Whipped cream smeared the corners of her mouth.

"Thanks," Amanda said. "Really."

Mouse shrugged again, an action that comprised roughly half of their conversations.

Amanda suddenly felt an overwhelming urge to get out of there, certain that if she spent another minute watching Mouse gobble down food, she'd vomit. "Here," she said abruptly, pulling a twenty-dollar bill out of her wallet. "This should cover the check. I've got to go."

"Whatever." Mouse's hand darted out and seized the money, tucking it away quickly.

"So . . . same time next week?" Amanda said as she stood.

"Yeah." Mouse didn't bother glancing up as she left. Amanda got the distinct feeling that the waitress wouldn't be getting much of a tip this time.

Teo sat silently in the back of the van. By now he knew everyone's name. There was Remo, a skinny kid whose jet-black hair hung over his eyes, and Janiqua, a girl who looked far older than her seventeen years. Crystal, Danny, and Hopper were all around his age. He hadn't gotten much of a chance to talk to them, but they seemed all right.

And of course, Daisy. Back in Oakland she'd slid into the van and sat beside him, so close their thighs were touching the entire ride. Although that might have been by accident; they were hunkered down as far as possible from the back of the van.

Once they'd left the farm, the atmosphere had cheered up

considerably. The kids passed around a bag of chips and cans of soda and teased one another about how freaked they'd all been by the dead guy.

Teo didn't join in. It was still bothering him. Remo and Janiqua had helped Noa and Zeke unload the body. Ten minutes later they were back, which definitely wasn't enough time to bury someone. He couldn't stop obsessing over what they had done with it, but didn't want to ask. He had the feeling he wouldn't like the answer.

Daisy bumped against him every time the van took a turn. She was smiling and laughing along with the others now, which just made him feel even more left out.

How could they all act like nothing had happened? They'd been forced to ride in the back of a van for hours with a dead body. Not that he felt sorry for the guy, exactly—after all, he'd been hired to deliver Teo to people who would kill him.

Teo wrapped his arms more tightly around his knees. The way the others were acting reminded him a lot of his house growing up, before Child Services took him away. His mother had a similar high, frantic energy as she babbled on, like words alone would keep his dad from beating on them. It never worked.

"Want some?"

Teo lifted his head; Daisy was rustling the bag of chips at him.

"No, thanks," he muttered.

"You okay?" she asked.

"I get carsick."

"Oh, crap, sorry." She pulled the bag away. "That sucks."

"Yeah."

They sat in silence while everyone clamored around

them. Teo had noticed that it was pretty quiet in the front seat, though. Noa's mouth had been set in a grim line as they hauled out the body.

"Why are we going to Phoenix?" he asked to get his mind off it.

"We're gonna raid one of the facilities," Daisy said. Her voice was low, but excitement hummed through it. "We'll rescue more kids, and shut the operation down. Noa and Zeke are really good with computers, they'll get information off them, then make them crash. It'll be awesome."

"Yeah?" He regarded her thoughtfully; her eyes were shining. "So you've done it before?"

"No, not me," Daisy clarified. "I mean, I've only been with them a few weeks, you know? But I heard all about the raid they did in San Diego."

"It sounds dangerous," Teo pointed out. "Especially if we don't have guns."

"Oh, they always have a plan to handle the guards so no one gets hurt," Daisy said dismissively. "It'll be fine. You'll see."

"Guards?"

"Rent-a-cops," Daisy explained. "Zeke says they're better than most, but still pretty easy to trick."

"Oh," Teo said faintly. "So who else has done one of these before?"

"Janiqua," Daisy said, indicating her with a tilt of her chin. "And Remo and Danny. I think Turk did all of them."

Her voice dropped a notch when she mentioned Turk, as if even saying his name was a bad idea. Teo was finding it hard to repress a growing sense of anxiety. He scanned the animated faces around him; it struck him forcefully that they were just a bunch of kids. Not a real army, not trained to fight guards with guns. All those stories that had impressed him so much . . . this was the reality. They took chances, and they'd been lucky—so far. But what if they weren't this time?

"It's always okay not to go," Daisy said, eyeing him with concern. "They're totally cool with that."

Teo flushed, feeling like a coward. "Yeah? How do you know, if you haven't done one of these before?"

"Janiqua told me," she said with a shrug. "Chill. It's really not a big deal. And think about the kids in there. Don't you want to save them?"

"Yeah, sure," Teo said. But the truth was, he didn't really care about some kids he'd never met. He shuddered, remembering the stack of trash bags at the back of the van, that weird heavy thud they'd made against the back door whenever they hit a bump. He wasn't going to end up like that. Teo decided he'd slip away as soon as they got to Phoenix, like he'd planned.

Peter slammed shut the laptop, frustrated. A full day of monitoring Mason's computer, and he had nothing. Less than nothing, really. The guy had done one Google search for a restaurant in the North End, and that was it. No emails sent or received, nothing private at all. He wasn't even surfing porn sites.

And if Mason had an iPhone or Blackberry, he wasn't syncing it with the desktop, something Peter had counted on. He was probably conducting most of his nefarious business on that device. Short of developing pickpocketing skills, Peter had no way of accessing that.

Which meant he'd have to break into Mason's apartment again and install the other surveillance tools. They were scattered across the desk in front of him—a couple of really cool tiny cameras that were supposed to provide a 180-degree view, although they didn't record sound, so he wasn't sure how useful they'd be. He had bought sound bugs, too, although those were trickier; Mason's apartment was huge, and Peter had no idea which rooms he spent most of his time in. The last thing he wanted was an earful of whatever happened in the bedroom. The office and living room would be the best places, he decided.

But to do it he'd have to get inside again, an additional risk he hadn't counted on. Peter reflected on how close he'd come to being discovered the last time and shivered. If Mason had caught him . . .

But he didn't, he reminded himself. And now that he had his bearings, he should be able to do the whole job in under five minutes. Maybe he could get Amanda to keep watch outside the building. . . .

Just as quickly, he dismissed the idea. Amanda had already had one bad encounter with Mason. He couldn't set her up for another. And what if she had an episode on the street?

Peter tilted back in his chair. It was late, nearly midnight. He'd drifted through his classes today in a reverie, wholly absorbed by the Mason problem. During study hall he'd made some headway on narrowing the search parameters for the Pike & Dolan data, but the software program was still returning massive amounts of information. And every day another heap of it was added to the top of the mountain. He'd spent a few hours sifting through emails and reports, but most turned out to be innocuous, about a new line of conditioner they were bringing to market, and the expansion of vaccine lines.

Nothing related to Project Persephone. In fact, he'd specifically searched for the files he and Noa had found months earlier, when they first hacked into the company's systems. Not a trace of them remained, so either his bricking had been more successful than he'd dreamed, or someone had systematically eliminated anything incriminating.

The bummer was that it meant those files might be housed on an entirely different server, one maintained separately from their computer mainframe. And if that were the case, those servers would probably be in a more secure location, where he couldn't just waltz in pretending to be a visiting tech genius.

Peter stared gloomily out his bedroom window. The bottom line was, all the risks he'd taken might have been for nothing. He hadn't heard from Noa, either. He wondered if the hostage had told her anything. More importantly, would she share the information if he had? It felt like they were operating at a growing remove from each other. Sometimes this all seemed like some terrible, inescapable nightmare he'd been sucked into. And he was in it all alone. He felt a flash of resentment. Where was his army? Instead of a trusted member of the team, he was starting to feel like the guy they kept on payroll to maintain the nuts and bolts of the operation, someone who sat alone at a desk mostly forgotten.

But it didn't have to be that way, he reminded himself. The Northeastern division of Persefone's Army was located right here in Boston. He'd met the leader once, a kid named Luke who seemed okay. Maybe he should try to get more involved with their operations.

Peter pushed back from his desk and started to pace. He had class in the morning, which meant he had to be up in six hours. But he felt too wired to sleep. All he did now was go to school, and spend time in front of a monitor trying to help Noa. His friends had pretty much given up on him, and he couldn't remember the last time he'd done anything that qualified as fun.

That wasn't entirely true, Peter thought, dropping back into his desk chair. The movie the other day had been fun, until Amanda did her spooky walk around the parking lot. He was still torn about whether or not to share his suspicions that she was in the early stages of PEMA. There was no treatment yet, nothing that could be done for her anyway. And what if he was wrong? He'd even toyed with the idea of telling her parents, but that felt like a betrayal. If the situation were reversed, he'd want his parents kept out of it entirely.

He'd left her a couple of messages today, but she hadn't called back yet, which made him nervous. Kids with PEMA exhibited all sorts of strange symptoms, including walking in circles and narcolepsy. She didn't drive anywhere, but still; what if she spaced out while crossing the street? Or zonked out in a place where a creep could take advantage of her?

He couldn't let that happen. Next time they met up, he'd talk to her about it. Maybe even see if her roommate had noticed anything weird. After all, that incident in the parking lot might have been something else, he told himself. Like stress from all her classes and volunteering. Maybe he'd exaggerated this whole thing because he'd become obsessed with PEMA.

Peter couldn't make himself believe it, though. He'd spent a lot of time on a PEMA ward watching his brother waste away. He knew exactly how the disease manifested itself. And Amanda had been exhibiting classic symptoms.

Which meant that she was going to die sometime in the next year. The realization hit him hard. His initial reaction had been rage at Mason for hurting her; the end result hadn't really occurred to him until now. Amanda was basically walking around with a death sentence on her head. And there was nothing he could do to save her.

The legs of the chair dropped down hard, jarring him as they hit the floor. Peter blinked back tears. Amanda was the first girl he'd ever loved; no, the only girl he'd ever loved, he corrected himself, although an image of Noa flickered, unbidden, through his mind. Amanda was one of the most amazing people he'd ever met: kind, caring, passionate, and fierce. She should have been destined for a long, productive life. Instead, she wouldn't even get the chance to graduate from college.

Well, if he couldn't save her, at least he could punish the man responsible for making her sick. With renewed determination, Peter flipped the laptop open again and started digging through Maurer Consulting's records. There had to be something here that would tell him Mason's weakness, and how he could be hurt. And he planned on finding it, even if it killed him.

CHAPTER SIX

"I count three guarding the perimeter, which means there are probably at least three more inside," Zeke said, squinting through the binoculars.

Noa was slumped down in the passenger seat; she could just see over the dashboard. "Can I look?" she asked, holding out a hand.

He passed her the binoculars, and she peered through them. They were parked on a small rise overlooking the warehouse facility. The building appeared abandoned; the only thing close by was a desolate office park a mile down the road.

The rest of the group was in a foreclosed-upon house in a half-finished housing development on the outskirts of Phoenix. Yesterday had been a long day of driving; after dumping the body, they'd decided to do it in one long stretch. Which hadn't been easy; she, Zeke, Remo, and Janiqua had all taken turns at the wheel, and they'd only stopped twice to buy snacks and let everyone use the restroom. But consequently they'd gotten here in record time, arriving a little after seven a.m. They'd spent the morning scouting for a new safe house, then hunkered down to rest up. A little after dusk, she and Zeke drove out to case their target.

"Phoenix is kind of perfect," Zeke noted. "Lots of places in foreclosure. I bet they had no problem finding an empty building to rent."

"Yeah, the bad economy has really been a plus for Project Persephone," Noa said drily.

Zeke issued a short laugh before adding, "It's pretty close to the highway, too, so we can get in and out quick. We can head straight to the Forsythes from here."

"That would be great," Noa said with a sigh. She could use a few days off. They hadn't been back to their home base in Santa Cruz, California, in nearly a month. It was one of the few places where she felt safe. The people who had first rescued Zeke lived there, an older couple who had stumbled across what was going on a few years ago. Horrified, the Forsythes had assembled a small group of like-minded people to try and stop Project Persephone. When all their efforts to publicize the experiments were quashed, they resorted to raids, although in a far less dramatic fashion. According to Zeke, they'd mainly snuck into loosely monitored labs in the dead of night, smuggling kids out in maintenance vans. Of course, the Forsythes weren't exactly young, or trained as fighters; they had been scientists who made a fortune and retired early. And most of the help they'd corralled came from adults with similar backgrounds. So when Zeke and Noa offered to take over the raids and kidnapping intercepts, the Forsythes had accepted with what Noa couldn't help notice looked a lot like relief.

"So what do you think?" Zeke asked. "Same plan as San Diego?"

"They'll be expecting that," Noa said, scanning the scene below through the binoculars. Even at this distance, the sight of the warehouse turned her stomach. It was a nondescript, dusty-brown building that could have doubled as an airplane hangar. No windows visible, and a single door at each end. It looked a lot like the place where she'd woken up after they'd operated on her. No matter how many rescue missions they did, she'd never gotten used to seeing a facility in person. "I think we need to try something new."

"Yeah, but what?" Zeke asked. "We don't have enough cash for anything fancy. Unless you want the Forsythes to send a money order . . ."

"We won't need anything fancy," Noa said. Her jaw clenched as she watched two of the guards chatting as they smoked cigarettes. They appeared relaxed, casual. Like they could care less about the fact that kids were being sliced open a few dozen feet away. "I've got an idea."

"Awesome." Zeke flashed her a grin. "I love your ideas."

She snorted.

"No, seriously," he added in a softer voice. "You're the brains of this operation. We wouldn't have gotten anything done without you."

"You were doing plenty before we even met," she reminded him, shifting uncomfortably. If anything, sometimes she thought that her involvement had only made things worse on everyone. Maybe it would have been better if they'd been quieter about bringing the fight to Pike &

Dolan. But no, she'd gone trumpeting about her little army all over the internet. A flash of the commando's dead body swept through her mind, and she winced.

"You're crying," Zeke said with surprise.

Angrily, Noa wiped the tears away with the back of her hand. She hardly ever cried. She'd always thought it was a ridiculous display of weakness, a physical tic that didn't accomplish anything. So why was it happening now? "I'm fine," she sniffled.

But Zeke was already reaching across the long van seat for her. She stiffened as his arms wrapped around her. "It's okay," he said soothingly, drawing her to him. "Just relax."

At the feel of his breath on the back of her neck, Noa experienced a flash of panic. The tears were one thing, but as he held her and murmured something unintelligible into her hair, she felt . . . something else. Something even more unsettling. She liked this, she realized. She wanted to lay her head against his shoulder and wrap her arms around him, too. She wanted . . .

Abruptly, she pulled away. Noa ran a hand through her hair and slid all the way to the opposite side of the van, pressing herself against the door. The air seemed thick, cloying, like there wasn't enough of it to fill her lungs.

"What's wrong?" Zeke asked, his voice filled with hurt and confusion. His eyes, usually so unreadable, were suddenly bottomless enough to drown in. "I was just trying to—"

"I know," Noa interrupted, wiping her cheeks again to get rid of stray tears. "Thanks."

"Yeah, sure," he said, still staring at her fixedly. "Anytime."

"We should go," Noa said. Suddenly, she had no idea

what to do with her hands, or where to look. She felt hot and flushed, like she'd suddenly developed a fever. "The others are waiting."

Still, he didn't move. Noa avoided his eyes, focusing on the building below them. Without the binoculars it was hard to discern details; it was just a mass of brown, nearly indistinguishable from the sandy lot surrounding it.

Another minute passed, the silence heavy and palpable. Noa's mind raced. She was being ridiculous. Zeke was her friend, maybe even the only person on the planet she could trust completely. She'd overreacted—he'd just been trying to make her feel better.

Noa turned to say that she was sorry, but Zeke had shifted in his seat to stare blankly out the windshield. His jaw was set, and he looked angry. As she opened her mouth to speak, he turned on the ignition and threw the van in reverse, spinning it around and tearing back toward the highway.

They drove in silence through the dusty landscape, wide stretches of desert punctured by saguaros, strip malls, and golf courses. Noa rubbed her bare wrist to comfort herself the entire way.

Peter opened the front door wearing pajama bottoms and a plain white T-shirt, his hair rumpled from sleep. "Hey," he said uncertainly. "What's wrong?"

"Everything," Amanda said, stamping her feet against the cold. "Can I come in?"

"Yeah, sure," he said, keeping his voice low.

Silently, Amanda followed him through the darkened foyer and up a flight of stairs to his room. Peter's house was so enormous she'd always found it slightly overwhelming. Even though they'd shared long rants about how over-the-top and ostentatious it was, deep down she felt a slight twinge of envy as she mounted the main stairway. Carved of wood and set with inlaid marble, it was like something out of a movie. Amanda had never admitted it to Peter, but she loved the plush Oriental rugs, the insanely expensive furniture, and the enormous kitchen stocked with every possible amenity. Her family wasn't poor, but they could never afford a house like this.

Peter held the door to his room open, then eased it shut behind her. Not that he needed to worry—his parents' bedroom was in a whole other wing of the house. Still, he seemed unusually jumpy tonight.

"Everything okay?" Amanda asked, standing awkwardly in the middle of his room. As usual, it was messy: Clothing spilled out of the closet and drawers, the bed was unmade, and there were stacks of papers and computer equipment everywhere. The walls were covered with vintage movie posters: *Star Wars*, *Indiana Jones*, *Star Trek*. A few months ago she would have dismissed them as immature, but now she found them oddly charming and sweet. The room had that particular teenage boy musk, too, which should have been unpleasant but wasn't.

"You tell me," he said, dropping down on his bed and cracking his knuckles. "It's the middle of the night, Amanda. What's going on?"

Amanda stared at her hands. She knew this was nuts. Part of her was tempted to make up some lame excuse, then bolt for the door. The entire T ride here, this had seemed like the right thing to do—the only thing to do. She didn't trust anyone but Peter with this.

But now that she was standing in front of him, she didn't know what to say.

"Sit," he said, patting the space beside him. "And take your coat off. You might as well crash here tonight, the T won't be running again until morning."

"But, your parents—"

Peter snorted. "Yeah, like they care. Please. If you want, I'll make sure they're gone before you leave."

Amanda pulled off her hat and sank down on the bed beside him. As Peter helped her out of her coat, his hand brushed hers. Usually when that happened, one of them ended up yanking it away. But this time, unless she was mistaken, his hand lingered.

Amanda carefully laid her jacket on the bed beside her. Crossing her hands in her lap, she tried to figure out where to start. "I'm sorry if I woke you."

He waved a hand, his light-brown eyes fixed on hers. "Don't be. I was up."

"More Noa work?" she asked, unable to contain the sharp edge in her voice.

Peter hesitated, then said, "I was working on something else tonight, actually."

He didn't seem to want to discuss it further, which was odd—she'd assumed that over the past few months, he'd been sharing everything with her. A terrible thought suddenly struck her—maybe he hadn't been working at all, maybe he'd been talking or texting with a girl. It would explain why he was suddenly being so secretive. Not that she should care, Amanda reminded herself. She'd broken up with him four months ago. Peter had the right to date whoever he wanted.

But she did care, Amanda suddenly realized, taking in his sleepy eyes and wavy brown hair. A lock of it hung over his left eye; looking at it, she remembered how surprisingly soft it was, how she used to love running her hands through it.

"Amanda," he said gently. "Tell me."

After seeing Mouse yesterday, she'd gone home and fallen into bed. Even though it had only been five p.m., she'd felt completely drained, and figured she had time for a nap before dinner.

A slant of light in her eyes woke her. Groggily, she checked the clock: It was eight a.m.; she'd slept for nearly fifteen hours. On the plus side, she felt great, well-rested and hungrier than she'd been in weeks. She devoured breakfast in the student union and headed to class. Maybe she'd had a low-grade cold that had finally run its course, and didn't need to go to the medical center after all.

The next thing she knew, it was dark outside. It was like she'd blinked on the path to class, and been transported to an entirely different world by the time she opened her eyes again. She was standing in front of the diner, staring at the CLOSED sign hanging on the front door. Amanda had no idea how she'd gotten there, or how long she'd been standing on the deserted street. Checking her cell phone, she saw that it was nearly midnight. It was only slightly comforting to see that at least it was the same day.

A lot could happen in fifteen hours, and Amanda fought rising panic as she flashed back to months earlier, when she'd woken up on a park bench with a warning scrawled across her back in black marker. So she'd rushed into the bathroom of a fast-food restaurant a block away, tore off her jacket, and pulled down her shirt.

She craned her head in the mirror to check: Her skin was unblemished. If she had been abducted again, this time there was no sign of it.

Which should have been a relief, but she couldn't shake

the feeling that this was something else. Maybe something even worse.

The diner wasn't far from the green line. She'd purposefully marched into the station and caught the last train out to Brookline, making a beeline for Peter's house.

Amanda still wasn't quite sure why. Maybe because Peter was the only person who knew about her previous abduction, so she could trust him with this. Plus, he would know better than anyone whether this was the sort of thing Mason would do.

Or maybe it was because she felt terrified and alone and wanted to see him. Wanted to feel his arms around her, if she was honest with herself. Maybe wanted even more.

And now she was here, and Peter was sitting next to her on the bed, his eyes filled with sympathy. And she found that part of her didn't want to tell him, because the very worst thing would be for him to pity her. She didn't want to feel like a victim; she wanted to feel something else for a change.

So she leaned forward and pressed her lips against his.

Peter froze for a second, then his lips relaxed, and he kissed her back. His hand reached up to stroke her cheek, then he ran it through her hair and pulled her head closer. And suddenly the kisses were deepening, and she had her hands up under his shirt, feeling the muscles of his back tauten, and they were lying down. . . .

A cell phone rang. Peter abruptly pulled back, a puzzled expression on his face. "That's not the iPhone," he said reluctantly after it rang again. "I need to get it. I'm really sorry, Amanda."

"Okay," she said breathlessly. "Just . . . be quick."

She watched him cross to his desk, straightening his shirt as he went. Peter dug a TracFone out of his backpack. Her eyes narrowed. *Of course—Noa.* A knot of resentment formed in the back of her throat. She knew that most of their communication involved coded messages exchanged on that Quad message board only hackers knew about. So if Noa was calling, there must be some sort of emergency.

Still, Amanda felt irritated. When Noa called, Peter jumped. He'd never been like that with her; at least, she didn't think he had.

Peter checked something on the phone, then dialed a long string of numbers. Amanda propped her head on one hand as she lay on her side, watching him. Noa must have answered, because he said something in a low voice, his head tucked down. Still, it was impossible to miss the spark in his eyes, and his slight smile as they spoke.

Something inside her shriveled. She was suddenly glad that she had no idea what Noa looked like—Peter had always been vague about it, so she was probably stunning. And based on the awe in his voice whenever he mentioned her, she knew he admired her. She'd suspected there might be more; and seeing his reaction now, it was clear. She'd lost him.

Amanda flopped over on her back and stared up at the ceiling, wrapping her arms around a pillow. Peter was speaking in such a low voice, she could only make out fragments: "Phoenix" and "Mason" and "blueprints."

"Be careful, please," he said, just loud enough for her to hear. Then he hung up.

He looked worried as he came back over to the bed. "They're going through with the Phoenix raid," he said before she asked.

"I figured," she said, trying not to let the peevishness show in her voice. "When?"

"Soon." Peter sat down. His eyes were a million miles away from her—or, more accurately, about two thousand, somewhere in Phoenix, with Noa. "It's kind of a genius plan, actually."

"Of course it is," Amanda snapped. "Noa came up with it."

That caught his attention. Peter frowned at her. "What's wrong?"

"Nothing," she muttered. "I should go."

"Wait, what? You can't." He sounded genuinely perplexed. "The T stopped running an hour ago."

"So I'll call a cab." Angrily, Amanda sat up and tugged her hat back on, fighting back pinpricks of tears.

"That's ridiculous," Peter said in an infuriatingly reasonable voice. "Stay. I'll crash on the couch, you can take the bed."

"No," she said obstinately. "I'm going."

"Amanda." He grabbed her wrist, stopping her. Amanda paused, still facing the door. She was torn between a wild desire to get away from the look in his eyes that no longer had anything to do with her, and the conflicting urge to fall into his arms and start sobbing.

"Please," she said in a small voice. "Just let me go."

"No," Peter said firmly.

She turned. Peter was gazing up at her, his brown eyes full of concern. "You don't love me anymore," she said quietly.

He looked dumbfounded. "What?"

"You heard me." She tugged hard, but his grip on her wrist tightened. "Let go."

"You can't just say something like that, then run away," he said angrily.

"I'm sorry I said anything," Amanda said, meaning it. What had come over her? Now she really wanted to flee.

She'd walk back to her dorm if she had to. "Just forget it."

He released her hand. Amanda fumbled with the buttons on her coat, stumbling and nearly falling in her headlong rush for the door.

Her hand was on the knob when he said, "I never stopped loving you."

Slowly, she turned to stare at him. Peter was standing next to the bed, hands hanging loose by his sides as he gazed back at her. "Never, Amanda. Not for one minute."

She crossed the room in three strides and threw herself into his arms. Peter pulled off her cap and dug his hands into her hair, then tilted her head up to meet his. The kiss ran through her whole body, familiar and yet different at the same time. It felt warm and safe and right. Amanda wrapped her arms around him, pulling him closer. In spite of herself, she felt a slight twinge of victory as Peter murmured her name in her ear.

"Any questions?" Noa asked.

No one said anything. The atmosphere in the room was keyed up and tense. Noa had just laid out her plan for breaking into the lab. They'd get in, deal with the guards, and save as many kids as they could. She'd gone through it step by step, laying out the role each would play in the assault.

Hopefully, this time there would be some kids left alive for them to save.

She glanced across the room to where Zeke stood with his arms crossed over his chest. He hadn't looked her in the eye since they'd gotten back. She wished she'd handled it better. It had been years since she'd been able to rely on anyone, and he'd been there for her through this whole crazy thing.

And if she was honest with herself, that's why she'd drawn

back. Not because she hadn't wanted to kiss him—she had, for a long time, she suddenly realized. But she was terrified that falling for him would jeopardize everything else. What if it didn't work out? Would she end up doing this all on her own?

Noa suddenly realized that they were all staring at her expectantly. Zeke caught her eye and threw her a questioning look. She cleared her throat and said, "The radios should work while we're in there, so make sure to maintain contact with one another on channel twelve."

She scanned the room. Everyone looked back at her steadily—except for Teo. A fine sheen of sweat covered his face, and he looked like he might throw up. Noa sighed internally. He seemed like a sweet kid, well-intentioned. But they'd had others like him join the group, and they never worked out. They just didn't have the stomach for walking into dangerous situations. Maybe they were the smart ones, she thought wryly. With that in mind, she added, "No one has to come if they don't want to. Same deal as always, if you stay behind, we understand."

"But we could use all of you," Zeke interceded. Noa threw him a look, but he ignored it and kept talking. "I mean it. We don't know how many guards are inside the building, or what kind of security measures they'll have. And without Turk, well . . ." He looked uncomfortable. "It'll be a lot harder," he said, mumbling the last bit.

Noa chewed her lower lip. He was right. Despite his faults, when things came down to the wire, Turk had always risen to the occasion. It was going to be a lot tougher without him, especially in a situation like this, where they didn't know exactly what they were up against. "Any questions?"

A few heads shook—no one spoke up. Relieved, she said,

"All right, chill out until then."

As they filed out of the room, she bent over the warehouse blueprints that were spread across the kitchen table. She sensed Zeke at her shoulder, and caught her breath.

"Sorry about earlier," he said in a low voice.

"That's okay," she said, relieved. "I'm sorry, too. I just kind of . . . freaked," she finished weakly.

He laughed quietly. "I know, Noa. Not your thing."

"What's that supposed to mean?" she asked, frowning as she turned to face him.

He shrugged. "Just that you're not so comfortable with the emotional stuff."

Flushing, she opened her mouth to retort, but he was right. She was sixteen years old, and could count on one hand the number of times she'd been kissed. Half of those hadn't been voluntary, either.

But that wasn't strange, right?

Zeke stepped closer, and Noa forced herself to hold her ground. Standing like this, they were nearly eye to eye.

He trailed a finger down her bare arm, making her shiver. "You know how I feel about you," he said softly.

Noa felt like her face was on fire. A familiar ball of panic settled in her chest, and she had to fight the urge to run, as far and fast as she could. "I don't know how to do this," she finally said.

"So we take it slow." Zeke leaned in and brushed his lips lightly across her forehead. The sensation made her inhale sharply.

Then he turned and walked away.

Teo had planned on taking off before the raid, but so far, he hadn't had an opportunity. The house they were camped out in was in the middle of nowhere, with nothing but desert and other abandoned houses all around. It was some sort of upscale development that had fallen apart; the closest signs of life were a few miles away. Phoenix wasn't what he'd expected; based on what he'd seen driving in, it was all strip malls and weird cookie-cutter housing developments like this one. There had to be a downtown somewhere, but how would he get there? And so far, he hadn't seen a single panhandler, which didn't bode well for surviving on his own.

Still, dying in the desert might be better than what was in store if he went along with them. Noa had announced that they were going in tomorrow night, even though they'd pretty much just arrived. He might be wrong, but it didn't seem like they'd taken time to get a sense of what they were rushing into. All the details on how many guards there were, and where they might be, seemed awfully vague for his liking.

Daisy smiled at him. "Damn, you look nervous." The two of them were hanging out in what probably used to be the master bedroom. Now it was bare, save for huge dust bunnies and a ragged carpet fragment they'd found in the garage. Daisy's blue hair was tied back in a loose ponytail, and she was wearing short shorts and a halter top.

"Me, nervous?" Teo said with false bravado, conscious of the embarrassed flush spreading across his face.

"It'll be fine," she said confidently. "Noa and Zeke have done a bunch of these, and they never have any problems."

There's always a first time, Teo thought, but he kept it to himself.

"You're coming, right?" Daisy whispered, nudging him.

Her skin was warm and soft against his arm. Teo felt himself go even redder. He kept his eyes on her bare feet; her toenails were painted with chipped neon-green polish. He wanted to ask her to come with him; they could slip away tonight, long before everyone piled back into that damn van. But he had the feeling she'd say no. And worse, she'd think he was a coward.

"Yeah," he said. "Course I'm going."

"Good," Daisy said in a low voice. She wrapped her fingers around his and squeezed. "We'll take care of each other. And when it's all over, we'll celebrate," she promised with a wink.

Teo's heart leapt. He was right; she had been flirting with him. Hopefully she meant what he thought about celebrating later. He'd wanted to kiss her ever since he first saw her; maybe she'd even let him do more.

Of course, Teo realized, he wouldn't get to "celebrate" unless he stuck around. Which meant going up against armed guys just as tough as the one they'd held captive. The good feeling quickly dissipated. "Yeah," he said desolately. "It'll be a hell of a party."

CHAPTER SEVEN

Peter impatiently blew hair out of his eyes. He'd gone too long between haircuts and now it was annoying him, blocking his vision. He should've worn a hat, anyway. What if Mason noticed a strange brown hair on his carpet? *Stupid*, Peter thought. At least he'd remembered to bring gloves this time.

He glanced at his watch: He'd already been inside the apartment for ten minutes. So much for get in, get out. He might as well pop open a soda and kick back on the couch for a while.

Angrily, he tried again to get the bug positioned, chastising himself the whole time. He should have practiced with one of these at home. The spy store salesman had sworn that these listening devices took less than a minute to install and activate, but maybe that time frame only applied to actual spies. For nearly five minutes Peter had been struggling to attach one to the underside of Mason's desk, behind the lip so it wouldn't be visible unless you were on your hands and knees looking up. But every time he thought it was secured, the bug dropped onto the rug.

Of course, the free-floating frustration he was feeling might not just be due to the bug. He'd awoken before dawn with Amanda curled up in bed beside him. Instantly, everything that had happened the night before snapped into his mind. He'd meant what he said, telling her that he loved her. At least, in the moment he had. But as he watched her sleep, conflicting emotions fluttered through him. Their breakup had hurt him badly. It was hard to feel like he could trust her anymore.

And then there was Noa.

Which was crazy, and ridiculous. But even though nothing had happened between them, and there was a good chance he'd never see her in person again, she occupied most of his thoughts. And his dreams, if he was honest. What he felt for Amanda was . . . different. There was a time when getting a text from her had made him light up, and he could have spent hours just holding her. Even after a year, whenever they were together he'd seek out physical contact with some part of her—his hand on the small of her back, or his fingers wrapped around hers.

He still cared deeply for her. But lying beside her that morning, he realized that he just didn't feel *that* way anymore. He didn't want to bury his face in her hair while wrapping his arms around her waist. Part of him was tempted to sneak out of the house before she woke up, but if he did that, she'd go ballistic.

So he waited, staring up at the ceiling, itching to get his

laptop so he could start working. When she finally woke up around seven, he tried to act normal. Gave her a kiss and a hug, helped her sneak out the back so his parents wouldn't see her. And when the door finally closed behind her, he heaved a sigh of relief, then immediately felt guilty about it.

He could tell that Amanda knew something was wrong, but she didn't say anything. Which just made him feel even worse. So he got dressed in a rush and came here, counting on the fact that Mason would be a creature of habit, and the apartment would be empty.

Stupid risk. But he'd gotten lucky—no one was home.

That luck didn't seem to be holding, however. Peter swore as the bug fell again, then sat back on his heels. He could practically hear the minutes ticking past, like a bomb countdown. He forced Amanda and Noa out of his mind, gritted his teeth, jabbed another piece of Velcro onto the damn thing, and tried again.

Finally, it stuck. Making a mental note to never go anywhere again without a tube of industrial strength Krazy Glue, Peter returned to the living room. The second and third bugs installed more easily: He tucked one under the kitchen counter, and after a tortuous few seconds of debate, installed the final one in the bedroom. Maybe Mason liked to lounge around on his bed chatting to P&D CEO Charles Pike like a high school girl with a crush. Hopefully, that was the only sort of activity he engaged in there. Peter had no desire to sift through hours of boudoir activity, but he was more afraid of missing something that might help save Amanda.

Peter scanned the room. He hesitated, then went back to the library one last time to make sure the damn bug hadn't fallen on the carpet again.

All clear. Nervously, he double-checked that there was no

sign he'd been in the apartment, then headed for the front door.

Halfway down the hall, he heard the distinct *click* of a dead bolt turning.

Amanda tucked her chin deeper into her turtleneck and hunched her shoulders. The temperature had plummeted overnight, and the faint sunshine barely made a dent in the biting air. She was late for her shift at the Runaway Coalition. Not that it really mattered, but lately she'd gotten the sense that Mrs. Latimar was watching her more closely, and she didn't want to do anything to rouse suspicion.

It had taken nearly an hour to get back from Peter's house; more than enough time to mentally review everything that happened. In the dark, Peter had been so sweet. She'd drifted off to sleep in his arms, feeling like they were finally together again, and everything would be fine from here on out.

But then she'd woken up to a stranger. Peter had been so weird and awkward, avoiding her eyes, going out of his way not to touch her. She could've sworn he even grimaced when he kissed her good-bye.

At the memory, Amanda fought back tears. She wasn't an idiot. Maybe he'd only used the *l* word last night because he felt sorry for her.

That got her angry. *Forget him*, she told herself. Between school and volunteering, she didn't really have time for a boyfriend anyway. Before Peter, she'd hardly dated; weekends, she'd hung out with friends. It had been nice, drama-free. Well, she'd just get back into that mindset. It was almost funny, that Peter was so hung up on a girl who wasn't even around anymore. At the thought, Amanda experienced a sharp flare of rage. She tamped it down, clenching her jaw to contain it, and quickened her stride. Just a few more blocks to the Coalition.

Amanda was so preoccupied by those thoughts that she was barely aware of her surroundings; someone suddenly stepped in front of her. She automatically mumbled, "Excuse me," shifting right to pass him.

But he moved with her, blocking her path. Annoyed, she jerked up her head. It was Mason.

Peter froze, his heart shuddering to a halt in his chest. As the doorknob turned, he got hold of himself and edged back down the hall as quickly and silently as possible. In the living room he stopped, his hands sweaty and shaking. Mason would kill him if he found him here. And he could probably dispose of a body in a hundred different ways without anyone finding out. Peter would simply vanish. His parents would assume he'd run away again. Amanda and Noa might search for him, but eventually even they would be forced to give up.

He had to get out, now.

His eyes frantically scanned the room for a hiding place. The curtains? No: too obvious, and they didn't reach all the way to the floor. Maybe he could make it back to the bedroom? And do what, hide under the bed? Was there even a closet in there? Crap, he couldn't remember.

Think! he berated himself.

There was a door off the kitchen; he'd noted it on his first pass through the apartment. As footsteps approached down the long hallway, Peter darted toward it. He was out of time and out of options. If it turned out to be a cabinet, he was screwed. Drawing a deep breath, he turned the knob and opened the door as silently as possible.

When Peter saw that it led not to the broom closet he'd

been hoping for, but to something even better, he nearly passed out from relief. He ducked into a small corridor with a trash chute and service elevator, easing the door shut behind him. Before pressing the call button for the elevator, he hesitated—what if it was loud? Mason might hear, and come investigate.

Better to wait a few minutes, Peter decided. Hopefully Mason wasn't staying long. This time of day, he probably had someplace to be, right?

The sound of keys hitting the counter, and a lower noise. Was Mason *humming*? Peter thought, flabbergasted in spite of everything. He would've been less shocked if the door suddenly sprouted a mouth and started talking to him.

Suddenly, a heavy tread approached. Peter stepped back, panicked. It was too late to call the elevator—there was no way it would arrive before the door opened. He frantically surveyed the room, but no windows or exits magically appeared. For a brief second he considered the trash chute, but it was roughly a foot wide; there was no way he'd fit.

The footsteps stopped right on the other side of the door. Peter swallowed hard. This was it. He was about to be caught. A hundred terrible scenarios whirled through his mind. Should he scream? Maybe someone downstairs would hear him. He could call 911 . . . and say what, exactly? That he was trapped outside the apartment he'd just broken into?

At least he could send Amanda a text. He fumbled his iPhone out of his pocket and stared at the screen, unsure what to type. *I'm at Mason's and someone's about to kill me(!) Good-bye, it was nice knowing you.* :(

Short and sweet, he decided. Give her Mason's address, and tell her to get in touch with Noa. While he was at it, he'd include a link to the packet sniffer. Peter berated himself for not sharing that data with her already—what had he been thinking? Noa had no idea that he'd inserted a back door into Pike & Dolan. Even if the Project Persephone files were on an entirely different server, there might be useful information there.

But no, he'd selfishly kept quiet about it.

The knob turned. He'd run out of time.

Peter ducked behind the door as it popped open, sucking in to make himself as narrow as possible. A hand tossed a small bag into the hall. Peter held his breath. It landed with a crackle a few feet away—white plastic knotted at the top, with the outline of cardboard containers inside. *Great*, he thought. His death could be blamed on Chinese takeout.

If Mason took one more step into the hall, he'd be seen. . . .

The door slammed closed. Peter waited a few beats, then exhaled.

Inside the apartment, a phone trilled. It was picked up after two rings. A woman started chattering in rapid-fire Spanish. He heard a sink turn on, then the sound of cabinets opening and closing.

Peter slid down the wall, dropping into a crouch. *Not Mason—his maid.* He had to repress a giggling fit at the realization. So he wasn't about to die, which was a relief. But he still had to get out of here, ideally without being seen.

He pressed his ear to the door, hearing the persistent whine of a vacuum on the other side. He'd have to chance it. Stepping quietly to the elevator, Peter pushed the call button.

The doors slid open silently. Peter stepped inside and jabbed the button for the bottom floor, then repeatedly pressed the one that closed the doors. As they slowly slid shut, he kept waiting for a hand to force them back open, then reach for him. . . .

The doors finally shut, and he collapsed against the rear wall. It was a service elevator, much drabber than the one used by residents: a chipped linoleum floor, gray walls scarred by streaks of paint. But as far as Peter was concerned, it was the most beautiful elevator he'd ever taken in his life.

He emerged in the basement. Took a second to get his bearings, then mounted a stairwell that ejected him into the alley behind Mason's building. He checked the street: It looked clear. Trying for nonchalance, he strode out of the alley with his hands jammed in his pockets. It took all his resolve to keep from breaking into a run.

After sliding behind the wheel of his Prius, Peter sat for a minute. His hands shook, echoing how his whole body felt. He was not cut out for this spy stuff. That had been a crazy risk he'd just taken, where the best-case scenario involved an arrest for breaking and entering. From now on, he'd stick to keeping track of things from the safety of his keyboard.

Feeling resolute, Peter turned the key in the ignition and pointed the car toward home.

Amanda could barely breathe. Mason was dressed in an impeccable gray suit with a wool overcoat, a Burberry scarf knotted around his neck. Despite the cold, his cheeks were pale as ever. "Amanda Berns," he said evenly. "What a coincidence. I was just heading to the Runaway Coalition."

Amanda opened her mouth, but nothing came out. Her whole body had frozen with terror. She stared at him dumbly for nearly a minute; the whole time, his gaze never faltered.

She finally snapped out of it. Smiling weakly, she said, "I'm heading there, too," and moved to pass him.

He fell in step alongside her. "Well, then we should walk together."

Everything inside her raged against the suggestion, but she couldn't come up with a valid reason to refuse. Amanda wanted to shriek at him for abducting her, marking her skin with a creepy warning, and stealing the lives of so many vulnerable teens. But she had no proof. And if she came out and started shouting at him in the middle of the sidewalk, she'd just end up looking like a crazy person.

Plus, Mason would know she was onto him. And everything she'd been doing at the shelter, stealing those names and passing them to Mouse, would have been in vain.

She swallowed hard, trying to get her throat working again. Kept her head ducked low, praying that he wouldn't talk to her.

But he did. "So," he said. "I believe we have a mutual acquaintance."

Amanda looked up sharply, suddenly panicked that somehow they'd been discovered. Had he done something to Mouse? She pictured her wan form laid out on a metal table; the thought made her ill. "Really?" She struggled to keep her voice even as she asked, "Who?"

"Peter Gregory."

A flash of relief, immediately followed by more panic. Did Mason know that he'd been helping Noa? "He's my ex," she said, fighting to sound dismissive.

"Ah, young love." Mason's mouth creased into a smile that didn't extend to his eyes. "Lots of ups and downs, right?"

She didn't answer. They were a block from the Coalition. The light was about to turn red; she broke into a trot to cross the street anyway. Mason matched her pace, although he managed it at a walk.

"I understand Peter is planning on attending Harvard next year," he said casually.

Amanda looked at him sharply. "How do you know that?"

"Oh, his parents and I are old friends." That smarmy smile again, really more of a leer.

Her heart drummed in her chest; it felt like she was running even though they'd resumed an even walking pace. The entrance to the Coalition was a hundred yards away—she was so close. All she had to do was play it cool until then. Drawing a deep breath, Amanda said, "I didn't know that."

"Well, we have certain business interests in common." His tone sounded overly casual. She couldn't repress the sense that there was a much deeper conversation underlying everything he said. "Peter seems like an intelligent young man."

They were almost at the door. She was terrified that at any minute a van would pull alongside and she'd be shoved into it, or that Mason would jab a needle into her neck and she'd wake up in a terrible place. Her lungs felt strained, like there wasn't enough air to breathe. "Yes," she said, although it came out as a hiss.

"Too smart, some would say." Without warning Mason grabbed her arm, jerking her to a stop. Amanda went rigid; it was like those dreams where something horrible is attacking, and you simply freeze and stare at it with awe.

"Wh-what do you mean?" she managed.

"I mean," Mason said, leaning in, "he is once again sticking his nose where it doesn't belong. I'm hoping you can clarify things for him."

Amanda hesitated. Should she scream for help? Perversely, part of her didn't want to give him the pleasure of seeing how terrified she was. Peter's blank gaze that morning as he basically chucked her out the door flashed through her mind. Her jaw tightened, and she yanked her arm free. Coolly, she replied, "Like I said. We broke up."

Mason's eyebrows lifted; clearly that wasn't the response he'd been expecting. After a beat, he said, "Well, then. I guess I'll have to speak with him myself."

Amanda put her hands on her hips and demanded, "About what, exactly?"

It wasn't what she'd intended to say. She'd planned on announcing that she was late, and ducking past him. But the words had slipped out of her mouth, and it was too late to take them back.

"Interesting," Mason said, eyeing her. "You surprise me, Amanda Berns."

The way he said it made her shudder. It was like hands roving over her body, creepy and invasive. She stuttered, "I-I really need to get inside. My shift started ten minutes ago."

"By all means." Mason stepped aside and bowed with a flourish. It was a ridiculous gesture, yet somehow he made it look natural. Amanda walked past him, keeping her pace steady even though she desperately wanted to break into a run. She paused with her hand on the door and looked back.

The street was clear. Mason was gone.

PART TWO
INFILTRATION

CHAPTER EIGHT

"**R**eady?" Zeke asked quietly.

"As I'll ever be," Noa muttered. Her hands ran over the tools and weapons hidden under a voluminous black jacket, checking for the hundredth time that they were all there. She had the Taser, and pepper spray for good measure. Zip ties and a box cutter. A pocket flashlight. A precious flashbang grenade, recovered during one of their earlier raids. She was dressed in black with a checkered scarf wrapped loosely around her neck, positioned so that when the time came, she could pull it up to hide her lower face.

Although chances were, everyone in that building knew exactly who she was.

"All right." Zeke peered through the night-vision binoculars again. It was late, nearly midnight. The same three guards were outside. Two played cards on a set of camping chairs by the main door, huddled beneath the security light. The other had made a few listless tours of the perimeter.

"They're tired and bored," Zeke said with satisfaction. "Piece of cake."

"Don't jinx us," Noa warned.

He turned and winked at her. "You and your superstitions. Chill."

Noa shifted. She was always tense before a raid, but tonight her fears were amplified, and she was at a loss to explain why. *It's just paranoia*, she thought. Coming on the heels of what had happened in Oakland, that was understandable.

At that moment, a set of headlights appeared on the road leading to the facility. The lights bounced as the truck rocked over uneven pavement. Loud club music spilled out the open windows, a faint bass line discernible from their position nearly a half mile away.

"Here they come!" Zeke said, an undercurrent of excitement in his voice.

Noa leaned past him. They were on the bluff overlooking the warehouse, near the spot where they'd shared that awkward moment yesterday. The others had dropped them off an hour earlier, then left with the van to execute phase one of the plan.

The headlight beams slid away from them as the truck turned up the final approach to the warehouse. The guards had gotten to their feet and were staring at it as if a UFO had just materialized out of the sky.

It was starting.

Teo sat next to Daisy in the back of the truck, trying his best to not completely freak out. Daisy was holding his hand; her palms were sweaty, slick against his.

Why hadn't he bolted when he had the chance?

The truck abruptly braked, throwing them against each other. Their heads bumped, and Daisy yelped. Teo was about to apologize when a sharp male voice outside made him fall silent. Not that it would have mattered; the music was blasting so loud he could hardly hear himself think.

"What the hell is this?" The guard sounded like he was a foot away, separated from them by a thin metal panel.

Teo held his breath. Beside him, Daisy got very still.

"Yo, dude. Cool if I park it right here?" Remo called back from the driver's seat.

"What?" The guard sounded puzzled, and annoyed.

Remo continued, "I could swing around back instead. Depends on where the rig is gonna set up."

"Rig? Christ, I can barely hear you. Turn that music down!"

The volume faded by a few decibels. In spite of everything, Teo repressed a smile.

"What the hell is going on?" a deeper voice demanded; the guard in charge, maybe? "Why is there a taco truck here?"

"Dunno," the first guard replied sullenly. "He's asking where he can park."

"Park?" Boss Man sounded incredulous. "Listen, son, this is private property. No trespassing, like it says on the signs. So turn around and get out of here."

"No can do, man. I got a contract to fill." Teo couldn't get over how calm Remo sounded—in his position, facing off against surly armed guards, he would've been crapping himself. But Remo was convincingly playing the stoned driver of a taco truck. "I gotta get it all set up before the party, you know?"

"What party?" the first guard asked, at the same instant

that Boss Man barked, "Aw, hell. What now?"

Teo pictured what they were seeing: a long line of cars streaming down the road toward the warehouse. If everything was going as planned, there should be dozens of them.

One of the guards swore—Boss Man again, from the sound of it. The click of a walkie-talkie, then he barked, "Control, we got a problem out here. Gonna need backup."

In the dark depths of the truck, Daisy squeezed his hand. Teo caught the glint of light off her teeth—she was smiling.

He wished he could share her confidence.

Footsteps moved away from the truck as more music drifted through the open front windows, an eclectic mix, all blaring equally loudly.

In the front seat, Remo tapped his fingers against the steering wheel, keeping time with the bass line. "All right back there?" he asked without turning around.

"Yeah," Daisy said. "We're cool."

Teo didn't say anything. He felt as far from cool as he'd ever been.

"Good." Remo's hands fell still as he announced, "Time for phase two."

Noa scurried along behind Zeke, bent double as she ran. The moon was a narrow sliver overhead; it was so dark she wished they'd invested in night-vision goggles. She tripped and nearly went sprawling a dozen times, just barely managing to stay on her feet as they crossed the half mile of desert in a little over ten minutes.

They stopped behind a saguaro cactus that tilted sideways, as if engaged in a slow free fall. Together, they took in the chaotic scene.

"Bet they're wishing they'd rented a place with a fence

right about now," Zeke chuckled.

The lack of a fence was precisely what had given Noa the idea for the raid. And on his end, Peter had come through spectacularly. At least three dozen cars and trucks were parked at all angles around the facility, most with their head-lights on and music blasting. Kids scantily clad in club gear were milling around; five overwhelmed security guards wove between them, yelling for them to leave. A few of the kids were openly mocking the guards. A cluster had gathered around the taco truck, where Daisy and Teo were frenetically passing out free tacos and beer to the gathering crowd. Still others were circling the building, looking for a way in.

Noa couldn't help but smile. So far, so good—everything was going according to plan. Peter had posted a message on every Phoenix party board he could find, claiming a squat-ter party—an underground techno music festival—would be happening after midnight at the warehouse. To sweeten the pot, he'd hinted that a famous LA DJ would be spinning.

Noa had worried that not enough people would show up. But a few hundred kids thronged the grounds already, and a steady stream of headlights approached from the highway. The response was better than she'd dared hope.

"Perfect," Noa breathed.

"Yup," Zeke said. Still, he eyed the guards warily. "Think they'll pull their guns? We don't want anyone to get hurt."

"No chance." Noa shook her head. "The guards won't risk an incident—P&D would flip out."

"And they can't call the cops either, obviously." Zeke tapped her shoulder. "I ever tell you you're a genius, Torson?"

"Not lately, no," she said, flushing at the praise. Even better, the awkwardness between them seemed to have com-pletely dissipated.

"So what're we waiting for?" he asked. "Let's get in there."

They slipped into the parking lot and were quickly immersed by the mob. Noa could see the taco truck parked about twenty feet from the front door. Zeke nodded at her, and they made their way to the entrance.

"Open the door!" someone called out. The cry was picked up and repeated, until hundreds of voices were chanting, "Open up!" A few girls screamed the name of the DJ.

As if on cue, a pulsing bass line started throbbing from inside the building. The crowd roared its approval.

"Right on time," Zeke shouted in her ear.

Noa grinned. *Way to go, Peter.* One of the things he'd discovered in the building blueprints was an intercom system that could be hijacked wirelessly. Using it, he was able to blast club music from every speaker in the building. It was tinny, and wouldn't fool the crowd for long—they'd be expecting a real sound system, the kind a professional DJ employed. But this seemed to be working just as well. The crowd was quickly being whipped into a frenzy.

She checked her watch. The music had been playing for two minutes. They were banking on the fact that the guards would react slowly, with no clue how to handle a mob of unruly teenagers. Still, she'd told Peter that once the music started, they'd have to get inside quickly.

Just as she was starting to grow concerned, someone yelled, "The door just opened!"

"Yes!" Zeke whooped beside her.

Noa offered a silent thanks to Peter. She could picture him hunched over a keyboard in a parking lot somewhere, sifting through the building schematics until he reached the grid that controlled the electric door locks. The warehouse was outfitted with lots of bells and whistles—some starry-eyed developer must have hoped it would one day house Department of Defense contractors. All that technology had probably been what attracted Pike & Dolan to the property; on the surface, it appeared far more impenetrable than the basic building where she'd been held.

Of course, Pike & Dolan hadn't factored in hackers when they selected it. *Too bad for them*, Noa thought. A high-tech building was a godsend, especially one with locks that could be controlled remotely.

"They've come for a party," Noa muttered. "Let's give them one."

The crowd surged toward the open door, a bottleneck forming as kids pushed and shoved one another in their haste to get in. She and Zeke broke into a trot, swept along by the tide of partiers. What they were wearing didn't really qualify as club gear, but no one seemed to notice.

"Everyone should be in position," Zeke said directly into her ear, one of his arms forming a protective barrier around her to fend off the worst of the shoving.

Noa nodded. "Five minutes, in and out," she said.

"All right." Zeke set his jaw and swiped a hand through his lank black hair. "Let's do this."

Peter sat in his car with his laptop open, the monitor casting the interior in a luminous white glow. Occasionally the screen wobbled as his leg started reflexively bouncing, a nervous habit he'd had since he was a kid. He had to repeatedly concentrate on stilling it.

He was parked in the neighbor's driveway again. As a concession to the freezing temperatures, tonight he was running the heater.

The controls for the Phoenix warehouse dominated the

screen. He'd created a mirror of the mainframe, so he was seeing everything the security guard in the control room was privy to.

And if he was that guy right now, Peter reflected, he'd be seriously freaking out.

He'd scoped out this system earlier, once Noa had announced that she was moving up the raid. Disseminating the party message had been the easy part; the DJ had been his idea, too. Based on everything he'd promised, the grounds should be swarming with club kids.

He was pumping techno through speakers situated throughout the building, and both the front and rear exit doors were locked in the open position. Whoever was manning the real control room kept frantically trying to close them again; every few seconds the computer would ask for approval, and he'd click the button denying it. "Sorry, dude," he said out loud. "As the new administrator, I'm going to have to say no to your request. Loser."

In another open window, he was monitoring the Phoenix police department's radio transmissions, making sure the guards hadn't called in outside help. So far, no patrols had been summoned to the area. He doubted they would be; Pike & Dolan was unlikely to allow the authorities anywhere near their illegal lab. But he kept an eye on it anyway, figuring it couldn't hurt to cover every angle.

Aside from frustrating some jerk in a uniform two thousand miles away, Peter didn't have much to do. He tapped his index finger beside the trackpad. He'd love to be able to see what was happening right now. The security cameras Noa had spotted on her recon must all be closed circuit, because he hadn't been able to find any evidence of them on the mainframe. Which was a shame. It would've been helpful to be able to see throughout the building, so he could direct them better. His thoughts drifted back to the spy store. Maybe next time, he could persuade Noa to wear some sort of minicamera. . . .

Imagining her reaction to a helmet cam, Peter laughed. He'd have a better chance of getting her to stage a raid while wearing a prom gown. A red light flashed on-screen, and he tapped the button to deny access again. "Nope, still not happening for you, man."

He really hoped the guy in the control room was tearing his hair out. He'd constructed a whole fantasy where it was Mason losing it, jumping up and down as he pounded at controls that refused to respond, his normally slicked-back hair sticking out in all directions.

An override button appeared on his screen, and Peter let out a low whistle. "Ooh, nice," he said. "Trying to circumvent the main computer from a different terminal? Great idea, man. Inspired." Peter tapped a series of buttons, then hit the return key with a flourish as he said, "Unfortunately, you are once again . . . denied."

Teo had slipped into autopilot mode, mindlessly filling red plastic cups and passing them across the counter as fast as possible.

They'd already gone through one keg and were well on their way to emptying another. He was kind of floored by how many people had shown up. When Noa outlined her plan, he'd thought it was ridiculous. He'd never even heard of a squatter party—hell, in the past year he hadn't been to anything that qualified as a "party." It was a little overwhelming to face a swarm of fresh-faced kids, all smiling and laughing and teasing one another. For a minute, he felt almost normal. Like he'd slipped into an alternate version of his life, where he was the cool guy handing out free beer.

Daisy was moving just as fast, doling out the tacos they'd bought in bulk. Her cheeks were flushed, and every time he caught her eye she gave him a broad grin.

"This is fun, right?" she said at one point, hollering to be heard over the din.

Teo nodded back. She was right, it was fun. So fun he'd almost forgotten the real reason they were here.

Remo had slipped away as soon as they'd opened the side panel to start serving food. He'd probably already met up with the others at the back of the building. Noa and Zeke were supposed to enter through the front with the crowd. The plan was for both groups to infiltrate, neutralize (Noa's term, not his) any remaining guards, and search for captured kids. Then everyone would exit out the back, where the van would be waiting.

Noa had explained that in the confusion, the guards would waste valuable time trying to get a grip on the situation. By the time these kids realized there was no awesome party head-lined by a famous DJ, their team would be miles away.

At least, that was the plan.

Teo was grateful that his part in it was limited to passing out beer. Just a few more minutes, then their orders were to pack up fast and drive to the meet spot.

Teo allowed himself a flicker of hope. If most of the raids went like this, then they didn't seem all that dangerous. In the van that night, Noa hadn't said anything, but there was a look of absolute calm on her face. She seemed totally con-fident and collected—and he'd finally understood why they all followed her. Why he'd go along tonight, too, even though he was terrified. Because despite the fact that they were all just a bunch of kids, she made them an army.

Suddenly, a meaty hand grabbed his wrist. Startled, Teo dropped the cup he'd been holding. A guard in a khaki security uniform had reached across the counter; he held Teo's wrist in an iron grip. He was older, in his forties maybe, his face and bald spot bright red with rage.

"Stop passing out booze!" the guard yelled, glaring at them.

Teo recognized his voice: Boss Man. Daisy leaned over the counter and flashed him a broad grin. "Want a taco?"

"You need to leave!" With his free hand, Boss Man straight-armed a bunch of kids who were trying to get around him. "Now!"

"Sorry, sir," Teo said, trying to mimic Remo's casual tone. "They're paying us to do this."

"Who's paying you?" Boss Man's eyes narrowed.

Luckily, they had a cover story for that. "Gila Sound System."

"Gila what?" The guard growled. Meanwhile, the kids around him were getting restless. Apparently unimpressed by the fact that he was armed, they jostled him harder. A few shouted for him to get out of the way.

These kids sure like their free beer, Teo thought. He shrugged. "That's all I know, sir. Just doing my job."

"Listen, you little punk." Boss Man's face went a few shades redder. "You and your little girlfriend better get this truck out of here or—"

Whatever he was about to threaten them with was abruptly cut off by a muffled boom from within the building. The crowd fell silent.

The guard's head snapped around. He released Teo's hand and scrambled through the crowd, forcing his way toward the building.

Daisy's eyes had gone wide. "What was that?"

"I don't know," Teo said, puzzled. There hadn't been any mention of an explosion in the plan, and that's what it had sounded like—a big one, too.

"Should we go?" she asked uncertainly.

Teo hesitated. Noa had given them strict instructions to get out of there immediately if anything went wrong. And the crowd had started dispersing, which wasn't good. He overheard mutters about "bombs" and "cops." "Let's give them another minute," he finally said.

Daisy nodded, no longer looking like she was enjoying herself.

CHAPTER NINE

Peter frowned—a red light had just popped up on the warehouse monitors. *Fire alert?* Noa hadn't mentioned anything about starting a fire.

He hurriedly clicked through a few panels to make sure the local fire department wasn't automatically contacted by the building's systems. Fortunately, he couldn't detect any sort of outgoing signal—Pike & Dolan had been smart enough to sever the links to emergency crews. Still, red lights flared across the screen now, indicating that the warehouse was rapidly filling with smoke.

Peter sat back helplessly. Now more than ever, he wished he had some way of knowing what was going on. Disturbing images flashed through his mind: Noa hurt, trapped in a smoke-filled room. Mason's minions swooping in and capturing her again.

Peter's legs jiggled. Noa was too valuable to be running these raids. Pike & Dolan had already proved they would stop at nothing to capture her again.

He breathed out hard and went back to the main screen. Now the whole thing was flashing red—based on that, it would be amazing if the building survived. "Noa," Peter murmured aloud, "get the hell out of there."

The chattering crowd swept Noa and Zeke down a narrow corridor. Fluorescent lights burned brightly overhead, glaring off the white walls and floors. This facility was more reminiscent of a hospital than the warehouse where Noa had been held.

Still, it made her shudder. She'd experienced a similar reaction during prior raids. An oppressive sense of claustrophobia, the walls closing in. Her wrist itched where her bracelet used to rest, and a tide of panic rose in her chest.

She fought it back down.

"All good?" Zeke asked, eyeing her with concern.

Noa nodded and said, "Yeah," even though she felt faint and nauseous.

The stream of teens slowed as they wound deeper into the building. Around them, kids were starting to protest; this wasn't the club scene they'd expected. No black lights or neon decorations, and the music sounded tinny and fake. The hallway was lined with doors on either side. Noa checked one as they passed: locked. She swore under her breath. Peter had promised to override the interior locks—hopefully he'd succeed by the time they reached their target.

And then: a loud boom from the depths of the building.

The crowd abruptly stopped moving and fell silent. "What was that?" Zeke asked.

Noa shook her head, puzzled. The whole building had shaken, and there had been a distant *whomp. Like a bomb*, she thought with a frown. But her team was only armed with Tasers and pepper spray. A needle of fear wormed inside her: Had the guards counterattacked? Were her people okay?

Noa felt a tremor beneath her feet. The teens in the lead suddenly surged back, screaming. They were chased by a wave of dark, noxious smoke.

The hall rapidly descended into a melee: people pressed into them from behind, forcing them deeper into the building, while, simultaneously, panicked kids tried to push back toward the front door. Noa gasped as she took an elbow to the ribs—then something slammed into her back and she went down, hitting her head hard against the wall.

She was lifted forcibly by the elbow. Woozily, she looked up: Zeke. It took a second for her to make out what he was shouting. "We have to get out of here. Now!"

The hallway was rapidly filling with smoke.

Her parents had died in a fire. And for a moment, she was back there with them: strapped into a car seat, staring at a jagged window as smoke writhed and coiled around her, heat searing her skin. . . .

Noa fought for air as her throat closed up. She could hear Zeke yelling, and felt the press of bodies all around her, but they seemed far away.

She barely reacted as Zeke hauled her along. They were suddenly next to one of the locked doors off the hallway. Zeke's hand released, and Noa dropped down, her knees crumpling beneath her.

Cool air. She opened her eyes.

They were in a utility closet filled with metal shelving stocked with plastic jugs of bleach, floor polish, and cleaning rags. Noa blinked, trying to clear her vision. Her head throbbed, but she didn't think it was a concussion; she was just a little stunned. Zeke was beside her, panting hard. He still held her arm.

"I'm okay," Noa said, fingering the lump on the side of her head.

"Yeah?" He regarded her with concern. "Because you just froze. I've never seen you like that."

"I hit my head," Noa said. "But I'm fine."

Zeke threw her a skeptical look, but she wasn't about to explain the rest, at least not now. Noa swallowed hard—her throat tasted sooty, and she wished she'd brought along a water bottle. "What happened?"

"Damned if I know," Zeke growled. "Someone set a fire."

"Apparently," she said drily. The noise in the corridor was abating; most of the club kids had probably made it out by now.

"So." Zeke looked at her expectantly. "What now?"

Noa glanced at her watch. Four minutes had elapsed since they'd entered the building. "Remo?" she said into her radio. "Do you copy?"

No response.

She exchanged a worried glance with Zeke, then tried to raise Teo.

Nothing but static.

Noa chewed her lip. Had the radios stopped working again?

If the other team had stuck to the timetable, they should be returning to the van, where Crystal was waiting. But without radio contact, she had no way of knowing where they were.

"We should just get out," Zeke said. "Leave through the

back, cut across the desert if the van is gone. Hell, the fire department might actually be on the way—"

"They're not," Noa interrupted. "P&D wouldn't be that stupid."

"The doors were all still locked, Noa. I had to pick this one. Checking the other rooms would take hours." He bent down beside her. "We're going to have to call this one a wash."

"Three minutes," she said firmly. "If we don't find anyone by then, we're out of here."

Reluctantly, he nodded. Noa pushed off the wall, easing back to her feet. The air in the small room was smoky—she wondered how much worse it had gotten in the hallway. She experienced a moment of self-doubt; was she nuts, insisting they go ahead with this even though the building was on fire?

Probably, she thought. Still, she pulled her scarf up over the lower half of her face and motioned for him to open the door.

Peter focused intently on the monitor as his fingers flew across the keyboard. As soon as the fire had started, some sort of override kicked in and every interior door in the place had rebolted. Which meant that if Noa and her team were still inside, the chances of them salvaging anything out of this mission were just about nil.

At least his adversary in the control room wasn't trying to stymie him anymore. "Couldn't handle the heat, huh, buddy?" Peter muttered as he worked. "Maybe Mason isn't paying you enough after all."

He clicked through a series of commands, trying to reset the parameters so that the doors would open. The building's systems were battling his efforts: Someone had done a decent job with the initial software, making sure that in the event of an emergency everything locked down. While Peter could appreciate the wisdom behind that, it was making his life a lot harder.

And Noa's, he reminded himself. She was in there some-where. What the hell had happened? Had Noa's team set the fire intentionally, to create a distraction? Or had something gone wrong?

A flashing window in the upper-right corner caught his eye: Crap, the doors had locked again. Peter forced himself to focus, digging back into the controls to unlatch them again.

The corridor was devoid of people, but filled with a dark, heavy cloud of smoke, which billowed down the hall, descending halfway to the ground. Noa felt the primal terror rising again, threatening to overwhelm her. With great effort, she tamped it down and said, "That's the way we have to go, right?"

"Based on the blueprints, yeah." Zeke's voice was muffled by his scarf. "You sure about going through with this? Daisy and Teo are probably still out front. Last chance to bail."

In response, Noa dove into the wall of smoke.

Immediately, her eyes started tearing. The heat was so intense she could practically feel her skin crisping. The front door was probably still propped open, and the fire raced toward it as the most accessible oxygen supply. It was impos-sible to see more than a few inches in any direction. Noa pressed her right hand against the wall and used it to guide herself along, moving at a slow jog.

Based on the building schematics, this corridor should dead-end at another that ran perpendicular to it. And accord-ing to the wattage usage, also courtesy of Peter, two sections of the building consumed the bulk of electrical power. One was the control room.

The other was a suite of rooms set in the exact center of the building, along the hallway they were approaching. Smart money said that all that power was being gobbled up by medical equipment.

But would there be anyone left alive in there?

Her hand suddenly slid off the wall into open air. She'd reached the adjoining hallway.

Zeke bumped into her from behind; he was coughing hard. The smoke seemed to be dissipating, although she could still hear the fire raging deeper in the building. It was easier to breathe through the bandanna, though, and her eyes were able to focus blearily.

Doors were set on either side of the hallway, identical to the ones they'd passed on their way in. "We need to check each room," she said.

Zeke was barely visible through the shimmering smoke cloud, but his head shifted slightly and he stepped away from her.

Every breath left a sharp, bitter aftertaste in her mouth. Ash coated the back of her throat, which felt swollen and sore.

While approaching the door, Noa slipped her jacket sleeve over her hand, remembering that you were supposed to do that in case the handle was hot. Not that the thin cotton offered much protection, but at least she'd be able to yank her hand back without leaving a layer of skin behind.

She issued a short prayer that Peter had managed to unlock these doors.

The knob wasn't cool, but it didn't burn her. She twisted it to the right, and the door opened.

Noa peeked inside. No guards, which was good. But no one else, either. The room was bare, save for a stripped-down hospital bed and an empty IV stand.

She closed the door behind her and tried the next one down the hall, following the same drill: It was exactly the same. Empty bed, empty IV stand, no signs of life. By the fourth room, Noa was starting to despair. In most of their prior raids, there had been clear evidence that the facilities were active. They'd recovered at least a half dozen kids at each site. Some were too far gone to be saved, but they'd managed to get them out anyway.

Whatever patients had been held here were apparently long gone. Or maybe it hadn't even been used yet.

There are all those guards, though, Noa reminded herself. Overkill for a building in the middle of nowhere if there was nothing inside.

She heard a shout and reflexively dropped into a crouch, her hands darting to her Taser and pepper spray. Figures emerged from the smoky recesses of the hall.

Noa tensed, ready to strike. Before she could react, she recognized the person in the lead: Remo. Janiqua and Danny were behind him. They were covered in soot, their eyes startlingly white in contrast. And there was a grim set to their jaws.

Her shoulders sagged with relief. It was the team that had entered through the back of the building. But where had they been all this time?

"What the hell happened?" Remo demanded. "You didn't say anything about a fire."

"It wasn't us." Noa automatically checked over her team: They looked filthy and tense, but no one appeared hurt, which was a relief.

"Well, it wasn't us, either," Janiqua chimed in.

"We gotta get out of here," Remo said urgently. "Teo and Daisy probably already took off."

"I'm almost done," Noa responded. "Did you pass Zeke? He was going to check the rooms down the hall."

"Didn't see him, and we didn't find anything," Remo said. "There's no one here. C'mon, let's—"

A shout from behind interrupted him. Zeke staggered into view, carrying a girl in a hospital gown. Her feet trailed along the floor as he dragged her. "A little help!" he called out.

Remo and Danny rushed over. Two other kids emerged from the haze: a teenage girl and a young boy. Dressed in matching hospital gowns, they clutched each other's hands.

Noa felt a wave of relief. There were kids here, and they were alive. She'd done the right thing by going ahead with the operation.

As Remo and Danny lugged the girl between them, making a sling of their arms, Noa yelled, "Any others?"

The new kids stared at her. She realized how she must look, covered in soot with a bandanna over her mouth. She yanked it down and repeated, "Are you alone here, or are there others?"

"Just us, I think," said the girl. She was nearly as tall as Noa, sixteen or seventeen years old. The kid clutching her hand couldn't have been more than twelve. Blond hair hung over his eyes, nearly covering them.

"You're sure?"

A look that she couldn't read passed between the two of them, then the girl said with more certainty, "Yeah, it's just us."

"Okay." Noa had checked all the rooms on her side of the

hall. She'd have to trust that Zeke had done the same.

Remo paused at the intersection of the corridors. "Which way?"

"Probably still guards out front," Noa said.

"The fire's bad back the way we came," Janiqua said fearfully. "We couldn't get to the van, so we headed this way."

"Shouldn't there be sprinklers or something?" Remo asked.

"Maybe they turned them off," Noa said, not adding what she was thinking, that the goal had been to smoke them out. This might have been a setup all along.

Noa's mind raced to come up with alternate exits. If only she could call Peter. He was probably sitting in front of the schematics right now, with a clear view of their options.

"Wasn't there a loading bay?" Zeke asked.

"Yes!" Noa said, suddenly flashing on it. "It was near the control room, though, so we decided not to use it."

"Well, I don't think we have a choice now."

Noa took in their ragged little group. There were at least five armed guards clustered around the building. If the club kids had taken off, the van would stick out like a sore thumb. They'd left Crystal behind to man the wheel—hopefully she'd been smart enough to move it. If they lost that van . . .

First things first, Noa thought. She needed to know where the rest of her team was. She unclipped the radio from her belt. "Teo? Daisy? Crystal? Does anyone read?"

A pause, then Crystal said in a panicked voice, "What the hell happened? The whole building's burning!"

"Crystal, where are you?" Noa said.

A longer pause, then Crystal sounding abashed as she said, "I'm about a mile away. When all the cars took off, I followed them. I wasn't sure—"

"That's good," Noa said, relieved. "You did the right thing. Have you seen the taco truck?"

"Not yet. It was still there when I left."

Noa frowned. Teo and Daisy were supposed to pull up stakes immediately if anything went wrong, and to leave within five minutes of the building breach even if it hadn't. So what the hell were they doing out there? And why hadn't they answered when she radioed?

She hesitated for a second, frozen by indecision. Zeke met her eyes, and she could tell he was thinking the same thing. "Someone set that fire," he said in a low voice.

"It was us."

"What?" Noa spun.

The tall girl had spoken. Her hospital gown was too long; it draped past her knees. "I set fire to an oxygen tank. I figured it would create enough of a distraction for us to escape. But then the doors all locked again, and we couldn't get out. Until he showed up," she finished, jerking her head toward Zeke.

Noa felt a flare of admiration. It probably wouldn't have occurred to her to do something like that. The fact that the guards had nothing to do with the fire was a relief, too. Maybe they had a shot at getting out of here after all. "Crystal, I want you to drive back."

"What?" Crystal's voice crackled. "But—"

"Drive fast and go straight to the south side of the building."

"Are you sure? Because—"

"Just do it! We'll be there soon." Noa clicked off, ignoring the stream of protests still issuing from the handheld. She had to get them through this maze of corridors to the control room, then past that and out through a loading bay. All with an unknown number of guards between them and the exit.

Noa tightened her grip on the Taser and pepper spray. "All right," she said, trying to inject more certainty into her voice than she felt. "I'll lead, the rest of you stay close."

They didn't look happy about it, but no one protested. Noa tugged her bandanna up and dove back into the wall of smoke.

"Oh my God, oh my God, oh my God . . ."

Daisy wouldn't stop wailing. She was doing it quietly, but it was only a matter of time before the guards came back. Teo could hear gravel flying as cars skidded out of the parking lot. Soon, they'd be the only ones left.

They were sitting ducks.

"Daisy, c'mon!" he said, shaking her by the elbows. She was huddled on the floor of the truck behind the counter, arms wrapped around her knees as she rocked back and forth.

He checked his watch again. It had been eight minutes since the music started inside the building, so they should have left three minutes ago. But Daisy was supposed to drive the van. He'd do it instead, but he'd never learned how. As a foster kid, he hadn't exactly had a car and driver's ed at his disposal.

Daisy was still unresponsive, though, and any minute now those guards would be coming back. He had to do something.

Teo got stiffly to his feet and awkwardly climbed through the gap into the driver's seat. Keys dangled from the ignition, which was a good sign. But the stick shift was not. He had a basic grasp of how to drive an automatic, but a standard? He didn't know the first thing about that.

"Daisy?" he called pleadingly. "I really need you up here!"

No response, except for her continued murmuring.

Teo peered through the windshield. The parking lot was smoky, and nearly empty; the stream of kids from inside the building had slowed to a trickle. The last few were rushing toward the remaining vehicles looking frantic and terrified. The atmosphere of gaiety had vanished, and a pall as heavy as the smoke hung over the scene. No sign of the guards— maybe they'd gone back inside the building?

A strange crackling sound from the passenger seat. He frowned, perplexed, then suddenly realized: *the radio!* He picked it up and pressed the button on the side. "Um, hello?"

A faint voice emitted from the speaker. Teo fumbled with the unit, finally locating the volume knob and dialing it all the way up. This time, when Noa spoke, her words were clear. "Where the hell are you guys? We need you, now!"

CHAPTER TEN

oa cursed. Teo had finally answered the radio, but it didn't sound like any help would be coming from that direction. He didn't know how to drive, and apparently Daisy had gone catatonic. Crystal had driven nearly to the highway before pulling off the road to await further orders. *Not much of an army*, Noa couldn't help thinking. Sure, they weren't trained soldiers, but she hadn't expected a total meltdown at the first sign of trouble. It was her own fault—she should have had a better backup plan.

Her eyes flitted across the faces staring expectantly at her: seven teens, one of whom was unconscious. Not exactly an inconspicuous group. They didn't have a prayer of slipping out among the club kids, if there were even any left outside.

Which meant somehow getting past the guards who remained in the building. Her stomach knotted with tension and fear. The other raids they'd pulled off had all gone smoothly; they'd overwhelmed the few guards quickly, and no one had gotten hurt. Now she had to face the possibility that they might not all make it out of here. Worse yet, Project Persephone might catch her again. She could end the night drugged and dumped back on a table.

At that thought she drew a deep breath, resolve hardening in her chest. No way she was going to let that happen.

"Well? We going or what?" Remo demanded.

She could tell by the strain on his face that carrying the girl, even though she was tiny, was taking a toll. The rest of the teens wore expressions raging from concern to terror. Only Zeke gazed at her calmly, as if he had utter faith in her ability to steer them out of this mess.

"I'll lead," Noa said. "Zeke, you take the rear. The rest of you stay together. Remo, I need your hands free. Danny and Janiqua, take the girl."

Some grumbling at that, but if they did encounter any obstacles, Noa trusted Remo to keep his head. After a second they complied, with Janiqua stepping forward to take the weight of the girl.

"Damn, she's heavy," she grumbled under her breath. "Should we even bother? She looks—"

"We're taking her," Noa snapped. Even if the girl was suffering through the final stages of PEMA, they weren't going to leave her here to be subjected to more "tests." "Now let's go. Gear out and ready."

She gripped her Taser and pepper spray as she led the way toward the south side of the building. The next three short hallways should lead to the control room, and the loading bay was just past it. Maybe they'd even get lucky and find a vehicle there.

Noa trotted down the corridor briskly, trying to ignore the clock ticking off each second in her head. They'd been inside for at least ten minutes. The smoke was dissipating; a curtain of it shrouded the ceiling, but it didn't feel like every breath was piercing her chest anymore.

Their footsteps were painfully loud against the tiled floor. If guards were waiting up ahead, they might as well be announcing their approach with a bullhorn.

They made it down the first hall, then the second, without encountering another soul. The lights were still on, the fluorescent bulbs making the bright white walls and floor throb painfully against her sore red eyes. By the time they reached the turnoff to the third corridor, the smoke had completely disappeared.

Noa held up a hand, stopping the others. The control room should be right around the next corner. She had no idea what it would look like; the blueprints had only marked it by name, without detailing whether or not it was closed off from the hall, or facing it with picture windows. She knew which option she preferred.

Noa eased her head around. Her heart sank. Worst-case scenario: The white wall ended in an enormous plate-glass window that stretched from waist height to the ceiling.

Worse yet, the door stood open, with two guards directly in front of it. The smaller one was dressing down the other guy, waving his arms and shouting about screwups. The guy hulking over him had his head bowed. Both were wearing khaki uniforms and had guns in hip holsters. Standard rent-a-cops, the only distinction being that no patches or insignia identified the company they worked for.

The set of double doors behind them should lead to the loading dock.

Noa ducked back and considered their options. They could rush them, but even if they managed to quickly overwhelm one guard, the other would have plenty of time to draw his weapon. And there might be more guards in the control room.

Deciding, she waved Zeke forward and whispered in his ear. He grimaced when she told him her plan, but nodded. She leaned past him and hissed at Remo, "Stay here, we'll handle the guards."

Remo's brow furrowed, but he nodded and raised his Taser.

She and Zeke stood. "Ready?" she asked in a low voice.

"It's a good night to die," he muttered under his breath.

"Not helpful," Noa countered as she slung an arm around his waist. Together, they stepped around the corner into the hallway, in plain view of the guards.

Teo was undergoing the worst crash course in the history of driving. He'd managed to get the engine started, and was pretty sure he had one foot on the clutch, but every time he shifted into first gear there was a terrible grinding noise and the truck lurched forward, then stopped. They'd only moved a foot, and now the parking lot was entirely devoid of other cars.

Through the windshield he could see Boss Man striding purposefully toward them, his hand resting on the butt of his gun.

"Hey, Daisy?" he called desperately. "This would be a really great time to pull yourself together."

She sniffled, but didn't answer.

"Great," Teo muttered. Jaw tight, he pressed the pedal on the left to the floor again, and let it out slowly as he tried to shift into first.

The engine stalled again. *Crap.*

The guard was almost upon them, approaching the driver's side window. Teo raised a hand and forced a weak smile, but he could tell the guard wasn't buying it.

"Toss the keys out the window, son," Boss Man called, stopping a foot away and drawing his gun. His face was florid, and streams of sweat coursed down it. "You and me are gonna have a little talk."

"I-I've really got to get the truck back," Teo said weakly.

"Do you now?" The guy's eyes narrowed. "'Cause it looks like you don't have a clue how to drive that thing. Which makes me wonder how you got hired to work it."

"I usually just hand out tacos."

"Sure you do." He wiggled his fingers. "Toss me the keys. Then you and your girlfriend get out nice and slow with your hands on your head."

Teo sucked in a deep breath. So this was it. He flashed back on what the others had said about the fate of captured kids—he should have run away when he had the chance. At least Daisy had finally stopped wailing.

"I said get out!" Boss Man repeated, his nostrils flaring.

Slowly, Teo raised both hands off the steering wheel and reached for the keys. As he did, the radio beside him crackled again. "Hello? Teo?"

The guard's brow furrowed. "The hell's that?"

"Nothing, it's just—" Teo frantically searched for an explanation. "My boss," he finished lamely.

"Yeah? On a radio? Toss that out the window, too, boy." The guard extended a hand for it.

Teo scooped the radio off the seat beside him. As he moved to hand it over, a voice in his ear said, "Duck."

Obligingly, Teo dropped to the side. As he did, the guard's

eyes widened. Daisy's arm extended past him; she was holding something. Small barbs shot out from it and latched on to the front of the guard's khaki shirt. His eyes popped open even wider and he went completely stiff, then dropped to the ground. Taser wires trailed out the window to him.

"About time," Teo muttered.

Daisy nudged his shoulder. "Sorry. Now move, so I can get us out of here."

"Noa wants us to pick them up," Teo said, sliding over with relief.

"Pick them up? Where?" Daisy asked as she climbed behind the wheel.

Teo looked past her. Boss Man was lying on the ground twitching, his face contorted with pain. "At the loading dock."

"What about the van?" Daisy asked. "Isn't Crystal supposed to get them?" The engine sputtered to life. Teo watched as she depressed the brake pedal, then slowly released the clutch while shifting into first. As the truck eased forward, he thought, *So that's how you do it.*

"I don't know, there wasn't exactly a lot of time to talk."

"Well, did she say which side it's on? The building's huge."

Daisy sounded annoyed, which irked him. If she hadn't completely lost it, they wouldn't even still be here. He resisted the temptation to point that out, instead saying, "The south side."

"Well, that's helpful," Daisy grumbled. "You have any idea which way is south?"

Teo swallowed hard. "No."

"F'in fantastic." Daisy sighed. "I guess we'll have to circle the whole place." As they slowly rolled toward the warehouse, she glanced in the side mirror. "Crap."

"What?"

"The guard's getting back up. And he looks pissed."

Peter had given up on trying to keep his legs still. The power was fading on his laptop; the low battery alert flashed steadily, and he'd forgotten to bring a car charger. He was staring at the screen, trying to interpret what was happening in Phoenix.

Suddenly, the computer shut down.

He stared at the blank screen for a few seconds, then slammed the laptop closed.

According to the clock on his dashboard, it was 3:20 a.m. The raid had started nearly a half hour earlier. Noa and her team should be back at their safe house by now, but he hadn't heard anything. And he should've. Noa always posted an encoded message in their chat room after a successful mission, letting him know that everything had gone off without a hitch.

And now that his computer was dead, he had no way of checking.

Peter rubbed his eyes; they felt sore and gritty. He was supposed to meet Amanda for breakfast in five hours. He planned on finally sharing his fears about her condition, and he'd prefer to be relatively well rested for that conversation. But even though he was exhausted, he doubted he'd be able to sleep tonight. Worry chewed at him; the sense of impotence had never hit him more strongly.

Peter tapped his finger on the top of the laptop, considering. Maybe he could risk checking in from home. He'd take every precaution, routing through VPNs to hide his IP address. And he wouldn't log on for long, just check once an hour until he received confirmation that Noa was okay.

It'll be fine, he told himself. It was unlikely that Pike &

Dolan were monitoring his internet usage in the middle of the night anyway.

Peter turned on the ignition and rolled back down the driveway. He'd send Amanda a text asking to meet for lunch instead. Delaying it a few hours couldn't possibly make a difference, right?

CHAPTER ELEVEN

oa's heart hammered in her chest as they staggered down the hall. She clutched Zeke's arm and giggled; it came out sounding incredibly fake. He was looking down at her with grave eyes, an equally forced smile glued to his face.

They made it halfway before being noticed. "Hey!"

Noa looked up. Both guards were staring at them, their expressions puzzled and put out.

"Man, you're old," she said, stumbling slightly. "You here for the party, too?"

Zeke squeezed her arm, and she kept moving forward. It was a desperate charade; they were covered in soot, who would believe they were just a couple of stoned teenagers here for a rave?

"Hey, where's DJ Leo?" Zeke demanded. "He should be spinning by now."

Noa admired the steadiness in his voice. They were still ten feet from the guards—too far for the Tasers.

"You're not supposed to be here," the shorter guy growled. "How the hell did you get in?"

"How the hell did you get in?" Noa mimicked, then giggled again.

Zeke drawled, "Dude, chill. You know what you need? The little blue pill. Right, Jenny?"

"Oh, yeah," Noa agreed, nodding. "The little blue pills are, like, totally awesome." The nearest guard stood a few feet from the door, and the other one still blocked it. They had to get to the control room window; she needed to know if anyone else was inside before they acted.

"You don't get out of here now, I'm calling the cops," the guard ordered.

Noa lurched forward, closing the distance between them. She grabbed his arm to steady herself, simultaneously yanking his hand off the gun. He staggered under her weight—she was a few inches taller, high enough to see the hair plugs dotting his scalp. "Oops!" she said. "I think I'm gonna puke."

"Aw, man. She always does that." Zeke shook his head. "Hey, you guys got a trash can or something?"

Noa shifted her head right. Through her peripheral vision, she could see into the control room. A bank of monitors displayed rotating images of the building's interior and exterior. Her breath caught as a shot of their ragtag group appeared in the upper-right-hand corner. The room was empty, though. Thank God the guards had been talking, otherwise they would have known exactly what was coming their way.

163

"Get off me!" the guard snarled, jerking his arm back. "Crazy bitch. I swear, I'm gonna—"

His words cut off abruptly as Noa jammed the Taser into the soft tissue at the base of his throat. His mouth opened and closed a few times like a fish. She jerked back—any contact with someone who had 1,200 volts shooting through their system would render her helpless, too. The guard fell to her feet, still twitching.

"Hey!" the other guard protested belatedly. Turning, Noa saw that Zeke was already on him. The guy's eyes rolled back and he dropped like a stone.

"Nice job," she said. "Little blue pills? Really?"

"What can I say, I'm a huge *Matrix* fan." He shrugged. "We could've used the flashbang, you know."

"Too much noise. It might've brought the others running."

"Your call." Zeke turned and hissed, "All clear!"

As the others hurried down the hall to meet them, Zeke bent over the guards, securing their hands behind their backs with plastic zip ties. This part of the raid, at least, was rote.

Noa scanned the control room. Spotting a nearly full can of soda beside the console, she picked it up and dumped it liberally over keyboards and towers. There was a satisfying hiss as fluid seeped into the electronics. The images on the monitors wavered, then went black.

"Not exactly the best use of your hacking skills," Zeke noted.

"Well, we're in a hurry," Noa muttered. She would've preferred to gather data off the server, but there was no time. More guards were lurking around here somewhere.

"Kidding. Sheesh." He grinned at her, clearly enjoying

himself again. Taking out a few guards always seemed to cheer him up.

"Let's go." Noa led the way out of the control room. The others waited silently in the hall outside. She pushed through the double doors, which opened onto a dimly lit, cavernous room. The ceiling soared to the full height of the warehouse. Twenty feet into the room the floor dropped off, right in front of a cargo bay with an enormous sliding metal door.

"All right!" Zeke said. "Now that's what I'm talking about."

"How do we get the door open?" Remo asked.

Good question, Noa thought, walking to the edge of the platform. There was some sort of motor attached to the base on the right-hand side. Motors weren't really her thing, unless they were attached to a motherboard.

"I got this." Zeke vaulted easily off the ledge and bent low, examining it. He pushed a few buttons, and with a grinding sound, the metal gate slowly started rising.

Noa closed her eyes, nearly overwhelmed with relief. She was going to get them all out. By now, the taco truck should be waiting on the other side. . . .

"Stop!" a voice yelled.

Noa turned. Two security guards stood just inside the double doors, pointing guns at them.

Teo clung to the door handle with a death grip. Daisy was careening around the building at a speed that the taco truck was clearly not designed for. As she swung the wheel left, his whole side of the truck lifted off the ground. The tires slammed back down on the pavement, but the tail protested, swinging out wide.

"We're going to flip!" he yelled. "Slow down!"

"Can't," Daisy grunted. "He'll catch us."

Sure enough, in his side mirror Teo could see the guard chugging after them, his hair sticking out in all directions. He was definitely gaining. Worse yet, his gun was raised. . . .

Ping! Something metal smacked into the side of the truck. Instinctively, Teo ducked.

"What was that?" Daisy yelled.

"He's shooting at us!" Teo screamed back.

Daisy jerked the wheel again, swinging the truck from side to side. Teo braced his knees against the dashboard; it felt like his arm was being ripped from his shoulder. The plastic food bins were sliding around in the back; there was a dull thud as a pony keg flipped over. *Looks like we won't be getting that security deposit back on the truck*, he couldn't help thinking as another *ping* resonated, perilously close to the cab judging by the sound of it.

"Can you see them?" she hollered.

"No!" Frantically, Teo scanned the side of the building. It was one long mass of brown brick; there was no sign of a loading dock. "It's not here!"

"Great. Just great," Daisy growled.

The barrage was increasing. Glancing back again, Teo saw that Boss Man had been joined by another guard. He appeared to be in much better shape, closing the gap with long strides as he shot at them. "Crap."

"What?" Daisy demanded.

"Nothing. Just keep driving."

Something groaned behind him. Spinning in his seat, Teo saw that the rear door had popped open. Through it he had a clear view of the guard as he raised his gun to shoulder height, leveled it, and fired.

Teo jerked back. The bullet sheared past the space where

his head had just been and hit the windshield, splintering it into a spiderweb of glass.

Definitely not getting that deposit back.

Daisy swore. They'd reached the back of the building. Tearing around the corner, the truck tilted crazily again, only righting after she struggled mightily with the wheel. As they approached the next corner, Teo closed his eyes and started praying. . . .

"All of you, get on the ground!" one of the guards yelled. Noa recognized him as the one who had been walking the perimeter earlier. The guy at his shoulder glared at them menacingly.

The kids looked at the guards, then back at her. Like they were expecting her to save them. Like there was still some way out of this, for all of them.

"No," Noa said, surprising herself.

"What?" The lead guard took a step forward. "I know you," he said, peering at her through the gloom. "They're looking for you."

Noa didn't say anything. She could feel a chill night breeze on her neck. The door was still rising behind her, and she was only a few feet away. She could drop, roll beneath it, and run. Maybe there weren't any guards left outside.

Zeke caught her eye. She could tell he was thinking the same thing. The two of them could make it. They had a pretty good sense of the surrounding landscape, enough to get away on foot. But it would mean leaving the others.

The guard stopped next to Janiqua and placed the barrel of his gun to her skull. The girl's whole body went rigid. The unconscious girl she was holding slumped to the floor. "Don't make me shoot her," he warned. "Just climb back up here, nice and easy."

Noa chewed her lip. If she capitulated, it would be over for all of them.

A tear slid down Janiqua's cheek. Noa sighed. Slowly, feeling like each foot weighed a thousand pounds, she walked back to the platform and placed both palms flat on it, braced to lift herself up.

As her heels pushed off the ground, there was a tremendous crash behind her and the shriek of brakes. Whirling, Noa saw the front of the taco truck jutting onto the loading dock. Its roof had collided with the gate, which ground to a halt. Daisy and Teo stared slack-jawed at her through a shattered windshield.

Everything seemed to slow down. The guards had been thrown off balance by the crash. Remo took advantage—he threw himself at the one who'd threatened to shoot Janiqua. Danny and the new girl thronged the other one. Zeke charged forward to help them, while shouting something that took a moment for her to discern.

"Throw the flashbang!"

Her brain finally processed what he was saying. Noa fumbled in her jacket pocket and drew out the grenade. She tore out the pin and hurled it; the flashbang bounced in between the nearest guard's legs before settling into a slow spin like a top. "Cover your ears and get to the truck!" she yelled.

The world around her exploded in noise and light. Even though she'd anticipated the blast, Noa's whole head throbbed from the concussion. Dizzily, she stumbled forward and grabbed the unconscious girl under the shoulders.

"Help me!" she shouted, dragging her toward the truck.

The pressure on her shoulder eased—Zeke was there, helping her carry the girl. Remo's feet were disappearing through the truck's windshield—he'd dived in headfirst.

Janiqua and Danny pushed past, following him.

Struggling with the weight, she and Zeke managed to get the girl off the ledge. Teo threw open the passenger door and helped muscle her inside. Noa spun to check on everyone. The guards were still down on the floor looking stunned—the grenade had gone off between them. Chances were they still couldn't see or hear very well. One was tearing at his eyes; the other clutched his head.

The young boy they'd found inside was standing right in front of them, looking dazed.

"Come on!" Noa shouted, waving for him to join them.

He hesitated.

"Hurry, we got company coming!" Teo yelled.

Looking terrified, the boy didn't move. Noa raced back across the room, grabbed the kid by his shoulders, and propelled him toward the truck.

"We gotta go!" Zeke shouted.

Noa pushed the boy toward the open door—someone hauled him inside. She dove into the truck cab after him, bumping her knee hard against the shift. Daisy threw the truck in reverse, briefly pinning her to the dashboard.

The back of the truck looked like a cafeteria after a food fight; a half inch of beer sloshed along the floor, sweeping taco flotsam along with it. The rear door was open, providing a window into the enormous parking lot that surrounded the building.

Two more guards were less than fifteen feet away. They were approaching slowly, guns raised, as the truck screeched toward them.

And she was fresh out of flashbang grenades.

"Get down!" Noa shouted.

The truck jerked to a halt six feet from the men. Noa

pressed herself to the floor, although she couldn't tear her eyes from the guns.

The truck lurched forward again, momentarily throwing off their aim; but the guards were too close, and the truck wasn't picking up speed fast enough. All they had to do was start firing, and they'd hit at least a few of them.

Suddenly an explosion went off right beside her. Noa yelped, her hands automatically leaping up to cover her ears. Another blast followed, even louder.

Zeke was braced between the driver and passenger seats. He was holding a gun and firing off rounds at the guards.

Immediately, they dropped to the ground. Shots kept coming, but they flew wild. Zeke clicked on an empty magazine. Without meeting her eyes, he let the gun drop by his side as he slid into a crouch.

Noa was speechless. No guns, that was her rule. She'd insisted on it. Even Turk had treated it as the single edict that couldn't be broken.

But Zeke had brought a gun.

The van finally picked up speed, veering out of the lot and bouncing onto the road that led back to the highway.

"Everyone okay?" she asked, scanning the other faces.

They all looked shell-shocked. A few murmured that they were fine. The rest just nodded.

"Good," Noa said. "Radio Crystal and tell her to park the van and wait for us. We'll ditch this truck by the highway."

"Then what?" Remo asked.

"Back to the safe house, but we need to clear out tonight and get on the road again."

Grumbles at that. Noa couldn't blame them. She was utterly spent. After everything that had happened, even she could probably clock eight hours of sleep. But they needed to put as much pavement between themselves and Phoenix as possible. Of course, looking the way they did right now, they wouldn't have a prayer of maintaining a low profile. They all needed to shower and change clothes; she'd allow time for that. Then they'd leave town.

Noa braced herself by planting the bottoms of her feet against a cabinet. Her jeans were soaked through. She was covered in soot and ash and felt sore, bruised, and exhausted.

And angry. Very, very angry.

CHAPTER TWELVE

oa handed over the pile of clothes that she'd collected from the other kids. "Here."

"Thanks." The girl took them from her hands. She was standing outside the bathroom, waiting for the young boy they'd rescued along with her to finish showering.

"We didn't really have anything small enough for him," Noa said apologetically. "But if he rolls up the sleeves and belts the pants, they should fit all right. We'll stop at a Walmart to get you both something better."

"They'll be fine," the girl said. "By the way, my name is Taylor."

"Noa." She held out a hand, and they shook awkwardly. Taylor balanced the stack of clothes under her opposite arm. "Do you know the others' names?"

"The kid is Matt." A dark look flitted across Taylor's face

as she continued, "And the girl was out cold when I found her. How is she?"

Noa shrugged. "We made her comfortable. She might turn out to be fine. We'll take her to some people who can help her."

"Good," Taylor said. "Maybe she's just drugged."

"Yeah, about that." Noa shifted uncomfortably. She wasn't usually the one who debriefed rescued kids; Zeke had a gift for setting people at ease. But he was off sulking somewhere. She'd already tried to talk to him about the gun, but when she confronted him, he stormed off.

The rest of the group was avoiding her, too. Noa wasn't sure if that was because they sided with her on the gun issue, or if they were just shell-shocked and taking time to process it. Either way, now she was stuck doing what Zeke jokingly referred to as their "intake interviews."

Usually she'd allow Taylor and Matt time to clean up and eat something, maybe even sleep, but they were against the wire.

"You want to know what they did to us," Taylor stated bluntly.

"Yes," Noa said. "It's pretty standard. I mean, I know it can be hard to talk about, but—"

"Did they take you?"

The question was so direct, it took her by surprise. Taylor was examining her closely, as if expecting her to lie. "Yes," she finally answered. "They did."

"And what did they do?"

Noa shifted uncomfortably. She was supposed to be asking the questions. And the truth was, she didn't remember much. All she knew for certain was that they'd operated on her, inserting an extra thymus gland into her chest that was wreaking havoc with her system.

She didn't feel like sharing any of that with Taylor, though. Noa knew that the kids followed her blindly because they practically considered her to be superhuman. She'd never explained why, and none had dared ask.

Until now. "They did . . . Well, I'm not exactly sure," she hedged. "What about you?"

Taylor shrugged noncommittally. "I'm not sure, either."

"But are you cut anywhere?" Noa pressed.

"Cut?" Taylor's brow wrinkled. "Like, did they torture me?"

"No, like . . . any operating scars?"

Taylor looked interested. "Is that what they did to you?"

"This isn't about me!" Noa snapped. God, what would it take to get a straight answer out of this girl? And why did she seem so determined to find out what had happened to Noa? She forced her clenched fists to relax, took a deep breath, and said, "Sorry. It's been a long night. I'm just tired."

"Yeah, we all are," Taylor said coldly. The door to the bathroom opened. Matt was wrapped in a threadbare towel, his straw-blond hair glistening from the shower. "Here," Taylor said, thrusting the clothes from the top of the pile into his hands. "Get dressed. I'll see you when I get out of the shower."

She pushed past, leaving him standing in the hall blinking up at Noa. They considered each other for a minute. Noa knew that she should get some answers from him, too. But before she could ask anything, Matt's mouth gaped open in a cavernous yawn, making him look even younger. "C'mon," she said, putting a hand on his shoulder to lead him down the hall. "You can change down here, then I'll find you something to eat."

* * *

Peter stifled a yawn as he slumped down in the booth of the diner where he was meeting Amanda for lunch. He'd been up until nearly five a.m. The third time he'd checked The Quad, there had finally been a message from Noa that read, *Weather's here, wish u were gr8.* That code signified that everything had gone well with the operation.

Although clearly it hadn't, at least not based on what he'd seen. He was dying for a full rundown, but there was no way to get one. He'd posted something different from his usual reply, though, writing, *Awesome. I'd kill 4 a vacay.* Based on that, Noa would know that he wanted to talk when she got the chance. But even though he'd risked logging back in after he woke up at ten, there was no answer.

Noa was probably sleeping, he rationalized. And when she slept, she practically slipped into a coma. Either way, hopefully she'd call today. And until then, he had plenty to keep him occupied.

Amanda hadn't arrived yet, which was weird. She had a real thing about being punctual; if he dared show up even a minute late, she'd lecture about how it "conveyed the message that he thought his time was more important than hers." He'd gotten that dressing down more times than he could count.

Peter checked his phone again: no messages. He'd gotten here right on time, thirty minutes ago. He unlocked his phone and sent a quick text, asking, *Hey, u ok?*

But as he hit send, Amanda came through the front door. Relieved, he waved. She smiled faintly at him, tugging off her scarf as she approached.

Peter's smile faded as he took in her appearance. Amanda looked even gaunter than she had just a few days ago. Her clavicle pushed sharply against the outline of her V-neck sweater, and her wrists looked painfully bony. The circles under her eyes were pronounced. Even her hair looked like hell, sagging against her scalp.

Peter tried to sound normal as he said, "Hey, you made it."

Her brow furrowed. "We said twelve thirty, didn't we?"

"Nope." Peter held up his phone, showing her the text from this morning. "Noon."

"Oh. Sorry." She seemed distracted. Even though he was sorely tempted to throw the punctuality lecture back at her, he held his tongue.

"So," he asked cautiously. "Everything cool?"

"Of course. Why wouldn't it be?"

Peter shrugged. "I don't know. You look . . . tired."

A flash of irritation. "You, too?"

"What?" he asked defensively.

Angrily, Amanda dumped her purse on the table and started riffling through it, finally digging out a ChapStick and running it over her cracked lips. "Diem won't leave me alone, she keeps threatening to drag me to the health center."

"Really? Why?" Secretly, Peter was relieved that someone else had noticed her condition. Better still, someone who saw her nearly every day, and could keep better track of her than he could. Maybe he should try to talk to Diem about it, even though Amanda would flip if she found out.

"She thinks there's something wrong with me."

"Oh." Peter played with his napkin, tearing it into small pieces and stacking them on the Formica tabletop. "Well . . ." He hesitated, then said, "Honestly, I'm kind of worried too."

Amanda focused a baleful glare at him and said cuttingly, "I'm fine."

"Maybe, but you've lost a lot of weight. And you seem kinda . . . off."

"Off?" She half rose.

"Just chill, okay?" He raised his hands placatingly. This was exactly why he'd put off talking to her about it—he'd known she wouldn't react well. "I just meant, it can't hurt to get checked out, right?"

Amanda glowered at him, but sat back down. Leaning in, she said, "I gave Mouse a few more files."

"Yeah? Great." He tried to come up with a way to steer the conversation back toward her health. Maybe he could suggest walking her over to the medical center after lunch?

"So did they do the raid?" she asked, lowering her voice even further.

Before he could respond, they were interrupted by a harried-looking waitress who shoved sticky menus in their hands. Peter waited until she'd left, then said, "Yeah. Last night."

"How did it go?"

He shrugged, not sure how much to share. After all, it wasn't like he had any concrete details. "Okay, I guess."

"Good." Seeming satisfied, Amanda sat back to peruse the menu. Peter watched her with a flicker of amusement, knowing it was all for show. She'd order the same thing as always: a veggie burger with a side salad. And today, as a nod to her strong sentiments against eating any animal products, he'd do the same.

Peter sipped his coffee. He'd already had a full cup, and didn't want to overdo it. But God, he was tired. He eyed her over the rim. Whatever closeness they'd managed to rebuild recently had dissipated. She seemed more distant than ever.

"You don't look so hot yourself, you know," Amanda said without raising her eyes from the menu.

"Thanks," he said wryly. "I was up all night monitoring the raid."

She made an indeterminate noise, closed the menu, and set it next to her purse. "So what's next?"

"What do you mean?"

She shrugged. "Is Noa just going to keep doing this?"

"Probably. Why?"

Amanda pursed her lips. She looked like she wanted to say something else, but apparently decided against it.

The waitress took their order, then stomped off. Peter felt distracted and edgy—this wasn't going the way he'd hoped at all. He wondered if there was usually a long wait at the health center; would they even be able to see Amanda today, or would she have to make an appointment? He should spend the rest of the day with her either way, but that meant shelving everything else. He had yet to finish tweaking the sniffer's software program. He'd risked a lot planting it; there had to be something there. He also had to go through the sound recordings from Mason's penthouse, and God only knew how long that would take.

And on top of everything else, he had homework to finish this weekend.

"Are you in love with her?" Amanda asked, interrupting his ruminations.

Startled, it took Peter a minute to process what she'd said. "With who?"

"Noa. I mean, I know you two got pretty close. . . ." As her voice trailed off, Amanda avoided his eyes.

Peter didn't know what to say. Her eyes were glistening, like she was holding back tears. On an impulse, he reached across the table and took one of her hands in his. "Amanda—"

"I mean, it's okay if you are. I didn't treat you very well." She swiped a hand across her eyes. "I just—I wish we could go back, you know? To the way things were between us."

Seeing her like this, he wanted more than anything to tell her that they could, and everything would be just the same. But it would be a lie. Because even as he watched her cry, all he felt was a pang of regret. The other night, when she'd showed up unexpectedly at his house . . . a lot of things had happened. It had been comforting, and familiar, yet the whole time he couldn't suppress the sense that it just felt . . . wrong. He'd meant what he said. He hadn't stopped loving her. But the form that love took had changed. He felt protective of her, and concerned for her. But that wasn't really love, at least not the kind they used to share. "I'm sorry," he finally said.

"Yeah, me too." Amanda pulled her hand away and strapped her purse over her shoulder. "You know, I'm really not hungry."

"Please, don't go." He couldn't let her leave, not until she'd at least promised to consider seeing a doctor. "I want to talk about it some more."

"I don't. Good-bye, Peter. Don't call me." She slid out of the booth without looking at him and practically ran to the door.

Peter sighed. Girls should really come equipped with some sort of instruction manual. Computers were so much easier.

"You still gonna eat?" the waitress asked, suddenly reappearing.

"Yeah, I guess," Peter said dejectedly.

She dumped a plate in front of him: a veggie burger with

wilted lettuce jutting out from the bun. In a brusque voice she announced, "She'll get over it, honey. You'll see."

"Thanks," Peter mumbled. But he knew better.

"So then I saw the oxygen tank, and figured that if I started a fire, they'd have to open the door."

Noa shifted in the front passenger seat, irritated. Taylor had proven to be downright chatty once they got on the road. For someone who had initially been dodgy about sharing her story, she sure was laying it on thick now.

The kids crammed in the back of the van were riveted by her performance. Noa had wanted to step in when Taylor started talking, but couldn't figure out how to do it politely. And she wasn't sure the girl would have shut up, anyway— she clearly enjoyed having an audience.

Zeke was driving, staring moodily out the windshield. She'd offered to take the wheel, but he'd brusquely refused. They were already passing Joshua Tree, four hours into what would be a twelve-hour haul if they were lucky and didn't hit any traffic. A barren landscape of desert brush and crooked cacti swept past the windows. The gray early morning light made everything look eerie, like they were passing through a bombed-out landscape. Noa snugged her hands into her sleeves and tucked her neck deeper into her hoodie. She was freezing, even though the heater was blasting.

It had taken longer than she would've liked to clear out the safe house, even though they'd only been there two days. The group was alternately groggy and punchy from fatigue. Noa had a hard time corralling them. As she'd closed the door, she worried that they'd left something important behind. No time to check, though; the sooner they got on the road, the better.

"So how did you set it off?" Teo asked, sounding awed.

"One of the doctor's must've smoked," Taylor said dismissively. "I found a pack of matches in the trash."

"That was convenient," Noa interjected, turning around to look at her.

Taylor gazed back levelly. "Yeah, I got lucky."

Noa frowned. She didn't believe in luck. And why would anyone have thrown out a pack of matches? In one of the patient's rooms, no less?

She seemed to be the only one who doubted Taylor's story, though. Daisy pressed, "Then what did you do?"

"I set one match burning on the outside of the pack and put it next to the canister. Then I turned the table on its side and dragged it across the room. When the rest of the pack caught and hit the oxygen, it made one hell of an explosion. Didn't open the door, though, which was a bummer."

I'll bet, Noa thought, but this time kept it to herself. The whole stunt sounded like something that would only occur to a person with military training; how the hell had a street kid come up with that plan?

The fact that the others were oohing and aahing over her resourcefulness only made it worse. Noa shifted in her seat, jamming her knees against the dashboard as she slumped down. It was funny; she hadn't had this reaction to any of the other kids they'd saved, but something about Taylor rubbed her the wrong way.

"Then the door clicked open, so I went down the hall and checked the other rooms, where I found Matt and her." Taylor gestured toward the girl who was laid out on a makeshift mattress along one side of the van. She still hadn't regained consciousness, so they'd kept her in the hospital gown and covered her with blankets. Noa had examined her, but couldn't tell what was wrong, exactly. The girl didn't have any incisions, or other marks indicating she'd been operated on. Which was puzzling. Since Noa had apparently been their first successful test subject, wouldn't Project Persephone be trying to replicate what they'd done to her? In the other raids, every single kid had a scar in the exact same spot she did; none of them, however, had experienced the same symptoms. Which was really, truly weird. Why was she the only one who had reacted to the surgery that way? What had they done differently with her?

Or was she different for some other reason? At the thought, she shuddered. Zeke glanced over and opened his mouth as if he wanted to say something. Without meeting her eyes, though, he clamped it shut again and focused back on the road.

Taylor sounded like she was wrapping it up—*finally*, Noa couldn't help thinking. ". . . so we were going down all these halls, and it was getting smokier and smokier. And then we found you guys."

"Pretty smart, blowing up that tank," Teo said admiringly.

"Well, I grew up on army bases. My dad died in Afghanistan, and my mom died of cancer," Taylor said matter-of-factly. "Growing up like that, you learn a few things."

"Which base?" Noa asked, swiveling to face her again.

"Why?" Taylor seemed nonplussed.

"Just curious," Noa said, keeping her tone nonchalant.

"Fort Huachuca," Taylor replied smoothly. "At least, that's where I was when Dad died. But we moved all over. Are you a military brat too?"

"Nope."

"I figured." Judging by her tone, that was meant to be an insult.

"And you don't remember anything they did to you?"

"You already asked me that," Taylor said sharply. "No."

"Huh. Because almost everyone remembers something," Noa continued evenly. "Surgeons standing over them, bright lights . . ."

"I remember this nasty nurse who kept jabbing me with needles," Crystal offered. "Every time I woke up."

"Yeah, me too," Remo chimed in.

"Guess I'm lucky I don't remember, then," Taylor said, with what sounded to Noa like false sympathy. "But whatever they did, Matt and I seem to be okay, right?"

"Right," Daisy said. "Thank God."

The rest murmured their assent.

"So these people we're going to see. They'll be able to help her, right?" Taylor gestured to the unconscious girl.

"Sure," Crystal offered. "She'll be fine. Monica and Roy—"

"We don't share information about them," Noa interrupted sharply.

Crystal looked startled, but she clamped her jaw shut.

"Oh," Taylor said. "I get it. If you told me you'd have to kill me, right?" She burst into laughter.

And there it is again, Noa thought. Taylor seemed uncommonly interested in finding out more about the Forsythes. Which also wasn't the usual reaction of kids they'd saved. They either wanted to return to wherever they'd been snatched from, or to join Persefone's Army. But they rarely asked a lot of questions; it wasn't something kids who'd lived on the streets were conditioned to do. They knew better.

Not Taylor, though. And the more she pushed for details, the more Noa resisted giving them to her. The Forsythes were the only reason she was still alive. If they hadn't saved Zeke, he never would have been around to rescue her. And within days, she probably would've ended up back in that terrifying operating room.

She glanced sideways at him. Zeke's jaw was set, his full lips pressed into a tight line. Like he was the one with the right to be angry. The night before last he'd tried to kiss her. It felt like forever ago.

The hairs on the back of her neck prickled, and Noa turned to find Taylor staring squarely at her. As their eyes met, Taylor's mouth split in a wide grin. She pointedly shifted her gaze to Zeke and reached out, laying a hand on his forearm. He started at the contact, then relaxed. "I really have to thank you," Taylor said in a low voice, as if it was just the two of them in the van. "You saved my life."

"It was nothing," Zeke said. "No problem."

But a red flush spread out of his jacket collar, reaching all the way to his cheeks. Seeing it, Noa scowled. She sank even lower in her seat and closed her eyes. The others could think what they wanted. She'd learned to trust her gut, and she had a bad feeling about this new girl.

CHAPTER THIRTEEN

t turned out that Mason wasn't much of a conversational-
ist. Peter had spent hours listening to the tapes. The bugs
were sound activated, clicking on whenever they detected
noise. Unfortunately, 90 percent of what they'd picked up
was just that: noise. Mason making coffee. Mason tapping
away at a keyboard. Mason brushing his teeth for precisely
two minutes, twice a day. His dentist must be so proud.

The few phone conversations he had were extraordinarily
one-sided, his end consisting mainly of curt "yesses" and
"nos." One had initially excited Peter, because Mason was
being unusually talkative. Unfortunately, it turned out to be
a lengthy discussion of seams with his tailor.

The mirrored computer still hadn't produced anything,
either. Mason basically used his desktop to check the stock
market and read the *Wall Street Journal*. He was probably the

only person on the planet who didn't surf at all.

Obviously, Mason's illegal business was conducted away from home. Three hours in, Peter was ready to give up and move on to the financials. At least then he'd be typing at a keyboard, which would provide the illusion that he was accomplishing something.

An alert suddenly popped up on his screen. Peter frowned: He'd set it to ping whenever Mason did anything new on his computer. He clicked over, bracing himself for more deathly boring financial articles.

His eyebrows shot up when he saw that, for the first time, a Word document was being opened. This was new. Peter took a gulp of soda from the can on his desk and crossed his arms, waiting. He'd be able to read whatever Mason was typing in real time. Hopefully Mason planned on unburdening himself, writing a lengthy confession of all the terrible things he'd done.

Instead, a message appeared across the screen in all caps. When Peter read it, his blood froze in his veins. It said, *HI PETER. HOW DO YOU LIKE MY PLACE?*

"Amanda! What are you doing?"

Amanda blinked, disoriented. Her legs felt cramped, and her neck was stiff. Her mind was fuzzy, too, like she was still dreaming. . . .

But she wasn't, she suddenly realized with a jolt. She was sitting on the floor of the Runaway Coalition office, knees tucked beneath her, head propped against Mrs. Latimar's desk chair. The files she'd dug out of the bottom drawer, the secret ones she wasn't supposed to know about, were splayed out like a fan on the floor around her.

And Mrs. Latimar was standing in the doorway, staring

down at her in horror. "Where did you find those?"

"Um, I . . . They were . . ." As her mind spun, trying to come up with a plausible explanation for how half a dozen files that had been locked in a drawer happened into her possession, Amanda frantically tried to gather them up. Papers spilled out of them, mixing all the records together. Amanda's heart sank as she realized it must have happened again—she barely even remembered arriving at the Runaway Coalition that day, and had no memory at all of digging the files out of the drawer. And now, she'd finally been caught.

She was on the verge of stammering out an apology when suddenly something struck her: She wasn't in the wrong here. Drawing herself up, Amanda gathered all her fury and narrowed her eyes. "I think the real question, Mrs. Latimar, is what are *you* doing with these?"

Mrs. Latimar reared back visibly. "What do you mean? I'm the director, I'm in charge of maintaining the files. I—"

"So why were these files *specifically* set aside?" Amanda demanded. "I know the filing system better than anyone; I helped design it. And none of these were in the right place."

"That's really none of your concern," Mrs. Latimar said, but her voice wavered.

"Really? Because I'll tell you what concerns me, Mrs. Latimar. It concerns me that apparently you're selling these kids out, giving information they trust us with to people who slice them open and experiment on them!"

Amanda stood there, her shoulders heaving.

"How do you know about that?" Mrs. Latimar's voice was just above a whisper, her face white with shock.

"Does it matter?" Amanda tossed back, but deep down she had a sinking feeling. Belatedly, she realized that she probably shouldn't have let Mrs. Latimar know just how deep her knowledge of Project Persephone went. Sharing that put her in terrible danger.

Mrs. Latimar stumbled forward and fell into the chair behind her desk. She sank her head into trembling hands. "Oh, Amanda," she said, her voice thick with emotion. "You have no idea, child."

"I think I have a pretty good idea," Amanda said, but her bluster was fading.

Mrs. Latimar lifted her head and stared at her. Her eyes were filled with tears, and she suddenly looked much older. "What they'll do to me . . . to you!"

Amanda squared her shoulders. "I don't care," she said. "What they're doing is wrong. Someone has to stop them." After a beat, she continued, "And I can't believe you helped them!"

"I didn't have a choice," Mrs. Latimar said heavily. "They would hurt her. They promised not to harm her, as long as I helped them."

"Hurt who?" Amanda's mind spun. She'd heard rumors that Mrs. Latimar had started the Runaway Coalition because her daughter had ended up on the streets as a teenager. But those same rumors all claimed that the daughter had died some sort of horrible death; losing her had inspired Mrs. Latimar to try and prevent other kids from falling victim to the same fate.

"My granddaughter." Mrs. Latimar managed a weak smile. "She's a little younger than you."

"I didn't know you had a granddaughter," Amanda said, surprised.

"I don't tell many people about her," Mrs. Latimar said softly. "My daughter . . . Well, we weren't close, not at the end, at least." Her voice lowered further as she continued,

"Clementine is the last link I have to her."

"And they threatened her?" Amanda said. She was still angry, but the woman looked so bereft, she almost felt sorry for her. "Why didn't you go to the police?" she demanded.

"I did," Mrs. Latimar said defensively. "Of course that's the very first thing I did. But you can imagine how they reacted when I told them that my granddaughter was being threatened by some strange man who seemed to know everything about me."

"They thought you were crazy," Amanda said thoughtfully.

"Of course they did," Mrs. Latimar scoffed. "And I can't say I blame them."

"So where is she now?" Amanda asked. "Clementine, I mean?"

"She's in a private boarding school in New Hampshire," Mrs. Latimar replied after a moment.

"And how do you know for sure that she's in danger?"

"They send me photos. All the time, at least one a week." Mrs. Latimar shuddered. "And other things—copies of her class schedule, her progress reports . . . last week I even received a lock of her hair in the mail!" As she spoke, she became increasingly agitated. "I wanted to tell the authorities, but Mr. Mason convinced me they wouldn't be able to help. These people can get to her, no matter what I do. And the police would be powerless to stop them!"

Amanda opened her mouth to argue, but she remembered what Peter had told her. About how he and Noa had managed to summon the FBI to a secret lab in southeastern Rhode Island. How they'd found victims of Project Persephone's experiments there, their bodies horribly mutilated and stuffed in coolers. And yet, in the end, it had all been covered up. Mrs. Latimar was right, she realized; however they'd managed it, Pike & Dolan appeared able to operate above the law. "So you started giving them files," Amanda said slowly. "When?"

Mrs. Latimar focused on the floor in front of her, as if afraid to meet Amanda's eyes. She said heavily, "Two years ago. I thought . . . At first, they only wanted one or two names. I thought that would be all. But then, they kept pushing for more and more. And every time I threatened to stop, they sent me another photo of Clementine. And the money—"

"What money?"

"We had started receiving large donations from an anonymous donor. I thought that maybe all my fundraising efforts had finally paid off. We were in bad shape. I was almost forced to close our doors. But the money saved us . . . and then I found out it was coming from them. Mr. Mason said that if I told anyone, revealed anything . . . they'd say I was part of it. I would go to jail, and never see Clementine again."

"You *are* part of it," Amanda snapped, her rage flaring again. "You know what they're doing to those kids, don't you? You traded in dozens of lives, maybe more, to save your granddaughter."

"I know," Mrs. Latimar said wretchedly. "God, Amanda, don't you think this is tearing me up? I barely sleep nights." Her face crumpled. Tears slipped out of her eyes and cascaded down her cheeks. "I'm sorry," she whimpered. "So sorry. I was just terrified for Clementine."

Amanda battled conflicting emotions. In spite of everything, she had a nearly overpowering urge to wrap her arms around the woman and comfort her. Mrs. Latimar had been scared for her granddaughter's life, and rightly so. A man like

Mason wouldn't blink at dragging her off to one of P&D's illegal labs. But still, all those other kids whose lives she'd traded in exchange . . . It was unforgivable.

Still, if it had been her brother, Marcus, whose life was threatened . . . would she have done the same?

"What do we now?" Mrs. Latimar asked softly.

She regarded Amanda plaintively, as if she was suddenly the adult. It was a fair question. One Amanda had no idea how to answer. "You can't tell them that I know," she said. "That's the most important thing."

"No, of course not!" Mrs. Latimar looked horrified. "I would never put you in that kind of danger."

Amanda bit back the retort that she hadn't had a problem putting kids in danger up until now. She continued forcefully, "And you can't give them any more files."

"But he's supposed to come tomorrow," Mrs. Latimar said weakly. "I have to give him something."

The rough outline of a plan was forming in Amanda's head. It was risky, but might work. "We'll give him old files," she said slowly. "Kids we know are safe. We can change the dates on them, so they won't figure it out for a while."

"Which kids?" Mrs. Latimar asked, her eyes narrowing.

"The ones who never came back, from years ago. By now, they'll either be too old for the project, or—"

"Or dead," Mrs. Latimar said, nodding. "Good. That's a good idea. Of course . . . they'll realize soon, won't they?"

"Probably," Amanda conceded. "But it gives us some time. And we don't risk anyone else's life," she added firmly.

"Okay." Mrs. Latimar looked relieved. "I guess we'd better get started, then. The old files are in storage in the back."

"I'll get them," Amanda said. "I know where they are."

"Yes, of course you do." Mrs. Latimar wiped the tears

from her cheeks. "Thank you, Amanda."

"You can thank me," Amanda said through gritted teeth, "by doing everything you can to try and repair the damage you caused."

Teo bounced in place, trying to ease the pressure on his swollen bladder. They were at a gas station off Route 5, indistinguishable from a dozen others they'd passed on the road. Noa had allotted ten minutes to use the facilities and grab some food from the mini mart. He'd ended up last in line for the restroom.

He'd let Daisy go in ahead of him, and was now sorely regretting his chivalry. She was taking forever.

The door finally opened, and Daisy appeared, looking apologetic. "Sorry it took so long."

"No worries," Teo said, his voice strained.

She stepped aside, and with an overwhelming sense of relief, he slipped past her.

When he emerged a few minutes later, Daisy was waiting for him.

"Hey," she said earnestly.

"Hey," Teo replied. Daisy must've splashed some water on her face; she looked great, even though like the rest of them she'd barely slept. The unconscious girl took up a disproportionate amount of floor space in the van, and the addition of Taylor and Matt meant that the whole group was piled on top of one another. Teo had spent most of the day waking up from a restless sleep with an elbow in his back or a foot in his face.

Daisy looked fantastic, though. Her blue eyeliner was perfectly applied, and her lips looked shiny and full. And once he'd noticed that, he couldn't seem to stop staring at them.

Even her outfit looked put together: tall black combat boots, ripped tights, a sheer white shirt over a black tank, and layers of bracelets on her wrists. Like she'd just stepped off the pages of a hip magazine.

"I wanted to apologize for, you know . . ." Daisy's eyes drifted to the ground. She kicked a gum wrapper away with the toe of her boot. "How I lost it last night during the raid. I'm, like, totally embarrassed about it."

"No worries," Teo said, even though he felt a flash of irritation at the memory of struggling with the gear shift while she wailed in the background. "You did all right in the end."

"Yeah, but I almost got us caught." She raised her head. "And if anything had happened to you, I would've felt really awful. Anyway, I'm sorry."

Teo pictured Boss Man, his face contorted with rage as he shot at them. . . . It had been close. And it had, at least partly, been her fault. But he wasn't the kind of person who held grudges. "I know how you can make it up to me."

"Really?" Daisy's eyes widened. "How?"

"Teach me to drive."

She laughed. "Yeah, I guess you do kind of need to learn that."

"It would help," he said drily. "You know, in case you freak out again."

For a second he worried that he'd pushed it too far, but she took the teasing in stride. She poked him in the arm and said, "I can't believe you didn't strip the transmission last night, the way you were grinding those gears."

"I don't even know what that means," he confessed, smiling, and she laughed again.

"All right, I'll teach you. But we'll have to wait until Santa Cruz. I don't think Zeke'll trust you with the van."

"Sure," Teo said. "That's cool."

"What's Teo short for, anyway?"

He considered lying to her. Plenty of times he'd told people that it was from Mateo, because that sounded a lot cooler than his real name. But Daisy was gazing up at him with her enormous trusting blue eyes. He swallowed hard and said, "Teodoro."

The corners of her mouth tweaked and she said, "Like, Teddy?"

"Yeah," he said. "Like that."

"That's so cute!" She punched his arm playfully. "I love that, like you're a teddy bear! I'm *so* calling you Teddy from now on."

With his slight build, it was unlikely he'd be mistaken for a teddy bear; certainly, no one had ever accused him of being cuddly. But as far as he was concerned, Daisy could call him pretty much anything she wanted.

They stood there for another minute, the silence between them suddenly awkward. Teo didn't know where to focus— no matter what he tried, his eyes kept coming back to her lips.

Then, without warning, those lips were suddenly pressing against his. Teo's eyes widened. He wasn't sure if he'd been focusing so intently that he'd moved in unconsciously, or if she'd started it. The kiss felt strange at first, almost too rough. But after a few seconds she tilted her head slightly to one side, and suddenly it felt like the most natural thing in the world to be standing outside a filthy roadside bathroom, making out with a girl with bright blue hair.

A car horn sounded, startling them. They broke apart. Daisy's lips were slightly parted, and she was breathing hard. Her cheeks had flushed bright red. Teo's whole body was humming in a way he'd never experienced, like kissing her had thrown some sort of switch.

"Um, we should probably go," Daisy said when the horn blared again.

"Yeah, I guess . . . um, yeah." His brain was still thrumming so loudly he was barely capable of coherent speech.

As Teo followed her back around the corner, his mind did some sort of reboot, and with it came a flood of worries. He'd never kissed a girl before, not really, just pecks on the lips when he was a kid. And this . . . Well, it hadn't been anything like that. What did he say to her now? How was he supposed to act?

The onslaught of thoughts made him feel slightly nauseous.

Footsteps behind them; he turned to find Taylor trailing a few feet back. She was wearing a pair of Vans, a tight pink T-shirt, and jean shorts, all donated from the other girls— who were smaller than her, so the clothes clung tightly to her frame. *Which isn't necessarily a bad thing*, Teo caught himself thinking. He flushed again.

"Hey, Taylor," Daisy said, noticing her. "You get to use the bathroom?"

"Yeah, I'm just coming from there." The girl smiled breezily at them. "Nasty, wasn't it?"

Teo frowned. "What, just now?"

"Yeah. Why?" Taylor tossed her hair. "Are you the bathroom police or something?"

Daisy laughed, which threw him. He stared at the ground, feeling like an idiot.

"Ugh, I cannot wait to get to Santa Cruz," Taylor continued, making a face. "The van sucks, right?"

Teo wanted to say that considering she'd been strapped to a table the night before, the van was pretty comfy by comparison. But he simply nodded and said, "Yeah, it's pretty crowded."

"I hope we get some real food there, too." Taylor fell in stride beside them. They rounded the corner to the front of the station, where the van idled in front of the mini mart. "I hate junk food."

Teo couldn't help himself—his eyebrows shot up. You lived on junk food as a street kid; candy bars were cheap and easy to steal and had enough fat and calories to get you through the day. No one who had spent any time on the streets dissed junk food; it was their staple, the main thing keeping them alive.

"I don't know, I'd kill for some Cheetos and a Coke," Daisy said.

"Well, they probably have those inside," Taylor said. "Enjoy. I'm going to try to find a spot where I don't have to lie on anyone."

"Good luck with that," Daisy said breezily.

Teo watched Taylor slide open the van door and pick her way gracefully through the forms huddled in back. "Huh," he said hesitantly. "That was seriously weird, right?"

"Weird how?" Daisy asked.

"Well, I mean . . . she couldn't have been in the bathroom. We would've seen her, right?"

Daisy shrugged. "So what?"

She was looking at him like he was some kind of paranoid freak. Hurriedly, he said, "Yeah, you're right. No big deal."

Another long blare of the horn. Daisy rose up on her toes, pecked him on the lips, then winked and said, "Race you!"

She tore off, her combat boots chewing up the pavement between them and the van. Teo recovered and followed, watching her blue ponytail bounce against her back as she ran.

Peter was finding it difficult to breathe. The words on the screen seemed to pulse with malevolent intent. The hairs on the back of his neck prickled as if Mason was actually standing behind him. *How did he know about the break-ins?* Peter cursed himself. He must've triggered some sort of backup system. He should've known that Mason was too smart to be cavalier about home security.

Still, he didn't dare touch his keyboard. It was silly, but he could picture Mason's hand reaching straight through the screen and wrapping around his throat, like something out of a horror movie.

More words appeared. *I KNOW YOU'RE THERE, PETER. DO YOU THINK YOU'RE THE ONLY ONE WITH COMPUTER SKILLS?*

That gave him a start. There was no way Mason could have installed a Trojan horse on his laptop—it was never out of his sight. Peter even left it perched on the bathroom counter when he showered. *So what the hell?*

GETTING BORED HERE, PETER. THOUGHT YOU WANTED TO CHAT.

Peter drew a deep breath, then lowered shaky hands to the keyboard and typed, *It's creepy for guys your age to chat with teenage boys online.*

False bravado, but Mason didn't have to know that he scared the crap out of him.

OH, BUT WE'RE OLD FRIENDS, PETER. I CAN'T TELL YOU HOW SORRY I WAS TO HEAR THAT YOU HAVEN'T BEEN BEHAVING YOURSELF.

"Old friends my ass," Peter muttered, feeling a flare of rage as he pictured Amanda's gaunt frame. *GO TO HELL*, he typed back.

WE'RE ALREADY IN HELL, PETER. WE MIGHT AS WELL HELP EACH OTHER SURVIVE IT.

Peter hesitated, momentarily dumbfounded. What kind of game was Mason playing? He finally wrote, *I'd never help you.*

YOU ALREADY HAVE, Mason wrote, *BY TAPPING INTO THOSE SERVERS. OF COURSE, THERE'S NOTHING VALUABLE THERE.*

Peter's jaw nearly dropped. How could Mason know about *that*? Had he been followed this entire time? And if so, had he inadvertently put Noa in danger?

More words materialized on-screen: *DON'T WORRY, PETER. YOUR SECRET IS SAFE WITH ME.*

Peter considered claiming that he had no idea what Mason was talking about, but that seemed futile. It felt like the ground was dissolving beneath him, swallowing him up. *What do you want?*

I TOLD YOU, PETER. THERE'S A WAY WE CAN HELP EACH OTHER.

This had to be a trick. There was no way Mason would come to him for help; he had a seemingly limitless supply of goons at his disposal. But, Peter reasoned, there was no harm in finding out what he wanted, right? *How?*

After a beat, Mason wrote, *I WANT YOU TO HACK INTO SOMETHING FOR ME.*

Peter snorted. Pretty rich coming from the guy who'd stolen his iPhone and laptop months ago to keep him from hacking. Ironic didn't even begin to describe it. *Really*, he typed. *Trying to get out of paying taxes? Or did you get kicked out of the Evil Villains forum, and you want to see what they're saying about you?*

The worst part was that Peter could picture Mason smirking as he read that; and when the response came, he could practically hear the words being spoken in that oily voice. *SUCH A COMEDIAN, PETER. SHAME THAT YOU DIDN'T CHOOSE TO PURSUE THAT TALENT INSTEAD.*

"Yeah, right," Peter muttered. "I bet you're really bummed about that."

More words were already streaming on-screen. *I WANT YOU TO HACK INTO THE PROJECT PERSEPHONE FILES. I KNOW WHERE THE SERVER IS LOCATED.*

Peter sucked in a breath. What was going on here? His heart racing, he typed, *I got those files months ago, jerkwad.*

YOU'RE MISTAKEN, PETER. THERE ARE MORE FILES THAN YOU EVER SAW.

Peter cracked his knuckles, trying to ignore the shiver that was running up and down his spine. It felt like the temperature in his room had dropped at least ten degrees. He finally wrote, *What makes you think I'd get messed up with all that again?*

Rather than text, a jpeg link appeared on-screen. With a twinge of dread, Peter clicked on it, expecting to see a creepy shot of Amanda in her dorm room, or heading to class.

When an image of Noa materialized, it struck him dumb. For a second, his heart clenched with terror; had Mason captured her again?

No, he realized, examining it more closely. This was an older shot of Noa. The leaves on the trees behind her were red and yellow, obviously autumn foliage in New England. It must've been taken back when they were stalking her, preparing to kidnap her for their nasty experiments.

That ticked him off again. *WHY ARE YOU SHOWING ME THIS?!* he typed.

BECAUSE IF YOU DON'T HELP ME GET THOSE FILES, PETER, MISS TORSON IS GOING TO DIE.

PART THREE
INVASION

CHAPTER
FOURTEEN

oa got out of the van and stretched her arms high above her head. She'd driven the last leg of the trip, a four-hour stint, and her whole body felt sore and cramped. The rear doors opened and everyone spilled out, clearly relieved to escape the close quarters.

It had taken fourteen hours to drive from Phoenix to Santa Cruz. They'd made good time, all things considered. They were arriving a little past seven p.m. The sun had already set, and as she stood in front of the Forsythes' palatial compound, Noa could hear the distant sound of waves lapping at the shore. Fields and orchards stretched away from her, leading to cliffs that plummeted down to the Pacific. Lights glowed out of every window on the ground floor, warm and inviting.

The Forsythes' place was a sprawling complex, with barns,

sheds, and guesthouses strewn across fifty acres. The main house had six bedrooms on two levels; most were part of the original farmhouse. The Forsythes had remodeled, but retained the stone walls and original rough lumber ceilings. Noa knew that the place was probably worth a fortune, but you'd never guess the Forsythes had money. They dressed like aging hippies: tie-dye shirts, jeans, and what she considered to be an excessive amount of hemp.

The couple had never told her where their money came from, and Noa had never asked. Zeke had explained that they were both trained doctors who ended up working in biotech. Apparently they'd patented something that earned them a fortune, allowing them to retire in their early fifties. He'd never been clear on why they were so motivated to fight Project Persephone; but after meeting them, Noa figured they were the type who threw themselves wholeheartedly into a cause. They'd just happened to settle on this one.

The front door of the main house popped open, framing Monica Forsythe. She was drying her hands on a dishtowel, her face crinkled in a wide smile. Noa lifted a hand to wave, hoping that their arrival wasn't poorly timed. She'd tried calling to give them a heads-up, using a burner phone bought at the gas station. But they'd changed numbers again. Which wasn't surprising. With everything they'd learned about Pike & Dolan, the Forsythes suffered from a healthy dose of paranoia, which Noa could certainly appreciate. Knowing how careful they were made this the one place on the planet where she was almost able to relax.

As Noa walked across their gravel driveway toward the main house, the tension eased from her body. Even though she had spent less than a month here in total, it felt more like home than anywhere she'd been in the past eight years.

The main house looked like something out of a fairy tale: Vines wound along the outside walls, almost covering the windows. There were high-peaked dormers, and a round tower that used to be a silo. The second story of the tower had been turned into a bathroom with stained-glass windows surrounding an enormous claw-foot tub. Noa could already imagine sinking into it, a damp washcloth over her eyes as she used her toes to send more hot water coursing into the bath. She sighed. The terrible events of the past few days: the dead bodyguard, the debacle at the warehouse, the flight across several states . . . all of that receded.

"It's so good to see you!" Monica enveloped her in a tight embrace. Normally, Noa shied away from physical contact, but that wasn't really an option with Monica Forsythe. And for some reason, it never bothered her. She leaned her head against the shorter woman's shoulder, inhaling the scent of cinnamon and dish soap and lavender.

"Really happy to be here," Noa said, smiling back.

"Well, we're thrilled to have you home, safe and sound." She patted Noa's cheek as if she was an elderly aunt and Noa was ten years old.

Monica reached for Zeke next, but her eyes were already scanning the group; Noa could see her doing a mental head count. "Is everyone okay?"

"We lost Turk."

"Lost?" Monica's eyebrows shot up with alarm.

"Not like that, he's okay. At least, he was the last time we saw him, but . . . it's a long story." The thought of Turk brought exhaustion rushing back in.

"Oh, dear." Monica examined her closely. "You look like you're about to keel over, Noa. When was the last time you slept?"

It was a good question—Noa tried to remember. She hadn't had one of her "real" sleeps in a few days. And she needed those; if she didn't recharge at some point, she turned into the walking dead. She'd been staving off fatigue with mass amounts of caffeine, but she could feel the repercussions; her whole body seemed to be growing heavier and heavier. If she stayed upright much longer, it felt like she might start literally sinking into the ground.

Aside from Zeke and Peter, the Forsythes were the only ones who knew about Noa's "condition." Thanks to their science and medical backgrounds, they'd been trying to find a way to alleviate her symptoms and get her back to normal. *If such a thing is even possible*, Noa thought darkly.

"We've got a patient for you," Zeke said. He'd slung his army duffel over one shoulder, and was still studiously avoiding Noa's eyes.

"I can see that." Monica pulled on her glasses, her expression somber as she watched Remo and Danny carefully carry the girl from the van toward the house. "How bad?"

"She's been out cold since we got her last night," Noa said.

Monica's lips pursed. "That could just be from the medication. Remo, please take her to the back bedroom. I'll examine her immediately."

As they shuffled off toward the house with the girl, Monica's eyes flicked over Taylor and Matt. She walked forward, beaming as she said, "Well, hello."

"This is Taylor and Matt," Zeke explained. "We found them last night, too."

They rarely shared the exact details of their raids with the Forsythes. It was something they'd agreed upon on the outset; the less they knew, the safer they'd be if anything ever happened.

"Hi," Taylor said brightly. "Love your place."

"Why, thank you." Monica smiled.

Matt half hid shyly behind Taylor. Monica bent down and winked at him. "You know, I just took a pie out of the oven. It would be terribly naughty to have a piece before dinner, but I won't tell if you won't."

Matt hesitated, then squeaked, "Pie?"

"Apple pie. I hope that's all right," Monica said.

He nodded gravely, and she extended a hand. He took it and allowed her to lead him into the house. "Taylor, why don't you help me get Matt settled, then I'll check on your friend."

"Yes, ma'am," Taylor said brightly.

Noa saw Monica's eyebrows shoot up at that. Not many of the kids they brought here started out with "ma'am." Half of them basically ended up calling her Mom, which was understandable. Noa had never heard an unkind word come out of the woman's mouth. Monica Forsythe's warmth, empathy, and overt goodness had a way of bringing around the most resentful and withdrawn kids.

She and Zeke watched Monica hustle Matt and Taylor into the house.

"It's good to be back, huh?" she asked tentatively.

Zeke merely grunted in response. Without looking at her, he stomped after them.

Noa glowered at his retreating back. She'd be happy to clear the air, and discuss the whole gun thing like rational human beings. But if Zeke insisted on sulking, that was his choice. Maybe Monica could talk some sense into him. The older woman liked guns even less than she did.

Exhausted though she was, Noa decided to walk down to the water. It would be total chaos for the next half hour as everyone got settled. Zeke would be assigning everyone to bedrooms in the main house and outlying buildings, Monica would be setting out food and examining her newest patient, the house would be buzzing with noise and activity. . . . The thought of it made Noa shudder.

The chance for a few minutes to herself sounded like heaven. Ignoring the heaviness in her limbs, Noa ambled past the house and down the narrow sandy path that led to the water. The solar lights surrounding it gleamed faintly, illuminating swaying sea grass on either side, fields that the Forsythes had allowed to go wild. A slight breeze teased Noa's hair, which had grown long; she'd borrow some scissors to cut it while she was here. Spend a few days resting up. Eat as much as she could whenever she was hungry. Among her many talents, Monica was a terrific cook. Despite the short notice, she'd probably set out a spread that would put Martha Stewart to shame.

The path meandered past spindly trees bent nearly double from the wind, their long branches pointed accusingly inland. Noa wound through them, then came to a stop. She was at the top of a cliff, where the grassy slope ended in a sheer rocky precipice. Down below was a narrow strip of sand, a tiny private beach hidden on both sides by jagged rocks. It was only accessible by a set of wooden stairs carefully painted to match the dark gray rock face they rode down. The Forsythes had constructed them that way to guard against surfers who might try to sneak in and ride the point break. Not that they minded sharing, they explained, but once they'd gotten involved in the movement, they couldn't risk strangers roaming the property. Noa eyed the stairs, debating whether she had the energy to make it down to the water in the dark. She'd love to take off her shoes and feel her feet sink into the sand as waves rushed over her ankles. But even if she could get down, the thought of climbing back up was daunting.

Instead Noa plunked down on the grass, crossed her hands over her knees, and stared out at the water. It must be low tide; waves whispered faintly against the shore. Out at sea, the lights of fishing boats and sunset cruises bobbed up and down as they headed back to port. It was a rare clear night; the past few times she'd been here, the property had been shrouded by fog. Tonight she could see the stars plainly. She picked out the few constellations she knew: Orion, the Big Dipper. . . . She had a dim memory of her father pointing them out when she was a kid. They'd been lying in a field a lot like this one, but on the opposite side of the country, in Vermont. She'd nestled against the crook of his shoulder, her eyes drooping as he traced invisible lines across the night sky with his fingertips. . . .

The next thing she knew, there were hands on her shoulders. Reflexively, Noa rolled away, struggling into a fighting stance. It was dark and cold, and she felt disoriented. Consequently, it took a second to register that the shadowy figure facing her was Roy Forsythe. His hands glowed in the moonlight as he held them out reassuringly. "Sorry, kiddo. Didn't mean to scare you."

"Roy," Noa said with relief. "Hi."

"Hi." His teeth flashed white in the gloom. "Did you decide that a bed would just be too darn comfortable?"

"No, I just . . . I needed a minute alone. I must have fallen asleep." Noa tried to shake away the cobwebs. That was the biggest problem—ever since the surgery, even though she needed far less sleep, when she finally drifted off it was incredibly hard to snap out of; Zeke had nicknamed it her

"Noa coma." Even now, her eyelids threatened to close. "What time is it?"

"Late," Roy declared. "Past ten. Monica was ready to mount a full search party, but I figured I'd check here first. Noticed that it seems to be your spot."

"Yeah," Noa said, slightly embarrassed. "It's nice here."

They stood in silence for a minute. The waves had picked up while she slept, and the tide had inundated the small beach, each wave chomping fresh bites out of the sand. Standing here, it was almost possible to pretend that all the ugliness in the outside world didn't exist.

"Let's get you to the house," Roy finally said. "I don't want to have to worry about you rolling off the cliff in the middle of the night."

Noa smiled weakly and fell in step behind him, carefully picking her way back to the path. The solar lights were dimmer now; Monica always grumbled about how they barely held a few hours' worth of charge, but Roy refused to install anything that would drain more power from their generator. They lived almost completely off the grid, thanks to solar panels and a small windmill perched precariously farther along the cliff top. Noa had a lot of respect for that—she knew a thing or two about living off the grid.

"So. Any changes?" Roy asked as they made their way back to the house.

"Not really," Noa said. "The sleeping and eating are pretty much the same."

"But no new symptoms?" he pressed.

Noa shrugged, forgetting he wouldn't be able to see that in the dark. "My eyes are getting worse, bright light really hurts now. But other than that, no. I haven't tried to climb any buildings lately, so maybe my spider powers kicked in and I just don't know it."

He chuckled at that. They walked in companionable silence back to the house. Noa knew from past experience that unless she chose to bring it up again, this was the last they would discuss it.

When she and Zeke had first arrived months ago, she'd told the Forsythes the whole story. How she'd woken up on a table with an incision in her chest, how Peter's doctor friend had taken an X-ray that proved she'd been given an extra thymus. How for some reason, that had resulted in a variety of weird symptoms, from healing superfast to the eating and sleeping thing. She'd appreciated the way that Monica and Roy had just listened, their faces filled with sympathy, backing off from questions when it was clear they made her uncomfortable.

At the end of her first week, Roy had offered to perform some tests. He made it clear that neither of them wanted to put Noa through any more suffering, but there was a chance that with their expertise, they might be able to glean some answers. By then, Noa trusted them more than anyone she'd met in years, with the exception of Peter and Zeke. She'd given them blood samples, and DNA scrapings from the inside of her cheek. They didn't have anything as advanced as an X-ray machine on their property, but they'd done an ultrasound.

In the end, they hadn't been able to draw any more conclusions than Cody had. But they'd promised to keep working on it.

Noa wondered if any of that work had produced anything. It had been months now; on the last visit, she'd been too afraid to ask.

Roy suddenly spoke up. "Monica mentioned that you and Zeke had some sort of fight."

"More of a disagreement," Noa said, wondering how much Zeke had told them and how he'd framed it. She debated coming clean about the gun, but hesitated. She didn't feel right about ratting him out, not before she'd had a chance to talk to him first.

"Well, I hope you smooth it over. Hate to see you fighting," Roy said diplomatically. "You know that boy's crazy about you."

Noa shifted uncomfortably, glad he couldn't see her face in the dim light. She mumbled something unintelligible.

"The need not to look foolish is one of youth's many burdens," Roy said with a sigh. Seeing her raised eyebrows, he explained, "Updike."

"Who?" Noa asked. Roy was always doing that, quoting people she'd never heard of. And the quotes never made sense, either. But he was a nice guy, so she let it slide.

"Never mind," he said, sounding amused. "Just thinking out loud."

As they approached the house, a series of motion-detecting lights automatically clicked on. Caught in their beam, Roy turned to face her. He had the weather-beaten face of a farmer, despite his advanced degrees. A battered Grateful Dead baseball cap covered his close-cropped gray hair, and he was wearing a fleece jacket, jeans that were probably decades old, and battered black clogs.

He was pretty much indistinguishable from every other middle-aged guy who strolled the streets of Santa Cruz sipping a fair-trade latte. But Noa knew better. Roy and Monica were special. She hadn't met many people in her life who were truly good, all the way down to their core. The two of them had almost restored her faith in the rest of humanity. Almost. "It's really good to be back," she blurted out.

Roy smiled warmly at her. "Well, it's good to have you back, Noa. Too damn quiet around here with you kids gone. And Monica rides me something fierce when she doesn't have anything to occupy her. You know she's actually trying to get me to rebuild the old barn by hand? I swear, that woman will be the death of me. . . ."

He chattered on as they approached the house. Despite the late hour, warm light spilled from the windows. The smell of roasted meat and potatoes wafted out the door as Roy held it open, setting Noa's mouth watering and raising unexpected tears to her eyes. It looked and smelled like home, she realized. And she'd never expected to feel that way about a place again. Right on the heels of that thought came another, one conditioned in her by a lifetime of disappointments: *It can't last.*

Amanda fought back a yawn. After her confrontation with Mrs. Latimar, she'd almost skipped the two-hour study group for cultural anthropology class. But there was a test coming up in a few days, and she was woefully behind on the syllabus. She was hoping that one of her classmates would be willing to share notes, and then maybe she wouldn't disgrace herself with another bad grade.

She was regretting that decision now, though. They were sitting in a corner of the library, plopped in overstuffed chairs dragged into a rough circle. The heat was cranking, making it stiflingly hot. She'd stopped for green tea on the way here, but the caffeine had barely made a dent; she should have had an espresso, maybe even a double. Anything to help keep her eyes open.

No one else seemed to notice that she was barely participating, though. For the past ten minutes the group had been engaged in a heated debate. Amanda had lost the thread of the discussion a few minutes in, focusing all her energy on staying awake. She should have skipped this, and emailed Jessica for her notes; she took the best ones anyway, and wouldn't mind sharing if Amanda offered to trade last semester's psych flash cards. She would've been better off getting a good night's sleep; after all, tomorrow she had to figure out a long-term plan for Mrs. Latimar.

Amanda had almost called Peter as she was leaving the Coalition, figuring he might have some thoughts. And also, she admitted to herself, because hearing his voice would steady her.

Mason had already proved that he could get to her if he wanted to. But as the months had passed, that danger had become more of an abstract concept.

Not anymore. Mrs. Latimar was plainly terrified. And somehow, the responsibility for extricating her and her granddaughter from this mess had landed squarely on Amanda's shoulders.

Still, in the end, she'd held off on calling. After the way they'd left things in the diner, she worried that the conversation would turn into another fight. And right now, just thinking about him made her feel like crying.

Amanda sighed and surreptitiously checked her watch, repressing a groan when she saw that it was nearly eleven o'clock. She had a nine a.m. class, and she'd already missed it once this week. Plus she hadn't done any of the reading for her feminist history class. . . .

The mountain of obligations towering over her was overwhelming. Everything seemed to be slipping; she was falling so far behind, she might never catch up. A raw ball of panic formed in her stomach. She could feel it growing, slowly rising up her throat to choke her. . . .

"Amanda? Are you okay?"

Amanda tried to focus, but her vision had suddenly blurred. She opened her mouth to form the words *I'm fine*, but nothing came out. *I have to get out of here*, she thought, suddenly frantic. The walls were closing in, she was . . .

Amanda dropped to the floor, twitching. Horrified faces faded in and out, gradually replaced by others: men in dark jackets, hunched over her. She kept trying to say that she was okay, she just needed a minute to rest, but no one seemed to understand her.

She was lifted onto a stretcher and carried out into the night, a chorus of agitated voices following her. Amanda tried to protest, but her whole body felt rigid and locked, like it had suddenly become a prison she couldn't escape.

Red lights panned past overhead, and she dimly realized they were putting her in an ambulance. Which was so absurd, it made her wonder if she was dreaming. They didn't call an ambulance for people unless they were sick, and she was fine, just a little tired. Yes, that was it—this was only a nightmare.

Which was why she thought nothing of it when the ambulance doors closed and Mason's face appeared directly above her.

Peter lay awake in bed, staring at the ceiling. According to his phone it was nearly three a.m., and he had to be up in four hours for school. But the weird conversation with Mason was playing over and over in his mind.

Initially, he'd thought that Mason was threatening Noa.

You'll never find her! he'd typed, simultaneously wishing he could believe that was true.

I'M NO LONGER INTERESTED IN FINDING HER, Mason wrote. *I MERELY WANT ACCESS TO THE RESEARCH.*

Which was unexpected, and probably total bull. This had to be Mason's twisted way of getting Peter to give Noa up. But he'd never let that happen; he wouldn't contact her again, if that's what it took. Even though the thought of it made him cringe. *Why?*

THERE IS QUITE A BIT AT STAKE, PETER, AND IT DOESN'T JUST INVOLVE YOU, Mason wrote.

Peter shook his head as he retorted, *You're Pike's lapdog. You want the research, just ask him for it.*

Another beat, then Mason replied, *I'M DISAPPOINTED IN YOU, PETER. IF YOU'D DUG DEEPER INTO MY FINANCIALS, YOU'D REALIZE THAT I WAS RELEASED FROM MY OBLIGATIONS TO PIKE & DOLAN FOUR MONTHS AGO.*

Released? In spite of everything, Peter's face split in a grin. Mason had been *fired*? Something occurred to him, and he wrote, *Really hoping I had something to do with that.*

APPARENTLY MR. PIKE WAS LESS THAN THRILLED BY THE WAY THE SITUATION WITH YOUR PARENTS WAS HANDLED.

"Ha!" Peter said out loud. So he and Noa *had* accomplished something. Although if that was true, then why was Mason still following Peter? And why did he want those files? A suspicion formed in his mind. *So, what? You want to blackmail Charles Pike?*

IF THAT'S WHAT I HAD IN MIND, PETER, I

ALREADY HAVE AN EXTENSIVE ARSENAL AT MY DISPOSAL.

That wasn't hard to believe; Mason was definitely the type of guy who took "cover your ass" seriously. And Pike probably had something on him, too, to ensure Mason's silence in the wake of his dismissal.

So why did he want those records? And why would he expect Peter to help him? This had to be an elaborate trap.

Still, if Mason really knew where the other server was . . . that was tempting. If Peter got his hands on concrete proof linking Charles Pike to Project Persephone, he could disseminate it so widely there'd be no way to bury it.

But in the end, caution had won out. Peter had told Mason where to put his offer in the strongest terms his keyboard could manage, then closed the laptop. A second later he'd snapped it back open, realizing belatedly that he should have saved the transcript of their conversation. But poof: It was gone, like it had never existed.

Peter could reconstruct it from hard-drive data, but he quickly realized that would be useless. After all, what had Mason really admitted to? Getting fired by Charles Pike? Sure, he'd named the project, but hadn't said anything damning about it. And he never said that he'd kill Noa, just that she was in danger. To an outside observer, it might appear to be a relatively benign conversation. Even though Mason had asked for help hacking into a server, the only person Peter could go to with that information was Charles Pike himself, and he wasn't about to do that.

Peter groaned and flipped over in bed. As usual, his parents had the heat blasting, global warming be damned, and the house was sweltering hot. He batted his pillow into shape. He had to get some sleep before the alarm went off. He couldn't skip school again; his parents were already suspicious, and the last thing he needed was for them to start watching him more closely. Their complicity made him sick. They'd be sitting at dinner, or perched on the couch watching TV together, and the whole time he wanted to stand up and scream at them.

But he and Noa had agreed that he should act normal, like he also wanted the whole thing to blow over. So Peter sat there, gritting his teeth and making small talk. Once he left for college, though, he was never coming back. Peter had decided that the minute he'd discovered the full magnitude of his parents' involvement.

His iPhone chirped, and he grabbed it off the nightstand. There was a text from an unfamiliar number. Peter frowned. Was Mason messing with him again? "Learn to take no for an answer, dude," he grumbled as he unlocked the screen. But the message wasn't from Mason.

Amanda passed out in study group, they took her to the hospital. Thought you should know.—Diem.

CHAPTER FIFTEEN

oa splashed water on her face. By the time she'd gotten back to the house, most of the other kids had scattered, assigned to bunks in various outbuildings. That was one of the great things about the Forsythes' compound; they could comfortably house twenty people without batting an eye.

They'd offered Noa her usual room in the main house. It was linked to the tower bathroom, a luxury in and of itself. The house epitomized Roy and Monica's eclectic taste, or what Zeke called "design schizophrenia." Every room had a different theme. Downstairs there was the "Victorian Formal Room," with elaborate wallpaper, wainscotting, and a fireplace you could practically walk into. The kitchen was pure French farmhouse, and Monica had nicknamed Roy's study "The Gentleman's Club" due to all the red leather and heavy oak furniture. The bedrooms varied from "The Winter Palace," which sported a Russian theme, to "Gauguin's Tahitian Retreat." And as a nod to Roy's favorite band, a small study had been converted into the "Grateful Dead Opium Den," with tie-dyed wallpaper and rainbow-hued teddy bears everywhere.

Noa's favorite was the bedroom she always stayed in: "The Cowboy Room." All the furnishings had been purchased during one of the Forsythes' Sedona vacations. An old-fashioned cast-iron canopy bed dominated the small space. There were colorful throw rugs on the wide plank wood floors, a massive matching wooden bureau and chair, and framed prints of sunsets and horses. Noa would never have expected to feel comfortable in such an environment, but as she padded across the room in stocking feet, she felt as sated as a cat in a sunbeam. After a long, hot bath, the final kinks in her body had finally released, and her belly was full of meat and apple pie. She drew back the covers and slid between the sheets, groaning slightly at the feel of the four-hundred thread count. Thankfully, the Forsythes' passion for hemp didn't extend to their bedding.

She'd just dropped back against the pillows and closed her eyes when there was a soft rap at the door. Noa frowned and considered ignoring it. All she wanted was to zonk out for at least twelve hours.

Another knock. Sighing, she propped herself up on the pillows and said, "Yeah?"

The door opened. Zeke slouched against the frame, hands tucked in his pockets, his face cast in shadow. "Hi."

"Hi," Noa said, suddenly wide-awake. She scrambled upright. "Um, do you want to come in?"

"Yeah, I guess." Zeke crossed the threshold, carefully

closing the door behind him. He stopped a few feet from the bed.

"You can sit down, you know," Noa said, slightly annoyed.

Zeke didn't say anything, but he came over and sat on the edge of the bed.

It was funny—they'd spent almost every night of the past few months sitting, eating, and sleeping right on top of each other. But for some reason, having him at the foot of the bed felt too close. Noa was suddenly hyperaware of the fact that she'd stripped down to a tank top. It was probably too dark for him to see anything, but she crossed her arms over her chest anyway.

"I'm sorry about the gun," he said after a long moment had passed.

"That's okay," Noa responded quickly, without thinking. Silently, she reproached herself; she'd spent the whole day planning this conversation in her mind. She'd wanted to explain how betrayed she felt, since they'd agreed to steer clear of lethal weapons. How the fact that he'd been hiding something that big made her feel like she couldn't trust him. But instead, like an idiot, she'd come right out and forgiven him. Noa bit her lip, wishing she could take it back.

"I know you don't like them."

"No, I don't," she said more firmly. "I thought you didn't, either."

His shoulders rose and fell slightly. "I just figured that if we needed it, I'd rather have it than not have it."

Noa opened her mouth to protest, then closed it again. Part of her realized she was being a hypocrite. The people they went up against in these raids were dangerous, they were armed, and no matter how clever her plan was, there was always a chance something could go wrong. Like it had last night. They'd been incredibly lucky to get everyone out alive and unscathed. And Zeke was right, there was no saying how long that luck would hold. If someone had gotten shot . . .

Still, Noa couldn't suppress the sense that arming up made them just as bad as the people they were fighting against. She hated guns and everything they represented. "I get that," she said. "But I'd wish you'd get rid of it anyway."

"Okay."

"Really?" She squinted, trying to see if he was serious.

"Yeah, sure. But when my ass gets shot off, I'll be saying I told you so." His teeth gleamed white.

Noa smiled back at him. "And you'll probably be expecting me to sew you up."

"Yeah, right," he scoffed. "I got about as much faith in your sewing as I do in your cooking."

She slugged him on the shoulder. "I can cook."

"Sure you can. That's why we always leave you off the rotation."

"Hey!" Noa protested.

"Seriously, even Turk could do a better job with chili." At the mention of Turk, they both fell silent. The awkwardness swept right back in.

After a long pause, Noa asked hesitantly, "Do you think I messed up by making him leave?"

"No." Zeke shook his head hard. "He had to go. Can't trust a user, you know that."

"Yeah, but still . . ." Noa fingered the knots on the quilt. "He was one of us."

Zeke was silent for a long time. Finally, he said, "We can't save them all, Noa. You know that."

She acknowledged that with a tilt of her head. He was

right. Six months ago, all she'd cared about was saving herself, anyway. Which in many ways had been so much easier. "I'm tired of it."

"Tired of what?"

"All of it," she confessed. "Being in charge, trying to keep everyone in line, trying to keep them all safe. It's exhausting."

"Yeah, it is." Zeke moved up the bed toward her. His face was caught by a shaft of light, so that she could finally see his eyes. They were warm and brown, sympathetic. There was a catch in his voice as he said, "I meant what I said the other night. You're doing great. You know that, right?"

Noa opened her mouth to respond, but before she could he moved forward suddenly, and his lips met hers. A charge spread from her mouth all the way through her body. She let her head fall back in his hands, loving the way his fingers felt as they cradled her neck. His mouth abruptly moved away. Noa started to protest, but then he was nibbling her neck and ears, setting her nerve endings jangling.

Suddenly she was lying back against the pillows, and Zeke was beside her. His hands ran up her bare back under her tank top. Zeke's breath caught as she ran her tongue over his lips, then down his throat. He let out a small moan, grabbed her, and rolled on top of her, his mouth exploring hers again.

In the back of her head, a small voice was protesting that she should stop. Noa ignored it. Everything about this felt good—it was like suddenly discovering that she possessed a whole other set of senses. She couldn't get enough of his mouth on hers, the way his fingers felt as they lightly brushed the surface of her skin. She never wanted it to stop.

A knock at the door. At first Noa thought that her own heartbeat had gotten so loud it was echoing through the room, but no—that had definitely been a knock. They pulled apart. Zeke's chest was heaving, and his hair was mussed. They stared at each other in the moonlight, the spell abruptly broken.

The knock repeated, louder this time. Noa groaned inwardly. Why was her room suddenly Grand Central? "Yes?" she said, annoyed.

"It's Taylor."

Zeke had already slid off the bed; he ducked into the bathroom. Noa ran a hand through her hair, trying to gather herself. Tugging her tank top back down, she went to the door and opened it.

Taylor stood in the hallway. She was only wearing a camisole and panties, and had her arms crossed in front of her chest. "Where's Zeke?" she demanded.

"Why?" Noa said, not bothering to curb the irritation in her voice.

"We were supposed to meet in his room." Taylor peered past her. "Were you sleeping?"

Noa suddenly felt ill. "Why were you guys meeting?"

Taylor smirked at her. "Oh, you know."

"No, I really don't." Noa glared at her. "You don't look like you're dressed to meet anyone."

Taylor laughed. "Wow, I wouldn't have guessed you were such a prude. If you see Zeke, tell him I'll be waiting in his room." She turned and sauntered down the hallway.

Noa closed the door behind her and fell back against it. The nausea was getting worse, and she felt shaky. The bathroom door opened, framing Zeke in light. They stared at each other for a minute without saying anything. Noa finally managed to swallow. Her voice was thick as she said, "So. You were going to meet up with Taylor tonight?"

Zeke shrugged. "Yeah. She wanted to talk about something in private."

"I'll bet," Noa muttered.

"It wasn't like that," he insisted, crossing the room. "Honestly, Noa, we were just going to talk. I figured maybe she'd remembered something about the lab."

"Right. That's why she was basically naked."

"Hey," he protested, stopping in front of her. "I didn't tell her how to dress."

Noa kept her arms crossed in front of her chest and her head down. She stared at his bare feet, ghostly white against the dark floorboards. She felt like an idiot. "You should go."

"Noa—"

"I mean it." She raised her head, meeting his eyes. "I want you to leave. Now."

"C'mon, don't be like this," he protested. "What is it with you and Taylor, anyway?"

"Something about her is off. I don't trust her."

"But she hasn't given you any reason not to, right?"

Noa opened her mouth to retort, but he was right. All she really had to go on was a gut instinct. But in the past, that had always been enough for him. "I'm just saying, she's not hurt, or sick. Maybe we should send her off to the Northeast unit. They could use the help."

"You're just trying to get rid of her." Zeke snorted. "You know what? I think you're jealous."

"What?" Noa said, flabbergasted.

"Taylor's hot, and smart. And she doesn't just take your crap the way everyone else around here does."

Noa was struck dumb. They'd argued a few times over the past few months; living on top of each other in stressful situations, they'd had their share of disagreements. But

Zeke had never spoken to her like this before. Even worse, he thought Taylor was hot. "Well, enjoy your private conversation," she snapped. "Better get going; she's waiting for you."

Zeke made a noise in the back of his throat, then stalked toward the door. Without looking at her, he flung it open and disappeared down the hall.

Noa pressed the balls of her hands to her eyes, forcing back the tears that threatened to spill over. Her lips trembled as she pictured Taylor stretched out on Zeke's bed, and him lying down beside her. . . . Well, if that's how Zeke really felt, then they deserved each other, she thought angrily.

Holding on to that anger, Noa marched back to the bed, crawled in, and tugged the sheets up over her head. No matter who else came knocking tonight, she was done answering the door.

Peter barely remembered leaving his house. The drive was a blur—he'd probably broken the Prius's land-speed record getting to the student parking lot outside Amanda's freshman dorm room at Tufts. It was almost four a.m., and nearly all the windows were dark. He parked at an angle across two empty spaces and raced to the door. He yanked the handle, but it didn't budge. He suddenly remembered that it could only be opened with a key card, and he'd returned his to Amanda when they broke up.

Swearing, he dug out his phone.

He'd considered calling Amanda's parents, or the cops, but ended up rejecting both ideas outright. He didn't want to spook her folks unless he knew for certain that something bad had happened. And he still didn't trust the cops to help. In that way, Peter thought wryly, he'd been won over to

Noa's way of thinking. She didn't trust any authority figures, regarding them all as the enemy.

Besides, maybe Amanda was lying in a bed at Boston General, recovering from a fainting episode; she hadn't been eating regularly, she'd admitted as much.

But deep down, Peter knew that wasn't true. Mason had her again. And somehow, he had to get her back before something even more terrible happened.

He dialed Diem's number. It rang repeatedly, then went to voicemail. Irritated, Peter hung up, then tried again. On his third attempt, a sleepy voice said, "Hello?"

"Hi, Diem?" He drummed his fingertips against the door. "It's Peter."

"Peter?" She sounded confused.

"Yeah, you know. Amanda's . . . friend. You texted me?"

"Oh, right." Diem yawned. "What time is it?"

"Late. Listen, I'm outside the building and can't get in."

Another yawn. "I told you, I'm not sure which hospital they took her to."

"Yeah, I know. I'm just thinking that maybe someone else in the study group might know."

"I'm not in that class," she said, clearly annoyed.

Peter bit back his retort. Sure, she and Amanda weren't exactly friends, but he'd like to think that if his roommate was carted off on a gurney, he'd display a little more concern. "Can you buzz me in, please? I'd like to find out more about what happened."

Diem issued a deep, pained sigh, then said, "Fine."

A second later the door bleated, and Peter yanked it open. He took the stairs two at a time and tore down the hall, pulling to a stop in front of their room. It looked so normal, he thought with a pang. Battered wood, the only decoration a

mounted whiteboard with flowers scrawled below *DIEM &
AMANDA*.

Diem opened the door to let him in. She was wearing
boy's boxer shorts and a tank top, her long black hair draped
over her shoulders. As he pushed past, she snorted and said,
"Come on in. Make yourself at home."

"So who can we call?" he said curtly.

Diem rolled her eyes. "You know it's, like, the middle of
the night, right?"

"Yeah," Peter said. "But some people must still be up."

Seeing that he wasn't going to budge, Diem stalked across
the room to her laptop. "I think Jackson is in that class. Let
me get his number off the student directory."

Peter paced while he waited. Diem seemed to be moving
in slow motion. He watched with mounting frustration as
her fingers stumbled over keys, then hit backspace to correct
the errors. After what seemed like forever, she looked up at
him. "Got his cell here. He's on the other side of campus,
though, and probably asleep. You know, seeing how it's the
middle of the night and all."

Peter was already dialing, praying that whoever Jackson
was, he didn't turn off his ringer when he went to bed.

A male voice answered on the second ring. To his enormous relief, music played in the background. "Jackson?"

"Yeah?" The kid's voice was drawling, slow. Like he was
stoned.

Peter gritted his teeth. It was probably too much to hope
for a sober person to be up this late. "Hey, listen. I'm a friend
of Amanda Berns, and I heard about what happened in study
group tonight."

"You're a what?" Jackson interrupted.

Definitely stoned, Peter thought with irritation. "Amanda

Berns. They took her away in an ambulance?"

"Oh, yeah, man. That was wild. We thought she'd just, like, fainted, you know? But then she started twitching and everything, so—"

"Wait, what? She had a seizure?"

"Well, yeah, dude. And she didn't wake up. So someone called an ambulance."

Peter dropped heavily down on Diem's bed, ignoring her yelped protest. "Which hospital did they take her to?"

"Um, yeah, they didn't really say. Hell, I almost passed out too. But from boredom. Man, that class—"

"Can you try thinking a little harder?" Peter was holding the phone so tightly he half expected it to shatter in his grip.

"Sorry, man. Like I said—couple guys dressed in black, with, like, bags—"

"They didn't have any badges on their sleeves?" Peter interrupted. His friend Cody had been a paramedic before he was killed; that was how he'd been paying for medical school. And his uniform had been navy blue, with round white sleeve patches that read EMS/CITY OF BOSTON.

"No, they were definitely black. Pretty rad, for ambulance guys, y'know? Both of them were totally yoked, too."

Peter hung up, cutting him off.

"What?" Diem demanded, staring down at him with her huge brown eyes.

"Amanda had some sort of seizure. They took her to the hospital." *Except they didn't*, he added silently. Mason had seized the opportunity and whisked her away.

Diem laid a hand on his shoulder sympathetically and said, "Listen, Amanda will be fine. They're probably just keeping her overnight for observation, right? We can find out where she is in the morning."

"Yes," Peter said, his resolve hardening. He didn't feel tired anymore, or scared. He was just really, really pissed off. "I'm going to find her."

"Well, all right," Diem said, clearly taken aback by his tone. "When you find out where she is shoot me a text, okay? I'll send flowers or something."

"Sure," Peter said. "Flowers." He didn't bother adding that wherever Amanda was, he knew for a fact FTD didn't deliver there.

CHAPTER SIXTEEN

Amanda opened her eyes. A bright light was positioned directly above, forcing her to wince against the glare. She tried to lift a hand to shield her vision, but discovered to her consternation that her arm wouldn't move. She raised her head a few inches, trying to ignore the pounding in her temples. Her eyes widened. Her arms and legs were bound with restraining cuffs to the metal rails of a hospital bed.

Immediately, she flashed back on all the terrible things Peter had said about what happened to Noa. How she'd woken up on a table. How they'd performed some sort of operation that changed her; he'd never elaborated on that part, but she gathered from his discomfort that it had been serious and irrevocable.

And most of the other kids who ended up on these tables

were never seen again. Unspeakable things were done to them. They were chopped up and stuffed into coolers. . . .

Amanda fought back a wave of panic. She closed her eyes again and focused on getting her breathing under control. Keeping them shut, she took a physical inventory.

Aside from her throbbing head, nothing really hurt. She had a vague memory of study group, and dots suddenly swimming across her vision. Concerned faces overhead . . . and then . . . an ambulance? There had been cold air, strangers in dark uniforms. And . . . Mason?

Her eyes jerked open at the memory and she lifted her head again. The bed was surrounded by a hospital curtain on metal rollers. Still, aside from the IV drip running down into her arm, there was no other equipment in the room. That was a good sign, right?

Amanda tucked her chin, trying to get a good look at the gown she was wearing. A thin blanket covered her to the waist. Above it the gown was white with tight navy pinstripes. It didn't have any hospital information stamped on it, but maybe they didn't do that anymore. She hadn't spent much time in hospitals, so couldn't say for certain. It was awfully quiet, though. And she couldn't see any of those handheld devices that adjusted the bed or called a nurse. Not that she'd be able to use it anyway.

Amanda tugged desperately at the straps with both arms—nothing. She tried again with her feet, straining as hard as she could, but couldn't even lift her legs an inch off the bed. Whoever had tied her down made sure she was completely immobilized.

Amanda felt panic encroaching again, spurred by her helplessness. She gritted her teeth and fought back against it. Maybe she wasn't Noa, some streetwise teenager who could fight grown men. But she wasn't a coward, either. And if they were watching, she didn't want to give them the satisfaction of appearing terrified.

Unfortunately, she was incredibly thirsty. It felt like she'd swallowed a bucket of sand. They hadn't killed her yet, so maybe they were planning on keeping her alive. For now, at least.

"Um, hello?" she called out tentatively. "I'm kind of thirsty."

A moment passed, then shuffling footsteps approached. Dread rose up her throat, all her muscles clenching as she braced for whoever was about to appear.

The curtain separated with a whirring of metal beads. Amanda found herself staring at a kindly looking elderly woman whose hair was drawn back in a tight white bun. She was built like a fireplug, small and squat and crammed into pink scrubs patterned with dancing ducks. She beamed as if Amanda was the best thing she'd seen all day, then chirped, "Oh good, you're up! And how are we feeling?"

We? Amanda thought. "Um, okay, I guess. Except that I'm tied to a bed, and don't know where I am."

A shadow flickered across the nurse's face, but her smile didn't falter. "Of course, it must be very disorienting," she said sympathetically. "It's for your own safety, however."

"My safety?" Amanda snorted. "Yeah, right."

The nurse pursed her lips. "Well, let me get you some water. I'll be right back."

She disappeared, leaving Amanda to stare after her retreating form. She twisted her head, trying to see through the small gap in the curtains, but everything outside was shadowed. The nurse trotted back in with a plastic cup that had a straw jutting out of it. "There we are. Let me help you."

The nurse gently cradled the back of Amanda's head as she tucked the straw into her mouth. Amanda considered refusing to drink, but her thirst was so overpowering she ended up greedily sucking on the straw. She drained the cup, and the nurse eased her head back onto the thin pillow. "There," the nurse said, sounding pleased. "That must feel better, right?"

"Where am I?" Amanda asked.

"The doctor usually explains these things." The nurse was running a hand over the cup, betraying some inner agitation. "I'm afraid I'm not supposed to say anything, dear."

"So where is he?"

"Oh, he won't be in for hours yet. It's the middle of the night, you know." The nurse blinked at her again, still smiling.

Amanda had never considered herself to be a violent person. But at that moment, more than anything she wanted to wrap her fingers around the nurse's plump throat and squeeze until her watery blue eyes bugged out. "Where am I," she repeated in a growl.

The nurse flinched noticeably. "I could get something to help you sleep, if you like."

"If you don't tell me where I am right now, I'll start screaming," Amanda said calmly. When the nurse didn't react, Amanda opened her mouth wide. Hurriedly, the nurse raised a hand.

"Wait! All right, dear. I'll tell you." She stepped closer to the bed and lowered her voice. "But when the doctor comes through for rounds, please don't mention it, okay? He has a very . . . specific way he likes to handle new patients."

I'll bet he does, Amanda thought grimly, but she nodded her acquiescence.

"You're in a PEMA ward, dear."

"What?" Amanda cocked her head, trying to read the woman's face to see if she was lying.

But her eyes were warm as ever as she repeated in a voice filled with empathy, "A PEMA ward, Amanda. I'm afraid that you're really quite ill."

Noa picked moodily at the plate in front of her. She wasn't hungry. Last night she'd had one of her gorging sessions, which meant she wouldn't be able to eat again for a few days. During dinner, she hadn't been up for her usual charade of consumption. She was pretty sure the other kids suspected she had an eating disorder anyway, so why bother faking it?

It had been a long, relatively uneventful day. She'd spent some time in the makeshift "infirmary" that Monica maintained in the main house. The converted guest bedroom was better equipped than most hospital rooms. The girl they'd found in Arizona still hadn't regained consciousness, and Noa could tell by the worry lines creasing Monica's forehead that she might never wake up again. She had the same incision as Noa, and her blood work had tested positive for PEMA. The machines monitoring her stats showed a slow degradation of her condition. It wasn't the first time they'd encountered this. They'd rescued other kids during raids who'd suffered too long at the hands of the Project Persephone bastards. Many had deliberately been infected with PEMA, then subjected to the same operation Noa had undergone.

They'd buried far too many kids here, in a small plot of land overlooking the sea at the edge of the Forsythes' property. And she could tell by Monica's silence that soon enough they'd be digging a fresh grave for this girl, probably without ever learning her name.

The thought depressed the hell out of her. Sometimes Noa felt like Sisyphus, just rolling that damn stone uphill, only to have it come tumbling back down. Over the past four months, they'd managed to save a few dozen kids. And only about half of those had survived. Were they really accomplishing anything?

Noa pushed away her barely touched plate of lasagna. She was alone in the kitchen, at the massive oak table where they ate most of their meals. The rest of the kids had already decamped to the living room, an enormous space with cathedral ceilings, lots of comfy sofas and chairs, and a roaring fire, welcome tonight since the fog had rolled in. She could hear them teasing one another as they played a board game. It was funny—once they got here most of the kids seemed to magically turn into regular teenagers.

All except her. Somewhere out there, the Project Persephone people were looking for her. And Noa was equally certain that at some point, they'd catch her.

She heard Taylor laugh sharply. Noa scowled. She'd been surreptitiously watching the girl all day, but hadn't seen anything out of the ordinary. If anything, Taylor seemed to have made a point of hanging out in plain view, with Matt by her side like a small sullen shadow. They'd helped Monica in the garden, Taylor brightly asking about the different kinds of plants, oohing and aahing over how self-sustaining the farm was. She'd helped cook dinner, then volunteered to clean up afterward. Monica seemed to have taken a real shine to her, which bothered Noa more than she cared to admit.

Zeke had been avoiding her all day, too. Along with Remo, Janiqua, and Teo, he'd been helping Roy rebuild the barn. They'd only shown up for meals, tired and dirty. After the last plate was cleared, he'd headed to his room, barely grunting good night. Noa had seen Roy and Monica exchange a meaningful look, and her face had flushed.

Maybe Zeke was right. Taylor was the first kid who not only didn't seem awed by her, she wasn't impressed at all. And Noa had to admit that bothered her. Much as it made her uncomfortable, she'd gotten used to the other kids treating her like she was some sort of superhero. Perhaps because of that, she was perceiving a danger in Taylor that didn't really exist.

And the fact that Zeke found her attractive didn't help, either.

Irritated, she got up and cleared her plate from the table, rinsing it and stacking it in the dishwasher. She should go for a walk again, try to clear her mind.

Noa was about to leave the kitchen when Roy came in. At the look of concern on his face, her heart sank. Had they lost the girl already?

"Evening, Noa," he said, pulling out one of the kitchen chairs and dropping heavily into it. "Everything okay?"

"Yeah, I'm fine," Noa said. "Just needed a minute alone."

Roy nodded, but she could tell he was preoccupied. Running a hand over his face, he said, "There's something we should talk about."

"Okay," she said uncertainly. Whatever it was sounded serious, judging by his grave tone.

"Let's go for a walk."

"Sure," she said, although now that he suggested it, she was loath to leave the cozy confines of the house.

Still, Noa followed him out the back door. The solar lights hardly penetrated the gloom tonight. It was an unusual fog, thick and low to the ground. She could barely see ten feet in any direction, and was struck by the strange sensation of walking into a dream. Noa tried to shake off her dread, fighting to keep her voice steady as she asked, "So what is it?"

Roy avoided her eyes as he said, "We got your new test results back."

"Yeah?" It had become a matter of routine every time she came here; the first day back, Monica always drew a few vials of blood.

Roy walked on, headed toward the cliff top. Noa followed, her heart in her throat. "I'm not exactly sure how to tell you this," he finally said. "But we both thought you should know."

"Know what?"

"Your cells. They're changing."

"Changing how?"

"That's the thing. We're not exactly sure." Roy stopped and turned to face her. For the first time since they'd left the house, he looked her in the eye. "I know I already asked last night, but has anything changed lately? Are you feeling any different?"

Noa tried to suppress a rush of fear. Her heart was pounding insistently, and she could have sworn that the extra thymus pumped in time with it. She ran through the past few weeks in her mind. Had anything changed? She couldn't say for certain. "Not really. I mean, I've been more tired, but we didn't really get much sleep out there."

He nodded as if that's what he'd expected. "It could be nothing, it's just . . . unusual."

"Unusual?" Noa said, a quaver in her voice. "But I'm not sick, am I?"

"I don't think so, no."

His look of concern belied his words, though. Roy was an

expert on microbiology, and he clearly thought that something was very wrong. "When you say they're changing, I mean . . . what exactly are they doing?"

"They're dividing at an abnormally high rate," Roy said. "Which isn't necessarily a bad thing, but now they're breaking down, too. And we haven't seen that before."

Noa didn't know much about biology; she'd only made it through a few months before she bailed out of school entirely. Times like this, she wished she'd paid more attention. "So am I dying?"

A long pause before Roy said, "Honestly? We just don't know. We'd like to run some more tests tomorrow. It might be nothing," he hurriedly added, seeing her reaction. "But just to be on the safe side, we'd like to have as much information as possible."

"Of course," Noa said faintly. She suddenly felt dizzy; was that because her own cells were betraying her? "Information."

Roy laid a hand on her shoulder and squeezed. "Easy, Noa. If we're lucky, it'll turn out to be nothing."

Noa tried to muster a smile and failed. If she'd learned anything over the course of her life, it was that luck was usually against her. "Sure."

"Let's get back inside," he said, dropping his hand. "It's nearly time for bed."

Noa followed him in silence. She'd slept heavily the night before, clocking almost thirteen hours. Which meant she'd probably barely sleep for a few days. Usually she was grateful for that; it gave her extra hours to plan the next raid. Tonight, it would only provide time to dwell on this conversation.

"Try not to worry, Noa," Roy said as they approached the house. He was struggling to sound comforting, but she could hear the strain in his voice.

Noa was about to respond when she realized that he'd gone stock-still. "What is it?" she asked.

Roy was frowning. "I thought I saw—"

His words were cut off as something flared a hundred years away from them, casting the trees in silhouette. It took Noa a second to realize that a burst of flame had suddenly exploded from the house.

Peter dropped his head into his hands. He'd hacked into the databases of every hospital in a twenty-mile radius, and none of them had Amanda listed as a patient.

The fact that there was no sign of her confirmed his worst fears. Amanda must have fallen into Mason's hands again. And this time, he wouldn't be leaving her on a park bench. He hadn't sent any more messages, and when Peter tried to open a Word doc, there was no response on the other end.

Peter tried to calm down. He was back in his room at home. No point sneaking around anymore, hacking into places from a parked car. No wonder there hadn't been any-thing on Mason's laptop, and most of the phone conversations were so innocuous. Peter felt like an idiot. He thought he'd been so sly, like some sort of smooth secret agent. Instead, he'd bumbled everything. Had they managed to track Noa through him? He wanted to contact her, but didn't dare, now that he knew his every move was being monitored.

Still, even if Mason knew exactly where he'd been in the physical world, that didn't mean he'd been able to track him through the virtual one. Peter had always taken extraordinary precautions. Even with access to military-grade technology, it was unlikely they'd been able to monitor him online. And if Mason needed help hacking into the server, it suggested he didn't exactly have a crack team at his disposal.

Obviously, Mason was using Amanda for leverage, to get Peter to do what he wanted. And it was working. He didn't have another option. Mason would keep her alive, as long as she still had value as a pawn in his sick game.

But unless Peter figured out a way to gain the upper hand, Mason would get rid of Amanda in the end. She knew too much for him to let her live.

Peter collapsed on his bed. He'd never felt so tired in his life. He couldn't even remember the last time he'd slept for more than a few hours at a stretch. He wanted to close his eyes and pass out. Sleep for a few days, and maybe when he woke up this would all turn out to be a terrible nightmare.

But he couldn't. Amanda was counting on him—no one else even knew she was gone. He hadn't had the heart to tell her parents, and her roommate couldn't do anything for her. *Besides, the fewer people who know, the better,* he told himself. Maybe if he kept it quiet, Mason would let her live.

He toyed with the idea of contacting Noa. If she was following standard procedure, she'd be holed up somewhere. She'd never told him where her home base was located, but made it clear that it was with people she could trust. That in and of itself was a mystery to him; it was hard to believe there were people who'd known about Project Persephone for years, and had been fighting it before they ever came on the scene. But at least it meant there was somewhere safe Noa could go between raids. He hoped she was there now.

Peter peered out his bedroom window. It was dark, and cold; whorls of white frost ate away at the edges of his windowpanes. He set his jaw as he stared out past the trees, toward the lights of the city beyond.

His only play here was to cut a deal with Mason in person.

But first, he needed to cover his back. Noa was too far away, and he didn't want her involved anyway. But there was someone he could turn to for help—someone who had a lot more experience with this sort of thing. Peter flipped open his laptop and logged into The Quad, typing in the code for the Northeast chapter. After a pause, he wrote, *Mayday*, then hit Send. The team leader, Luke, was supposed to check the page every night. Peter had only met him once, but he seemed pretty capable—a seventeen-year-old who'd been living alone on the street for years. And his unit was almost as good as Noa's in terms of their capabilities.

Peter closed the laptop, feeling moderately relieved. Mason wouldn't expect him to have backup. And maybe if they worked together, they could bring him down once and for all.

CHAPTER SEVENTEEN

oy recovered quickly. A second after the explosion he was tearing toward the house, moving much faster than she would have guessed a man his age could run. Noa followed close on his heels. The lower floor of the house was on fire; the bomb, or whatever it was, had been in the dining room. Luckily, unless they'd moved, most of the kids were still on the other side of the house.

"What was that?" Noa yelled.

"I don't know," Roy shouted back grimly, circling around to the kitchen door. As they approached, it flew open. Teens spilled out onto the lawn, their faces masks of terror. Everyone was yelling, their voices sharp with fear and confusion. Noa scanned them quickly, doing a head count. Daisy and Teo were missing; so were Zeke, Taylor, and Matt. Monica wasn't there either; she was probably still with the unconscious girl. And the makeshift infirmary was in the front of the house, right beside the dining room. "Where are the others?" she yelled.

They stared at her blankly, as if too dazed to process what she was saying. She grabbed Remo by the arm and shouted, "Daisy and Teo, Zeke and Taylor and Matt. Where are they?"

"Uh, Daisy and Teo headed back to the bunks," he said, snapping out of it. "And I think Zeke and Taylor . . . um, they went upstairs. Haven't seen Matt, I thought he went to bed."

"We have to help them!" Noa yelled. "C'mon!"

Roy was already pushing through the cluster of kids, making a dash for the door. He stumbled on the bottom step and almost went sprawling. Catching himself at the last minute, he vanished into the smoke that rolled out the door in thick black waves.

Noa followed, with Remo at her heels. The kitchen was filled with smoke, tendrils of it wafting almost languorously toward the door. She pulled her scarf up over her face, instantly experiencing a wave of déjà vu; had it been only the night before last when they'd nearly burned to death in the warehouse?

Suddenly, the floor shook as another explosion rocked the house. Noa instinctively ducked as the glass windows lining the kitchen shattered. It sounded as if that one had ignited upstairs. . . . Where Zeke was.

"Go help Roy find Monica!" Noa said, waving Remo toward the front of the house.

He nodded and vanished through the door to the living room.

Noa took the stairs two at a time. It was much hotter upstairs, and the fire roared like a living thing. She fought off an inner wave of raw panic and terror, forcing herself to keep going. Zeke was up here somewhere. And no matter what the hell he was doing with Taylor, she owed him her life many times over. Noa staggered down the hall, struggling through rapidly increasing clouds of smoke. From the sound of it, the second explosion had hit the side of the house fronting the driveway. The fire had almost reached the door to Zeke's room; it was licking along the walls toward her. . . .

Noa squinted against the heat and smoke, tears forced from her eyes. Already her lungs felt charred, and her skin prickled from the heat. She pulled down her sleeve and touched the knob quickly: still cool. Noa turned it and hurled herself into the room, almost afraid of what she'd find.

Empty.

She backed up, puzzled. The front bedroom was engulfed in flames; if Zeke was in there, it was already too late. Which left her room.

She drew a deep breath and checked the knob: cool. Noa said a silent prayer and flung it open.

Zeke was standing with his back to her. And facing him, brandishing a small gun, was Taylor. At the sight of Noa, her lips turned up in a snide grin and she said, "Good, you're here. We've been waiting for you."

Teo had floated through the day. He'd spent most of it helping Remo, Zeke, Janiqua, and Roy fix up an old barn. At first he'd been hopelessly clumsy, repeatedly hitting his fingers with the hammer. But Roy was a really cool guy, patient and nice, and he spent a lot of time giving Teo tips. By the end of the day, he was securing boards in place with the same ease as the rest of them. The whole experience had been refreshingly novel: being outside in the sunshine, a cool breeze blowing off the ocean, and no cup in his hand. A full belly, working with kids who teased each other, but without the nasty undertones he was accustomed to. It felt . . . normal.

When they got back to the house, Daisy was waiting for him. Over sandwiches she bragged about staking tomatoes, proudly showing him the mud encrusted under her chipped nail polish, like it was a badge of honor. She hadn't bothered with the full Goth paint since they'd left Oakland, and her cheeks were slightly burned from the sun. He thought she was pretty much the most beautiful girl he'd ever seen in his entire life. The whole time they ate, she surreptitiously held his hand under the table.

And now they were lying side by side in his bunk bed. They'd been assigned to a converted shed a few hundred yards from the house, which Roy jokingly referred to as their "finest guest hut." It was actually pretty nice inside. Wood floors, a small bathroom, two sets of bunk beds on either wall, and a thick rug. And the bunk bed was surprisingly comfortable, with a really soft mattress and warm blankets.

Daisy had stripped down to a tank top and boy shorts before slipping under the covers. His heart was thudding so hard in his chest he was sure she could hear it. Daisy pressed closer to him. She dropped her head, leaned in, and kissed him.

Teo's breath stopped entirely as he kissed her back. Her lips were so unbelievably soft, and she tasted so good. He was suddenly hyperaware of his own breath. He'd brushed his teeth, but only with his finger because there'd been toothpaste but no toothbrush. Was she totally disgusted, and wishing she hadn't started this?

Daisy pulled away, smiling dreamily. She gently trailed her index finger down the side of his face. "I really like you, Teddy."

"I really like you, too," he said, embarrassed by how hoarse and raspy his voice sounded.

"So can we take this slow?"

"Slow?" The distance from his ears to his brain seemed to have widened into a vast gulf. "Yeah, sure. Slow is good."

"Good." She smiled, and snuggled up against him. Teo wrapped both arms around her.

Daisy made a small happy noise in the back of her throat, which he took as encouragement. Throwing caution to the wind, Teo started to draw slow circles with his fingertips, inching up her back gradually. She tilted her face toward him, and they started kissing again. . . .

Daisy pulled away, a small frown creasing her features.

"What?" he asked anxiously. "Do you want me to stop?"

"Do you smell smoke?"

Teo sniffed the air. It did smell like smoke, but nothing like the nasty, chemical burning smell at the warehouse the other night. "Probably just from the fireplace," he said dismissively. He parted his lips hopefully, pulling her back toward him.

"That's definitely too strong to be from the fireplace," Daisy stated bluntly, pulling herself up. "Something's wrong."

Teo sighed, wondering if this was just an excuse. Obediently, he sat up too, taking care not to knock his head on the upper bunk. He inhaled obediently, and frowned. She was right: It did smell unusually smoky. Crap.

"I'll go check it out," he said with resignation.

Teo shuffled over to the door, readjusting his clothes as he went, his toes curling in protest against the cold floorboards. He opened it and peered out into the night, then turned back to Daisy with a dumbfounded expression on his face.

"What?" she asked.

"The house. It's on fire!"

Mason had the nerve to look surprised at finding Peter on his doorstep. He was dressed for bed in a pair of navy pajamas and a dark robe. Somehow, even in that outfit he managed to look intimidating. "Well," he said after a beat. "Bit late for a social call, isn't it, Peter?"

"There's nothing social about this," Peter snarled, pushing past him into the living room. Inside, his entire body was quaking, but he wasn't going to give Mason the benefit of seeing that. He plunked down on the sofa.

Mason remained standing, arms crossed over his chest and a bemused smile on his face. "I see you're accustomed to making yourself at home here."

Peter snorted. "Honestly, first time I walked in, I figured this must be the wrong address. You decorate like a grand-mother."

Mason raised an eyebrow, but a stronger emotion flickered in his eyes. He settled languidly on the easy chair opposite. "So you came here to insult my decor?"

"You know why I came," Peter spat. "So, fine. I'll hack into the server. But if I do that, you let Amanda go. Unharmed."

Mason continued studying Peter speculatively.

"What?" Peter demanded.

Abruptly, Mason got to his feet, so suddenly it made Peter flinch. But he simply crossed to the kitchen and poured two glasses of water, then came back. "Well, then. I'm glad you changed your mind."

"Whatever," Peter mumbled. Mason held the water out to him, but he didn't take it. After a second, Mason set the glass on the coffee table between them and settled back in his chair. "I still don't get why you want *me* to do this."

Mason shrugged. "It came to my attention during our last . . . encounter, that you are quite skilled at what you do. Too skilled for your own good, obviously."

"Gee, thanks."

"It really is a shame that we got off on the wrong footing, Peter. If your parents had any grasp of your talents, they would have suggested bringing you into the fold themselves."

The thought of his parents enlisting him in the kidnapping and murder of other teenagers turned Peter's stomach. The worst part was that, considering the amount of money involved, they might've done it. If Project Persephone succeeded, and Pike & Dolan discovered a cure for PEMA, there were millions of dollars at stake.

Which was probably, he realized, precisely why Mason wanted those medical files. "So," he said carefully, "what am I looking for on the server, exactly?"

Mason narrowed his eyes. "Wondering what I'm after, Peter?"

"Yeah, actually." Peter reached for the water. The way Mason was looking at him had made his throat go dry. "You trying to rip them off?"

Mason waved a hand. "That's really none of your concern."

"Sure it is." Peter drained half the glass, then set it back down, perversely pleased when it left a ring on the table. "I mean, I've got to know what to look for, for one thing. I can't just pull everything off the server."

"Really?" Mason cocked an eyebrow. "You did just that last time."

Peter shifted uncomfortably. He didn't want to go into detail about how he'd managed to get the information off

P&D's servers before bricking them. "That was different. It's complicated."

"I see. You still have those files, I'm assuming?"

Peter shrugged. No harm in admitting that—obviously he wouldn't have gotten rid of them. He'd buried them deeply, though, scattered across a dozen servers in as many countries, with full backups in place.

"Good." Mason steepled his fingers, looking satisfied.

"So you just want me to hand those over?" Peter demanded.

Mason shook his head. "No need. That research only served to lay the groundwork."

Peter was confused. If the files were worthless, why had anyone bothered keeping tabs on him? "So, what, they had some sort of breakthrough in the past few months?"

Mason stared at him. Peter shifted, disconcerted. Mason's black eyes looked particularly creepy in the dim lighting.

"What?" Peter finally said, turning his palms up. "Is it some big secret?"

"Actually, yes, Peter. It is." Mason still hadn't touched his own water. "One that Charles Pike paid dearly for."

Something struck him. "Wait. Have they found a cure for PEMA?" In spite of the situation, his heart leapt. If he could get Amanda back, and a cure was about to be released . . . maybe she'd be all right after all.

"Close," Mason said. "But not entirely."

Peter's heart sank. "So why are we bothering to steal the files? Just because Charles Pike pissed you off?"

"He more than 'pissed me off,'" Mason said, his face twisting into an ugly sneer. "And what happened between us isn't your concern. Suffice it to say that there are people who will pay dearly for this research."

"It is about money." Peter snorted. "I already told you you're a jerkwad, right?"

Mason moved so swiftly, Peter barely had time to register it before being hauled bodily out of the chair. Mason held him by the front of his jacket, lifting him nearly off the ground. His shirt collar was gathered so tightly, Peter choked for air. They were face-to-face, inches apart. As calmly as if they were still sitting across from each other, Mason said, "You should watch yourself, Peter. I would hate for anything to happen to you."

Peter struggled, and Mason abruptly released him. His knees knocked hard against the rim of the coffee table as he hit the ground, making him wince. He swallowed, his heart still drumming against his ribs at about a hundred miles an hour. Mason, meanwhile, didn't even look flushed from the exertion; it was as if the encounter had never happened.

"We leave in five minutes," Mason said.

"Wait a minute," Peter stuttered. "You want to do this *tonight*?"

Mason was already strolling toward the bedroom. He called back over his shoulder, "While you're waiting, I'd advise wiping the water ring off my coffee table."

Noa couldn't help herself; her immediate reaction was to snap at Zeke, "Told you we couldn't trust her."

He grimaced. "Yeah, obviously. Sorry. Feel better?"

"A little." In spite of the situation, she felt vindicated. "Is that your gun?"

He didn't reply, which was answer enough. Noa sighed. This was exactly why she didn't like guns. It was far too easy for them to be turned against you. "So what's your plan?" she asked Taylor.

Taylor shrugged. "We wait."

"Really? Here, in a house that's on fire?" Noa threw up her hands, exasperated. "In a few minutes, this whole place is going to be burning."

"Oh, they'll be here before that," Taylor said confidently.

"Crap," Zeke muttered.

Noa could feel the temperature in the room rising, a shimmer in the air. "Not a great plan, I have to say. Personally, I'd have gotten out of the house after setting the fires."

"Actually Matt set them. He's quite the little firebug," Taylor said, a note of pride in her voice.

"So you were plants," Noa said. "You're working for Project Persephone." Which meant that the Phoenix raid had been a setup all along.

"We both were." Taylor looked smug. "Awfully sweet of you to break in and rescue us, though."

Noa shot a glance at Zeke, but he was avoiding her eyes. If Taylor was telling the truth, they'd led their enemies straight to the Forsythes' doorstep. That realization filled her with rage. She had to warn the others. The woods surrounding the property might already be swarming with mercenaries.

"But why help them?" Zeke asked, sounding perplexed. "They're killing kids."

A shadow flitted across Taylor's face, and her smile faltered. She tossed her hair and said, "I don't have to tell you anything. I just have to keep you here for a few more minutes until they take care of the others."

"What are they going to do to them?" Noa asked, dread blooming in her stomach.

"Well, they're not really useful anymore, are they?" Taylor said sweetly.

"So they're going to kill them? And you're okay with

252

that?" Zeke took a menacing step forward. Taylor lifted the gun higher, although Noa noticed her hands shaking. Seeing that, her eyes narrowed; it was unlikely that Taylor had much shooting experience. She wasn't exactly one of Mason's trained commandos. Probably just a kid they'd threatened, or offered money to. She took a step forward, too.

Taylor jerked the gun toward her, then back at Zeke, trying to cover them both simultaneously. "Stand still!" she warned shrilly. Apparently she'd just realized that the cavalry was running late. And that covering two people with a gun was no mean feat if you didn't know what you were doing.

Zeke took a step away from her, toward the windows. Noa moved in the opposite direction. "What are you doing?" Taylor demanded. "Stay together!"

"Where's Matt now?" Noa asked, edging forward another step. "I didn't see him outside."

Another flicker of uncertainty in Taylor's eyes. "You didn't?"

"Nope."

Taylor was clearly fighting to recover her bravado. "He probably went off to wait for them in the woods."

"Them? So you know how many are coming?" Zeke asked casually. He was also moving incrementally, widening the gap between them.

"Stop moving!" Taylor's eyes darted back and forth as she slowly backed up. Noa watched carefully, gauging the distance between her and the bed.

Zeke was almost at the windows. Noa was flanking her on the other side. The back of Taylor's legs hit the edge of the bed, and she glanced over her shoulder, her face a mask of shock, as if she hadn't even been aware of moving.

Noa seized on her momentary distraction and lunged

forward, arms extended. But instead of reaching for Taylor's hands, she knocked her hard in the right shoulder, sending her spinning toward the bed.

The gun went off, with a bang so loud it set her ear drums reverberating. Out of the corner of her eye Noa saw Zeke vault across the room, covering the distance to the bed in three long strides. She was struggling to pin Taylor down; what the girl lacked in size and strength she more than made up for in unadulterated rage. She snarled and kicked as Noa pressed her face into the comforter. The room was slowly filling with smoke. Noa's nostrils twitched and burned. She could feel the heat along the length of her back.

Taylor swung her arm wildly, trying to take another shot with the gun. She bucked hard, and Noa's grasp on her right arm slipped. She lunged for it again, but too late.

Bang! Another shot. Noa looked up in time to catch the look of surprise on Zeke's face. He pressed a hand to his side; it came away bloody.

CHAPTER
EIGHTEEN

Amanda had completely lost all sense of time. She'd drifted in and out of consciousness for what could have been days, weeks, or even months. The older nurse came and went, and sometimes other people dressed in scrubs wandered through. But she had a hard time focusing; as soon as they left, their faces slipped from her mind.

In a small corner of her brain, she understood what was happening; they were keeping her sedated, so that she'd be easy to manage. Yet the drugs had Amanda so removed from herself that she couldn't muster the energy to care. It was disarmingly pleasant, being turned into a sort of oversized rag doll. She was being fed through an IV line, and occasionally the nurses would fluff her pillows or slip ice chips into her mouth. Amanda placidly wondered if her parents had any idea that she was being kept here against her will. At the thought, she tried to summon some indignation, but that required too much energy.

Until suddenly, it didn't. Maybe they'd gotten her dose wrong, or forgot to replenish the IV drip. But Amanda finally opened her eyes, blinked, and knew exactly where she was, and what was happening. Close on the heels of that realization came a groundswell of rage.

Followed by elation, because not only was she fully conscious, but the straps that had been restraining her were inexplicably gone.

Amanda sat bolt upright, then clasped her head in both hands, nearly overcome by a wave of dizziness. She squeezed her eyes shut and took a few deep breaths, fighting back nausea. Cautiously opening her eyes again, she saw with relief that the room had stopped spinning, although it still swayed noticeably. She groped under her gown, checking her chest, belly, and lower back. Her panic ebbed slightly when she didn't encounter any bandages. Maybe they hadn't had time to experiment on her yet. Which gave her all the more reason to get out before they strapped her down again.

Moving slowly, Amanda carefully swung her legs off the bed one at a time. She flexed her feet and wiggled her toes: Everything seemed to be working, which was a relief.

The privacy curtains were still drawn, leaving a narrow passage of a few feet around her bed. Amanda eased the IV out of her arm, wincing. She pressed the surgical tape back down, clamping her hand on it to stop the bleeding.

She drew a deep breath, steeling herself, then pushed off the bed and stumbled toward the gap in the curtains. Amanda drew back a corner and peered out.

And frowned. Another set of curtains hung two feet

away. She stepped out and drew them back. What she saw made her choke back a gasp.

A young boy lay on a bed. His eyes were closed, and an IV line led from his right arm. He was restrained the same way she had been.

Amanda slid the curtain shut again. This must be what Peter had told her about; one of those illegal labs where they treated kids like guinea pigs. And she'd been dumped here as a punishment. Mrs. Latimar must have told Mason that she'd stolen those files. Or maybe they'd snatched her to punish Peter.

Either way, Amanda realized this was her chance. Now she would be the one on the front lines, saving kids from terrible fates. She had to act quickly, though. First she needed to find a way out.

Amanda stepped as quietly as possible along the narrow corridor created by the curtains, the floor icy under her bare feet. Right past the edge of her bed, the passage opened up. Her jaw dropped. There was a wider corridor, nearly fifty feet long. The floor was composed of plain white tiles, matching the bland fiberboard drop ceiling that hung low overhead. And a dozen curtained areas lined both sides. She padded silently to the section opposite hers, and drew back a curtain to discover yet another girl tied down and hooked up.

Were all of these beds occupied? If so, this was a much bigger operation than anything Peter had told her about.

In spite of everything, that thought gave Amanda a rush. She quelled it, telling herself that this wasn't about showing up Noa; it was about saving as many kids as possible. Although a small part of her could already picture the expression on Peter's face when he found out. This gave her a chance to prove she could accomplish anything Noa had, even if she was just a spoiled upper-middle-class girl from the suburbs.

Amanda slid along the main corridor as quickly as possible. It ended in a set of metal double doors. The entire room was eerily silent and still, although she could sense the presence of kids behind the curtains. It was as if they were holding their breath along with her.

Amanda said a silent prayer that the doors wouldn't be locked, then pushed on the right side: It swung open easily, and she broke into a grin. This was going to be easier than she thought.

Easing through the gap, Amanda found herself in another hallway. It was wide, with the same ceiling and floor tiles, but the walls were painted a cheery yellow and broken at regular intervals by doors. Amanda frowned. She'd been expecting something a little more ad hoc, like the warehouse Peter had described. But maybe because of the raids, Pike & Dolan were using a different type of facility now.

An illuminated sign at the end of the hall read EXIT. Amanda trotted to it and opened the door: a stairwell! And a few flights down, she could see a door rimmed by light.

Now she just had to start shuttling kids out of here. Hopefully they wouldn't be too hard to wake up.

She eased the exit door closed, flinching at the audible *click*. She'd have to prop it open with something.

On the way back to the double doors, she worked through the most efficient way to approach the problem: start with the kids closest to the door, unhook their IVs, and try to revive them. Two at a time was probably all she'd be able to manage.

She was so preoccupied with the planning that she didn't hear the footsteps until they were almost on top of her. Amanda spun at the squeak of a shoe against tile. The wizened elderly nurse was blinking up at her, hands on her hips and a stern expression on her face.

"Miss Amanda," she snapped. "What are you doing out of bed?"

Peter hunched down in the darkness outside the building. He'd never been so terrified. Mason had directed him to this deserted corner of the city, not far from the piers. As they pulled up in his Prius, Peter wondered if they were close to where Noa had been experimented on; that warehouse had been located in South Boston, the area they were in now.

No boatyard nearby, though, and these buildings appeared to be falling down. It definitely didn't look like the kind of place where a corporation would store vital servers; but then, that was probably the point. The streets were deserted. Peter tucked his head more deeply into his jacket, wishing for a hat and gloves. If he'd known that he'd be hanging out in a deserted parking lot in the middle of the night, he would've come better prepared.

Had Luke received his message? Even if he had, it was doubtful that the Northeast unit could have gotten to Mason's in time. Peter hadn't seen any sign of them as they left the building. Which meant that he was probably on his own. "How are we getting in?" he asked in a low voice.

Mason was leaning against the side of the building. He'd changed into black jeans and a turtleneck, and wore a sleek leather jacket over them. Despite the cold, he was pale as ever. And he appeared remarkably relaxed, which should've made Peter feel better, but didn't. "The server is on the second floor of that building," Mason said, indicating a dilapidated structure in the middle of a row of three.

"So, what? We just waltz right in?" Peter clenched his jaw

to keep his teeth from chattering. The temperature was in the low teens, but it felt even colder thanks to the wind.

"In a manner of speaking," Mason said in a low voice. "Ah, there he is."

Peter followed his line of sight. A man had emerged from the building. He was dressed just like the goons who had broken into Peter's house on that first night, except he wasn't carrying a gun, at least not visibly. The guy looked in both directions, then dropped a backpack on the ground at his feet. Leaning back against the closed door, he bent his head and lit a cigarette.

"Filthy habit," Mason said with disgust. "I never tolerated it when I was in charge."

Peter watched as the guy took a deep drag. "How many are in there?"

"I have no idea," Mason said blithely. "We'll find out soon enough."

"What?" Peter turned and stared at him. "Are you nuts? There could be fifty of them inside."

Mason didn't answer. He pulled back his sleeve to check a Rolex. "Almost time," he said softly.

"Time for what?" Peter felt like throttling him. This whole thing was insane. What were they even doing here? Mason didn't seriously expect him to go into a building filled with armed, trained men, did he?

As usual, Mason behaved as if he hadn't spoken. Peter gritted his teeth. He should just go back to the car. There was no guarantee that if he went through with this, Mason would let Amanda go, anyway. All he'd done was play right into his hands.

A muffled sound inside the building.

"What was that?" Peter asked, leaning forward to see.

"That was our cue." Mason pushed off the wall and started walking purposefully toward the guard manning the door. Peter's jaw dropped, and he hunched lower. Maybe Mason really was insane.

Mason stopped ten feet away, then turned and said impatiently, "Come along, Peter. We don't have all night."

Peter slowly got to his feet. Swallowing hard, he followed Mason. The guy was approaching the door like he owned the place.

The guard glanced up, spotting them. He hurriedly stubbed out the cigarette and grabbed the backpack off the ground by his feet.

Peter froze, waiting for him to pull a gun and start shooting. But the guy just stood there holding the bag. Almost like he was expecting them.

From a few feet away, Mason called out, "Any problems?"

The guard shook his head vigorously. "None, Mr. Mason."

"Excellent." Mason held out his hand for the bag. Peter watched, dumbfounded, as he unzipped it and extracted two gas masks. He handed one to Peter, saying, "Put this on."

Peter's hands automatically closed around the straps. The mask was heavier than it looked. He turned it over, staring at the thick eye lenses. "What the hell is this for?"

"For the gas, of course." Mason was already pulling it over his head. "Trust me when I say you won't want to breathe it in."

"Gas?" Peter said dumbly.

"A fentanyl derivative." Mason's voice became muffled as he adjusted the mask over the lower half of his face and secured the straps. "Nasty stuff. The Russians used it in a hostage situation more than a decade ago, but unfortunately it ended up killing more than just the terrorists. Ready?"

"Um, no, not really," Peter shot back, still holding the mask in both hands. "No way in hell I'm going in there."

"Of course you are. Otherwise, what will happen to poor Amanda?" The mask made him look and sound even more sinister than usual.

Peter swallowed hard and yanked his mask on. Immediately, he felt a wave of claustrophobia. He could hear his own breath, abnormally loud, like Darth Vader on steroids. The goggles shrank his field of vision to the size of a fishbowl.

"Stay with me," Mason said, then he nodded for the guard to open the door.

Teo and Daisy spilled out of the small cabin. A few hundred yards away, the house was burning.

"Oh my God! What happened?" Daisy shrieked.

Teo was no expert, but this didn't look like an accident. For one thing, two completely different sections of the house were in flames. Plus, the fire was raging hard, like it had been going for hours already. Or like someone had deliberately set it.

He flashed back on Taylor, the guilty look on her face at the gas station. He should have recognized it for what it was, probably would've if he hadn't been so goofy over kissing Daisy.

Daisy was frozen, both hands clamped over her mouth as if trying to force back a scream. Oddly, Teo felt calm. Like something had clicked in place inside him, and he knew exactly what had to be done.

He raced back inside, grabbed his jeans off the chair, and hurriedly pulled them on. Yanked a heavy wool sweater over his head and thrust his feet into a pair of sneakers. In less than a minute, he was back outside. He grabbed Daisy by the shoulders, turning her to face him. She'd gone full deer-in-headlights again, face pale, eyes wide with fear. As gently as possible, he said, "Daisy, you need to get dressed, fast. I'm going over there to help."

She blinked at him dazedly. "Should . . . Do I . . ."

"Stay here," he said firmly. In her state, she'd end up doing more harm than good if she got closer to the action. "I'll send everyone to you, okay? Just wait right here."

She nodded, a look of relief flitting across her features.

Teo squeezed her shoulders, then swiftly bent and kissed her hard on the lips. Then he raced toward the flames.

He didn't have a plan, really, beyond trying to help. Roy, Noa, and Zeke were probably already managing the situation, maybe manning hoses or something.

A figure darted out of the woods to his left, sweeping him off his feet with a flying tackle.

He struggled for a minute, flailing and punching. But his attacker was heavier, pinning him to the ground. Teo fought to twist out from under him.

It took a minute to realize that his assailant was fighting just as hard to get away from him.

"Danny?" he asked, managing to get him at arm's length.

"Teo, man, you gotta run!" Danny said hoarsely, his eyes panicked. "They're everywhere!"

"Who?"

But Danny had already struggled back to his feet and was tearing headlong toward the trees. Within seconds, he vanished into the fog.

Teo slowly got up. The calm had utterly dissipated, leaving behind a cold, hard core of terror. Danny had looked like a trapped animal, all wild eyes and flashing teeth. What could have put him in such a state?

Teo turned in a slow circle, conflicted. Should he still head for the house? Or follow Danny?

Daisy, he thought. He should go back to her.

Teo was running back toward the shed when another figure emerged from the fog, not far from where Danny had disappeared. But this one was dressed all in black, carrying a gun.

CHAPTER NINETEEN

"No!" Noa screamed. Taylor was already whipping her hand around, the gun pivoting in her direction.

But Noa was so enraged she barely noticed. A snarl escaped from her throat as she snapped her head forward, connecting with Taylor's forehead. The pain sent lights swirling across her vision, but she barely noticed. Taylor dropped back against the pillows looking dazed. Noa pinned her arms down with her knees, wrapped her hands around the girl's throat, and squeezed.

She'd never been so angry. All the frustration and heartbreak of the past few months exploded out of her. Noa was barely aware of Taylor gasping and straining beneath her, eyes bugging out, face turning purple. A small, distant part of her brain noted how small Taylor's neck was, and how naturally her hands fit around it. . . .

Dimly, she became aware of a voice calling her name, and of other sensations, the temperature rising in the room, her own throat closing as it filled with smoke. . . .

A fit of coughing brought her back to herself. Noa blinked, feeling like she'd just woken up. Zeke's mouth was wide. He was yelling her name over and over.

Looking down, she realized that he was trying to pry her fingers from Taylor's throat. The girl was limp, her eyes closed. The gun had fallen from her grasp.

Staring at the hands that suddenly felt like they belonged to her again, Noa abruptly released them. Her fingers were still tense, and sore from gripping so hard. Red lines wrapped around Taylor's throat like angry vines.

"Did I kill her?" she asked dazedly.

Zeke bent over Taylor, checking her. "Not yet, but close," he said grimly. Zeke tucked the gun in his waistband, then grabbed Noa by the elbow. "We've got to get out of here."

"Right, the fire," Noa said hollowly, turning her head. She still felt out of it. The seams around the door glowed with a flickering light, and smoke seeped along all sides of it. She imagined opening the door and staring out at a solid wall of bright orange and red. The fire would rush in and consume them, eagerly chasing down the fresh oxygen stored in the room like dry kindling.

"We have to get to the windows," Zeke said, tugging at her arm. "Noa, c'mon!"

Noa was still focused on Taylor. The girl's chest was rising and falling, although her breath wheezed in her throat. But that's not what she was staring at. Taylor's shirt had pulled down, revealing part of her bra, along with . . . "Zeke, look. That mark, on her chest—"

"We don't have time!" he yelled, physically hauling her off Taylor and away from the bed. He propelled her forward.

"Wait, weren't you shot?" she asked.

"Yeah, thanks for noticing. Can we get out of here now, please?"

Zeke had one hand clenched to his side; a slow tide of red oozed from under his fingers. His face was tight with pain and fear. The look in his eyes finally snapped her out of it. Noa rushed to the window and tore open the curtains, then unlatched the sash and threw it open. Zeke peered down with her. Her bedroom was on the back side of the house, facing the ocean. The second-story windows were nearly twenty feet above the ground, thanks to the vaulted living room ceiling below. Noa couldn't see or hear any of the others. She wondered if they'd already been captured or killed.

"We'll have to climb down the vines and hope they hold us," Zeke said, his voice strained. "Ladies first?"

Noa didn't answer. Her throat had gone dry. The only thing she hated worse than fire was heights.

"I'll go first," Zeke said. "Don't expect me to catch you, though."

"Wait." Noa put a hand on his arm. "What about her?"

He followed her eyes back to Taylor, who was still slumped lifelessly in the bed. "What about her?" he asked warily.

"We can't just leave her here."

"Why not?" Zeke said incredulously. "She was trying to kill us! And oh yeah, she shot me!"

"Zeke, she's one of us," Noa said. "She has the scar, too." She drew a line along her chest on the outside of her shirt.

His eyes widened as he realized what she meant. "But she said—"

"She lied."

Zeke eyed Taylor unhappily. "We'll have to lower her down with something."

Noa scanned the room. The bedsheets would take too long to knot together, and there was no way they'd be able to manage Taylor between them, not without falling. She hesitated. It had felt good, strangling her. If Zeke hadn't been there, would she have stopped?

Noa realized her fists had clenched again; she straightened her fingers. There had to be a solution. "The bathroom," she suddenly said.

"What about it?" Zeke was getting paler; he was bent nearly double. The blood had soaked his shirt and pants. The chances of him being able to climb down without help weren't good. Was she nuts to try to save a girl who'd betrayed them all?

Probably. But she was going to do it anyway. "We can use the curtain ties to make a rope, and lower her down that way."

Zeke looked dubious, but he followed her to the bed. Noa got her hands under Taylor's shoulders and lifted, taking the bulk of the girl's body weight. Zeke led the way into the bathroom, grimacing with each step. Through gritted teeth he managed to say, "For the record, I think this is a terrible idea."

"Noted," Noa grunted. Taylor was deceptively heavy. A few times, Noa checked her chest nervously, relieved each time to see it rise and fall.

Noa gently lowered the girl to the bathroom floor and closed the door. She quickly rolled up a towel and pressed it against the bottom of the doorframe. But the air was already smoky, and more seeped through the cracks by the minute. The floor felt hot, too. What if the house collapsed before they got out? Noa hurried to throw open the large window behind the tub.

"So how exactly do we get to the ground?" Zeke asked dubiously, leaning over the tub to take in the drop.

"Carefully," Noa muttered, getting to work. Monica had taken the theme to extremes here; the bathroom looked like the kind of tower an unfortunate princess might be locked away in. Marble floors, velvet wallpaper, and long, heavy curtains tied back with thickly woven gold braids.

Noa unknotted the closest curtain cord; it was at least four feet long. Her eyes darted around the room: There were eight other cords. Tied together, they should reach the ground, or at least get them close enough to jump without seriously injuring themselves.

Hopefully.

Zeke had caught on and was staggering around the room, slipping off the rest of the sashes and unknotting them. Noa started connecting them, tying a firm square knot at each end.

Taylor moaned softly, startling her. She glanced over; the girl's eyelids were fluttering.

"Great," Zeke said. "Maybe she'll wake up and try to kill us again while we're trying to save her life."

Noa ignored him. Taylor was unarmed now, and didn't seem like much of a fighter, anyway. If she woke up, it would make this a lot easier.

Noa tied one end of the rope to the claw foot tub leg, securing it with a few tugs. She examined Zeke covertly under her lashes while she did it; his face was twisted in a rictus of pain. "Are you okay?"

"No, I'm not. I got shot," he said peevishly. "Would you be okay?"

Satisfied that if he was still capable of being annoyed, it probably meant he wasn't dying, Noa threw the other end of the rope out the window. "You first," she said. "Then we'll send her."

"Yeah?" He eyed Taylor skeptically. "You still sure this is a good idea?"

"No," Noa said honestly. "But I don't want anyone else to die if I can help it."

Zeke looked at her for a second, then slowly nodded. Something in his eyes softened. "Careful, okay?" he said. "If you can't manage her, get yourself out."

"Yeah, okay," Noa said.

He looked like he was about to say something else, but at that moment he doubled over in pain. Noa lunged to help him, but he shook her off. "I'm fine," he said gruffly. "Just gotta breathe through it, right?" Zeke crawled across the tub, swung his legs over the window ledge, and grabbed hold of the rope with both hands. "See you down there," he tossed back before vanishing from sight.

The bathroom had to be a hundred degrees now. Sweat poured down her. Noa turned on the bathtub tap, relieved when it spewed a stream of cold water. She gathered up a handful of it and tossed it in Taylor's face. Nothing. Frowning, she repeated the action.

Taylor sputtered awake with a cry. Her eyes snapped open. Seeing Noa, she initially looked confused. Then a scowl furrowed her features. "You tried to kill me!"

"Yeah, well. Just trying to repay the favor." Noa jerked her head to the window. "And we've got about a minute left before we cook in here, so you better get moving."

Taylor's gaze shifted around the room, taking in the scene quickly. Seeing the rope attached to the tub, her eyes narrowed. "We're climbing out?"

"Yup. And if you're not down that rope in a few seconds, I'm going without you." Which wasn't technically true; she wasn't about to leave Taylor alone up here, free to untie the rope as she dangled from it. This way, by the time the girl got to the bottom, Zeke would be waiting with the gun. And after that . . . Well, she hadn't gotten that far along in the planning yet.

Noa stepped forward as if making good on the threat, but there was no need—Taylor was already scrambling to her feet. Clearly the girl had a finely honed sense of self-preservation. She gracefully stepped across the tub and straddled the window, then with a final glance back at Noa, started sliding down.

A loud *crack* in the bedroom made Noa jump. Probably the long mirror over the bureau, shattering from the heat. Noa felt a sharp pang at the loss of the room, and the house. She should have known better than to get attached to a place. None of her homes ever lasted.

Another *crack* as the bathroom door started to give. Noa swung her legs over the windowsill and tried not to look down. Misty sea air immediately chilled the sweat clinging to her skin, making her shiver. She let the curtain cord slide through her fingers as she rappelled down the side of the house, swinging away from a section on the right where the ivy was already in flames.

Her feet hit something solid and she exhaled deeply, releasing some of the tension knotted through her shoulders. Turning around, she saw Zeke and Taylor in a stand-off.

He was pointing the gun at her chest with his free hand, although to Noa's concern his arm was wavering.

Taylor seemed unfazed. She stood facing him, eyebrow cocked as she said, "So, what? You saved me just to shoot me?"

"You can go," Noa said.

"What?" Taylor spun toward her.

"Go." Noa nodded at the forest. "Run back to the people who operated on you. I'm sure they'll be happy to see you." She jerked her head toward the sea and said, "C'mon, Zeke."

He hesitated, then followed, staying half-turned to keep the gun directed toward Taylor. Noa sucked in lungfuls of fresh air while making a solemn oath to steer clear of burning buildings from here on out.

"You won't get away!" Taylor called after them.

Noa glanced back over her shoulder. Taylor was standing there, a pale figure limned by fog and darkness. She looked like the lost girl in some twisted fairy tale, like she'd tumbled from the tower and discovered when she hit the ground that there was no prince waiting to whisk her away.

Zeke let out a hiss of air and stumbled, nearly falling. Noa caught him, then slung one of his arms over her shoulder, propping him up as she helped him along.

"What about the others?" he gasped.

"I'll go back for them as soon as I get you somewhere safe," she said.

"Leave me. I'll be fine."

"I'm not arguing about this," Noa said. "So you might as well shut up and move faster."

"Great bedside manner as always." Zeke managed a strangled laugh. "Where are we going, anyway?"

"The beach." The plan formed in her mind as she said it. "We can swim out."

"Swim?" Zeke coughed, "Wow, you really are trying to kill me."

"Shut up and keep moving," Noa said. Their whole world was crumbling around them, literally. She had no idea where everyone else was, if they'd escaped or even now were being killed or herded away. And the closest thing she'd had to a home in nearly a decade was burning to the ground.

But she was with Zeke. And for some reason, that meant all was not lost.

They had turned the far corner of the house, and were in sight of the shelter of the trees, when her peripheral vision caught a flicker of movement from behind.

Noa spun, thinking for a moment that Taylor had changed her mind and decided to chase them down.

Instead, she saw Janiqua, cornrows streaming out behind her as she tore in their direction.

Right behind her were two men dressed all in black, wearing masks and carrying assault rifles.

The guy was wearing a helmet and a weird mask that covered the lower half of his face. He turned toward Teo, his gun panning along with him.

Teo looked down and saw a tiny red dot on his chest. He'd watched enough movies and TV shows to know that was never a good thing.

He bolted.

"Hey!" the guy yelled, but apparently Teo had moved too fast for him to react; or maybe he had orders not to shoot. Either way, Teo wasn't hanging around to find out.

He raced back to the guesthouse, praying Daisy was where he'd left her.

He was a hundred feet away when he heard her scream.

That spurred him on. The gray-shingled walls of the shed appeared through the trees. Teo put on an extra burst of speed as he rounded the corner toward the front door.

Another guy in black was pointing a rifle at Daisy. Still wearing only the thin tank top and boy shorts, she was shivering from cold and fear.

The look of terror in her eyes galvanized him. As the guy's head pivoted toward him, Teo sprang forward, slamming into his side. They both went flying. Teo flailed out with his fists. Most of the blows glanced off, but the few that connected made the guy grunt.

"Get off him!" Something jabbed Teo in the side.

The second jab got his attention—he spun so quickly, the guy behind him fell back a few steps.

Slowly, he got to his feet. Daisy was gone—hopefully she'd gotten away. The guy at his feet was groaning. Teo hoped that he hurt like hell.

The gunman squinted at him. "You're not on the list."

"What list?" Teo said.

The guy paused, then said, "Forget it, kid. Doesn't matter."

"Well, if I'm not on the list," Teo said hopefully, "maybe you can just let me go."

The guy scoffed. "Yeah, right. Nice try. Yo, Berinsky. You still breathing?"

The guy at Teo's feet shifted and cursed.

"If you're done getting your ass handed to you by a scrawny kid," the first guy sneered, "you mind getting up? We gotta get this one to the van."

Berinsky pulled down his mask and spit blood onto the ground. "I want five minutes with him first."

"Uh-uh," the first guy shook his head. "You heard the boss, we're not supposed to damage the merchandise. Besides, where they're headed"—he broke into a grin that made Teo's blood run cold—"trust me, man, they'll wish they got stuck with you and me."

The labs, Teo thought. *Somehow they found us, and they're rounding us up.* He prayed that Daisy was smart enough to hunker down and hide. And he hoped she'd at least think about him every once in a while.

Berinsky grumbled something as he lumbered to his feet, then bent to scoop up his rifle. Teo kept a wary eye on him the whole time.

"C'mon," the first guy said, gesturing to the right with his gun. "Van's that way. Start walking, kid."

Berinsky went first, limping slightly, and Teo reluctantly followed. They slogged through the woods. The smoke from the burning house had intermingled with the fog, creating a damp black curtain that snaked around them. It was so dark and thick he could barely make out anything a few feet away. For a second, he considered running for it, but the gunman must've picked up on a change in his posture; he snarled, "Don't even think about it. I'd love a reason to shoot you. And like I said, you're not on the list."

Teo wondered again what this list was, and how they'd gotten it. Had Taylor given it to them? If so, then he should've been on it, right?

Who else could have provided it?

Teo tripped on a tree root and went flying, landing hard on his hands and knees.

"Get up!" the guy behind him snapped.

Berinsky didn't seem to be paying attention to either of them. He just kept shuffling forward through the trees.

Which was lucky, because as Teo started to get up, he heard a loud *thwack*, followed immediately by a bullet skimming past his face.

"Run!" Janiqua shrieked. "They're coming!"

Noa whipped around, trying to drag Zeke with her, but he just slumped against her shoulder. "Leave me!" he rasped in her ear. "I can't run!"

"I'm not leaving you," she said through gritted teeth. Janiqua passed them and vanished, headed toward the beach. Noa followed at a snail's pace, Zeke's weight bearing down on them. Her own energy was flagging; it felt like her knees would give out at any minute. They'd nearly reached the woods when a shot rang out. A voice yelled, "Next one hits lower! Freeze!"

She hesitated, looking at Zeke. Their eyes met, then his gaze flicked down: He'd taken out the gun and tucked it under his arm. Noa nodded to show that she understood, then slowly turned.

The men's faces were covered in masks that lent them an oddly wasplike appearance. Other than that, though, they were indistinguishable from the commandos she'd wrangled with months earlier. Her mind flicked back to the café guy; she wondered if these were his buddies. And if they had any idea what had happened to him.

Noa forced the thought away. "He's been shot!" she called out. "He needs medical attention."

"Don't move!" one of them ordered. They edged forward, keeping the gun barrels fixed on their chests. Grimly, Noa found it a little flattering to be viewed as such a threat. They clearly weren't taking any chances.

"Hands where we can see them!" the same guy yelled.

"He's hurt!" Noa protested. "He can't lift his arm!"

"I don't care if he's dying, raise your hands and get on the ground or I start shooting!" the guy growled.

Noa slowly lifted her hands. As she did, something flashed beside her, followed by a bang so loud it made her wince. One of the commandos fell to the ground with a cry. The other's focus snapped toward his partner.

Noa tried to run, but Zeke's full weight sagged against her, forcing her to stumble. Ironically, his collapse saved them—she heard the whistle of a shot tearing past her ear as they fell. All the air was forced from her lungs as she landed hard on her side, with Zeke pressing down on her. Then he slid off, hitting the ground beside her lifelessly.

"Zeke!" she cried out, scrambling for him. Noa rolled him toward her. His head flopped sideways, and Noa fumbled along his neck, trying to feel for a pulse. But her fingers were trembling too badly. All she could sense was how cool his skin was, slick with mist.

"Good," she heard from over her shoulder. "He wasn't the one they wanted anyway. Probably would've just had to shoot him."

Noa lunged toward him with a growl, but her attacker had kept his distance and when she got to her feet, his rifle was fixed on her chest. "Stay back!" he warned. "Your friend is still breathing. You don't behave, that can change real quick."

Noa looked down; he was right, she could see the shallow rise and fall of Zeke's chest. Squaring her jaw, Noa raised her hands. The woods were at her back—she could run that way. Maybe even make it to the beach, if she managed to avoid the rest of them. But that would mean leaving Zeke, and this guy obviously didn't have any qualms about shooting him. She couldn't let that happen.

The gunman walked over to where his friend lay on his back and nudged him with his foot. "Shit, you smoked Costa. The boss isn't going to be happy about that."

Zeke was lying on his side with his eyes closed. It looked like someone had painted a wide swath of red across the belly of his white shirt. He'd fallen on his good side, but a growing pool of red spread out from his waist. He was losing too much blood. If she didn't do something, he'd die right here.

"Save him," she said, "and I'll come with you."

The guy snorted. "Save him? Yeah, right. You're coming with me whether you want to or not."

Noa pulled the gun out from behind her back, raised it, and pointed it at her temple. "No, I won't," she said with finality.

Above the mask, his eyes widened. "What the hell? Are you nuts?"

"I'll do it," Noa said, her voice steady. "Unless you help him. I'll walk with you to the van, you give him first aid. And then, when I see that he's going to be okay, I put the gun down. Not before that."

"Like I care if you shoot yourself," the guy said, his voice full of bluster. "I already got enough of you kids. They didn't say we had to get all of them."

"But I bet they said you had to get me. And alive, too," Noa said. "So yeah, I think you care."

A long silence as he weighed what she'd said. Noa didn't blink, and barely breathed. Everything depended on whether or not the guy in front of her was smart enough to follow orders. They must have demanded that she be taken alive.

But he might not understand just how important that was to them.

And if he didn't care . . . then this could end with both her and Zeke dead.

"Fine," the guy finally said, although he didn't sound happy about it. "I'll get someone to carry him back to the van. But after that, no—"

His words were cut off as he was suddenly tackled from behind. Noa started, nearly firing the gun. Two figures rolled on the ground in a tangle of limbs. Suddenly, the person on top jerked his head up—weathered skin, streaked with soot. Roy opened his mouth and yelled, "Noa, run!"

CHAPTER TWENTY

Acting on instinct Teo dropped, flattening out his body. A grunt behind him, and the sound of something heavy hitting the ground.

"Teo!"

Teo looked up. The guy with the rifle was lying prone. Daisy stood above him, brandishing a shovel in both hands. Flipping over, he saw that the bullet had whisked past him and hit Berinsky in the back. He lay facedown in the grass, motionless.

"Come on!" Daisy urged. She dropped the shovel, turned, and ran.

Teo scrambled to his feet and followed. They raced through the trees, dodging low-hanging branches. Belatedly, he realized that he should have grabbed the rifles. "Where are we going?" he gasped. "To the street?"

"Yeah," she said. "We'll stay off the road for a few miles, then try to hitch a ride into town."

Then what? Teo wanted to ask. Were they just supposed to pretend that none of this had ever happened? Go back to living on the streets, trying to forget about the kids they'd left behind?

He didn't feel comfortable with that. But what was he supposed to do?

The fog was so thick and pervasive, Teo quickly lost all sense of direction. He tried to reconstruct the layout of the property. A thick, twelve-foot-high hedge bordered three sides; the fourth dead-ended at the cliffs overlooking the ocean. The main house sat in the center, surrounded by an acre of open fields and gardens. The rest was heavily forested, and dotted with smaller guest houses and outbuildings. He hadn't walked the entire perimeter, but was pretty sure that only one main gate led to the road.

And right now, he had no idea which section of the woods they were in; he couldn't even pinpoint where the main house was anymore. Hopefully Daisy had a better sense of where they were going.

Voices to their left. Teo grabbed Daisy's arm and yanked her down as he drew into a crouch.

"Wha—"

He put a finger to his lips. Her eyes went wide, but she nodded.

Together, they pressed up against the trunk of a tree. Teo carefully leaned around the side.

Crap. They'd reached the gate; just past it, the driveway hooked right before meeting up with Route 1. But the exit was blocked by vehicles. More commandos everywhere, all bearing nasty-looking rifles. Teo's heart sank—it didn't look like there was a way past them.

Daisy must've realized the same thing. She shook her head and said, "The hedges have wires running through them, and the electricity is probably still on. We can't risk it."

Teo's heart sank. "So what now?" he whispered. "Hide?"

Daisy's pale face was dewy with droplets of moisture. She chewed her lower lip thoughtfully, then said, "The beach. It's the only other way out."

Teo figured this was a bad time to mention that he was barely capable of a dog paddle.

Yelling, followed by barked orders. Teo eased around the side of the tree again, staying low. A kicking and screaming Janiqua was being pushed toward a white panel truck by two men with guns. Her hands were bound behind her back, and her shirt was filthy and torn. She was raging and spitting. At the last minute, she tried to run.

One of the men casually cuffed her across the chin. Janiqua went flying, hitting the ground hard. They yanked her to her feet and threw her inside.

"How many more?" the other guy said.

His partner held up a sheet of paper. "Three, including the big fish."

"Good," the first guy muttered. "I've had enough of this crap for one night."

His buddy grunted assent as he slid the door closed. The truck rocked slightly as someone thumped around inside.

A tug on his hand. "Teo," Daisy whispered urgently. "We've got to go!"

"No," he said, surprising himself. "We're not leaving them."

Daisy opened her mouth as if to protest, then she slowly nodded. "Okay," she said resignedly. "But what can we do?"

Teo scanned the scene—too many guards for them to handle on their own. They needed to create a distraction somehow.

At that moment, another pair of guys marched along the driveway, just a few feet from where they were hiding. They were dragging Taylor between them. He ducked back down.

"Hey!" Taylor shouted. "Let go!"

"Get in the truck," one of them growled.

"I told you, you idiot," she snarled. "I'm not supposed to go with them. That was the deal. I told you where they were, now you're supposed to let my brother and me leave."

Brother? Teo thought. She must mean Matt. It all clicked into place. Taylor and Matt had been working against them the whole time. He flashed back on earlier that evening, when everyone had been sitting around a roaring fire in the Forsythes' living room playing a celebrity game. They'd laughed at him for not knowing any of the people they were talking about. It had been fun; Teo had finally felt like he was part of something.

And this girl had destroyed all that.

"Holy crap," Daisy gasped. "Taylor told them where we were?"

Teo nodded tightly, not trusting himself to speak. He'd never understood what people were talking about when they said they "saw red." Now he got it. It felt like waves of hot blood were surging through him, clouding his vision. His fists clenched into tight balls, and his whole chest tightened up until the contraction was crushing his ribs.

He hoped these bastards would do terrible things to her.

"Teo!"

He looked down and realized that Daisy was tugging urgently on his arm again. She was looking past him.

One of the guards had suddenly shifted toward them. Teo saw his eyes widen.

"Hey!" the guy shouted, pointing directly at them. "There's two more!"

Teo didn't think, he just reacted. He gave Daisy a shove and yelled, "Go!" then darted in the other direction, hoping to draw them off.

Branches tore at his skin as he stumbled through the woods. The mist was dissipating, which made it easier to find his way, but also increased the chances that he'd be spotted. The middle of his back itched; he couldn't stop picturing red laser sights zeroing in on it. . . .

The sounds of pursuit behind him. He shifted direction, darting left. His muscles responded with an extra jolt of speed, and for a second he felt the familiar surge he used to get during track meets, when it felt like he'd tapped into some secret reserve. He'd had regular meals and decent sleep the past few days, so he was physically in much better shape than he'd been just a week ago.

Hopefully, it would be enough.

Teo cut right, then left again. The crashing sounds in the woods behind him seemed to be fading. Unfortunately, he'd also lost all sense of where he was. Was the sea ahead, or behind him? He prayed that Daisy had made it there safely. And that maybe, in the chaos, some of the others had managed to escape.

A huge shape suddenly loomed up in front of him, and he had to backpedal to avoid hitting it: the barn! Which meant that the path to the beach was only a hundred feet away. As he ran past, Teo scooped up the hammer he'd left sitting on a sawhorse that afternoon. Not much use against a rifle, but better than nothing. He kept running.

Turning the corner, Teo nearly crashed into a figure running toward him. He pulled up short, gasping for air.

It was Taylor. Her eyes wild, she stared at him for a minute, then spun and started to sprint past him.

A second later, the guy chasing her flew around the side of the barn. At the sight of Teo, he raised his gun.

Teo whipped the hammer in a wide arc and slammed it into the side of the guy's head. His helmet flew off, and Teo drew the hammer back and swung again.

The guy grunted and sagged to the ground.

Teo stared down at him for a second, his shoulders heaving.

"Nice," someone behind him said.

He turned quickly—Taylor was standing there, hands on her hips. He saw her eyes flick toward the rifle on the ground. They lunged for it at the same time, but he got there first. Whipped it up and pointed it at her.

She laughed at him. "What, you're going to shoot me, Teo?"

"I might," he said. And realized to his surprise that he meant it. Any residual doubt in his capabilities had been swept away. He felt hard, sure of himself. He wondered if this was how Noa felt all the time. He was pretty sure she wouldn't hesitate to pull the trigger.

"Go ahead," Taylor said moodily as her shoulders slumped. "I'm pretty much dead now, anyway."

"You should be," he snapped. "You sold us out."

"I didn't have a choice!" she retorted. "You have no idea what they threatened to do to my brother."

"Yeah, well—nice job saving him. I bet he's already in the van with the others."

She looked stricken. Teo's finger twitched on the

trigger—he didn't have time to mess around with her. He had to get to the beach, and to Daisy. The woods were still full of bastards trying to catch them.

"Get out of here," he said, jerking his head to the side.

Taylor narrowed her eyes, as if suspecting a trick.

Teo kept the rifle up as he backed away, headed toward the beach path. Once he turned the corner, he wheeled and trotted off in the direction of the beach, the gun heavy in his hands.

CHAPTER
TWENTY-ONE

The first downed guard lay on the ground a few feet inside the building. His eyes were bugged out, and he was clawing at his throat.

Mason made a tsking sound and said, "Bad reaction. That's unfortunate."

Peter hurriedly checked to make sure the straps of his mask were tight. Swallowing hard, he carefully stepped over the guy and followed Mason down a long, dark hallway that looked like something out of a horror film. Wisps of gas hung heavy in the air; snaky tendrils of it wrapped around Peter's arms and legs as they moved slowly through the building.

Mason walked with purpose, as if he knew precisely where he was going. Peter had to trot to keep pace. The interior of the building was in even worse shape than the outside; the walls were cracked, and tufts of insulation poked through enormous gashes in the drywall. Between the damp, mold, and level of dust in the air, Peter couldn't imagine a worse environment for sensitive computer servers. Was this seriously the best place Charles Pike could come up with to hide his data?

Mason hooked right down the next hallway and led Peter up a flight of stairs. The top was blocked by a fire door. Mason flicked open a keypad on the side and punched in an eight-digit code, then pushed the door open with both hands.

Peter left the door open, in case they needed to beat a fast retreat. He followed closely, working it out in his head. Obviously, Mason had some sort of arrangement with the guard who had handed them the masks. Peter wondered how much money he'd been promised to betray the people he worked with. And if Mason would let him live long enough to spend it.

The second story was a dramatic departure from downstairs. Solid white walls extended the length of the hall on both sides. The floor was bare concrete, meticulously clean.

The air was still wreathed in tendrils of white gas, however. It poured from the vents above.

Halfway down the hall, a guard lay on the ground. Mason stepped adroitly over him as if he wasn't there. This guard's eyes were closed, his chest rising and falling as if he was simply deeply asleep.

Peter nearly stumbled over him. He knew it was psychosomatic, but he was having a hard time breathing. He wondered if the mask was really working; he felt dizzy, sick.

They turned right down another hallway, toward the center of the building. Mason stopped in front of a massive door that would have been right at home in a bank vault. He punched in another code, then swung the lever and wrenched it open.

Peter stepped inside. This room was strikingly similar to the one at Pike & Dolan's corporate headquarters, except it held only a quarter as many servers. They hummed along in the background. There was no gas, aside from what had followed them in; there must be a separate ventilation system.

Mason was watching him; the goggles accentuated the extraordinary blackness of his eyes.

"I didn't bring a data sniffer," Peter said, realizing that it would have been pointless, anyway. It wasn't as if their infiltration had been discreet; Charles Pike was going to know that someone had broken into his servers, since obviously the rest of these guards weren't on Mason's payroll. So what was he doing here?

"No need," Mason said, his voice muffled. "We'll be taking the hard drives. All of them."

He started along the aisle. Peter followed warily, watching Mason extract hard drives from the server banks. He looked around the room—there were over fifty servers in here. How long before the effects of the gas wore off, and the room was flooded with ticked-off guards?

Mason was carefully stacking hard drives in the open backpack. He glanced at Peter. "Care to help? We are in a bit of a hurry."

Peter hesitated, then went to the far end of the room. As he disconnected the cords on a hard drive, his mind raced. Mason could have brought anyone with him—this job didn't exactly require incredible hacking skills. So was he supposed to get the information off these drives afterward? Maybe they were encrypted, and that's why Mason needed him.

He was working on the third server when he felt a tug on the back of his head. Spinning quickly, he dropped the hard drives he'd collected—they clattered to the ground. Mason was standing right behind him. With another violent yank, he tore the gas mask off Peter's head.

"What the hell are you doing?" Peter demanded.

"I'm leaving you behind," Mason said matter-of-factly as he stooped to gather the hard drives off the floor. "Sorry for the confusion, but as it turns out, I won't be requiring your skills after all. Charles will be so delighted to have finally caught the ringmaster behind Persefone's Army. Sadly, your compatriots escaped with the hard drives. But one must accept losses in any business endeavor." He dropped the drives into the bag.

Peter took a step toward him, enraged. "You assho—"

Suddenly, the room cartwheeled. He staggered back, knocking his head against a hard metal server frame. His knees gave out, and he slowly slid to the ground.

Blearily, he watched Mason move away from him, sliding hard drives out and disconnecting them with practiced ease. This had been a setup all along. His eyelids felt heavy; there was less gas in here, thanks to the recycled air, but apparently it was still potent enough to knock him out. Peter remembered the first guard they'd encountered, the one having a "bad reaction." Was the same thing happening to him? His throat constricted, and his lungs battled for air. He felt like he was suffocating to death.

But he had no intention of dying alone.

Determined, Peter fought back the waves of darkness washing over his vision. Unsteadily, he lurched to his feet.

Mason paused and looked up. His eyes creased in a smile

as he said, "You should just relax, Peter. Fighting will only make it worse."

"Amanda," Peter croaked out past the blockage in his throat. "Where?"

Mason shrugged. Though his mouth was hidden, Peter could swear he was smirking. "I have no idea where Ms. Berns is now, Peter." He slid out a final drive, tossed it into the pack, and tucked Peter's mask on top of it. Slinging the bag over one shoulder, he said, "I do hope Charles isn't too hard on you. He has a terrible temper, you know. Shame that all of this will be falling on your shoulders, but it worked out quite well for me."

Amanda backed away from the nurse, stopping when she felt the double doors at her back. "Stay away from me!" she said, her voice low and threatening. "I don't want to hurt you."

"Of course you don't, dear," the nurse said soothingly, although her eyes were concerned. "Now, why don't you just calm down. You're feeling a little confused, that's all."

"I'm not confused!" Amanda nearly shouted—it took effort to keep her voice low, but the last thing she wanted was to bring someone else running. This nurse she could handle, but who knew how many armed guards roamed the halls. "You're kidnapping kids and operating on them!"

"What?" The nurse's brow furrowed. Amanda was disgusted that she actually had the nerve to look perplexed, like she had no idea what Amanda was talking about. "Now, dear, you must've just had a bad dream. That can happen, you know."

"So, what, the kids in there were just a nightmare?" Amanda retorted, jerking her thumb back over her shoulder.

The nurse shook her head slowly. "We've already explained

this to you, Amanda. Those children are ill, too—you all are. We're keeping you together because it's the best way for us to care for you."

"Yeah, I'll bet." Amanda snorted.

The nurse sighed. Her crocs squeaked against the floor as she took a small step forward, reaching out with her hand. "Listen, sweetheart—"

Amanda evaded her grip, dodging right and darting down the hall before the nurse could react. A startled noise behind her, then the nurse's voice rose to a high pitch as she yelled, "Security!"

Amanda sprinted for the exit. No way to save anyone but herself now. But she'd send help, make so much noise that it couldn't simply be swept under the carpet. She'd show Peter and Noa how it was done, she thought, her jaw hardening.

But first, she had to get out of here.

Without breaking stride, she burst through the exit door onto a concrete landing. A blocky 5 was painted in red on the wall.

Amanda took the stairs two at a time. Her legs felt shaky, and a few times she nearly fell. She was terrified that they'd simply give out and she'd pitch forward, tumbling the rest of the way down.

But adrenaline buoyed her up. She flashed past the third floor, then the second. And suddenly, the stairs ended in front of a door that was gloriously labeled EXIT.

Amanda shoved it open and skidded to a dead halt.

She was in a bustling hallway, filled with people. And most of them were wearing scrubs and lab coats. A nurse and doctor passed, conferring in low voices. A guy in his thirties was pushing a wheelchair down the hall. He glanced curiously at her as he passed.

But that wasn't what stopped her dead. It was the sight of the patient he was pushing. The guy was draped over, bent nearly double. And he was old. Really, really old.

Amanda turned in a slow circle. The wall behind her was covered in translucent tiles, each labeled with a name. Above it, a sign announced *Boston Medical Benefactors*.

She knew where she was. She'd been here once before, when her great-aunt fell and broke her hip.

This was a real hospital.

"There you are!"

Amanda turned. The elderly nurse was standing in the doorway to the stairwell, one hand over her chest. "Dear God, you nearly gave me a coronary, running like that!"

"Sorry," Amanda said reflexively.

The nurse squinted at her. "You won't be giving me any more trouble now, will you?"

"Where am I?" Amanda interjected.

The nurse sighed. "I told you, dear. You're in the hospital."

"That was a PEMA ward," Amanda said, realization dawning.

"Yes, I'm afraid so," the nurse said more gently. "Now should I call for someone, or will you take the elevator back up with me?"

She tentatively reached out her arm again. This time, Amanda took it.

"I'll come with you," she said dully.

"That's a good girl." The nurse patted her arm soothingly. "Your parents said they'd be back tonight to visit. That'll be nice, won't it?"

Amanda tuned her out as she chirped on, choosing instead to stare up at the elevator panel as the lights descended. Five, four, three, two . . . the countdown echoed in her mind.

PEMA. She'd suspected it, in the back of her mind, but had blithely refused to acknowledge what was happening to her. The lost time. The lack of appetite, and difficulty sleeping. The way her mind felt oddly lumpy and mushy, like a marshmallow left out in the sun.

"What stage am I in?" Amanda asked as the doors pinged open and they stepped inside.

The nurse hesitated, then said, "Stage Two. Don't you remember? You and the doctor discussed it this morning."

Amanda searched her mind, but there was nothing there. "I don't remember," she admitted. "I didn't even know my parents had been to visit."

"That can happen, dear." The elevator doors slid open again, and the nurse led her into the hallway. "Perfectly normal, nothing to worry about." They passed a nurses' station and turned a corner; there was the staircase door on the right, and the double doors farther along.

Amanda felt completely numb. She was pretty sure that once you entered Stage Two, you had less than a year to live. She tried to process that, and couldn't. It was too surreal.

"I can give you something to help you rest," the nurse offered. "Would you like that?"

"Yes, please," Amanda said vaguely. Rest would be good. Maybe when she woke up, she'd discover that this had all been a terrible dream.

Peter's face flashed through her mind, his concerned expression in the diner the other day. And her roommate Diem, eyeing her from across the dorm room. All those covert glances that she'd brushed off or ignored; they'd been right. There had been something wrong with her, and she just hadn't wanted to admit it.

Amanda let herself be helped back to bed. She held out

her arm, barely wincing as the nurse eased in a fresh IV needle. As soon as the drapes were pulled shut, she turned on her side and curled into herself. Somewhere, Mouse was probably wondering where she was. Mrs. Latimar was waiting anxiously for her to come up with a plan. And her parents . . . God, her parents were trying to wrap their minds around the fact that their only surviving child had just been handed a death sentence.

As she drifted off to sleep, tears slipped out of Amanda's eyes and soaked her pillow.

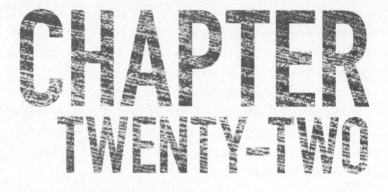

CHAPTER
TWENTY-TWO

Before Noa could react, the commando threw Roy off. The older man went flying, rolling until he smacked against the base of a tree. The commando growled and lunged for him, bent double. As Roy got shakily to his feet, the guy drove his head into his stomach, slamming him into the tree trunk. Roy grunted with pain. He raised both hands to try to ward the guy off, but he was no match for a trained soldier.

"Hey!" Noa shouted, suddenly realizing that she was still holding a gun, and the soldier's remained on the ground where he'd fallen.

He didn't acknowledge her, intent on drawing back his fist. There was a loud crunch, and Roy's head jerked back; his nose erupted with blood.

That did it for Noa. She strode forward and pressed the

barrel of the gun to the commando's ear. He froze.

"Step away from him," Noa said, her voice low and menacing. "Now."

The guy's whole body tensed, probably in preparation for pulling some fancy maneuver. She stepped back to put some distance between them, and his shoulders slumped. "Hands up nice and slow," she continued. "And maybe I won't shoot you."

The guy slowly lifted his hands, but spat, "Kid, you don't have it in you."

Noa didn't respond. Her hands were steady, even though she felt weak from rage. He was wrong. Right now, she wanted to pull the trigger more than anything.

"What happened to Zeke?" Roy said weakly as he pushed off the tree.

"He got shot," she said. "It's bad."

Roy swore under his breath and hurried to where Zeke lay on the ground. Out of the corner of her eye, Noa saw him stoop to examine Zeke's wounds. "Through and through," he said. "That's a blessing, at least."

"Will he be all right?"

"If we get him out of here, maybe," Roy said. "But we really need to get moving, Noa."

"Moving where?" she asked, the hopelessness of the situation suddenly overwhelming her. Zeke was shot. Roy was hurt. She had no idea where any of the others were. And from the sound of it, they were surrounded.

Roy stepped closer, lowering his voice to a murmur so only she could hear. "I stashed kayaks on the beach. They're half-buried at the south end, covered by driftwood. If we can get to them, it's not too long to Steamer Lane. You remember that beach? We drove there together one time, when you wanted to watch the surfers."

"I remember," Noa said. It had been a beautiful day. In truth, she hadn't asked to see the surfers, but Roy had insisted on showing them to her. Then he and Monica pretty much forced her and Zeke onto the carnival rides at the Santa Cruz Pier. She'd grumbled about what a waste of time it was, when they could be planning a raid. But now the memory of throwing up her arms and screaming as the rickety old roller coaster flung them around forced her to blink back tears.

"There's a truck stashed in the parking lot there," Roy continued, speaking quickly but quietly. "An old Ford F-150. Keys in the wheel well. The owner of the lot is a buddy of mine, he knows all about it."

"Why are you telling me this?" Noa said. The commando was watching them closely, clearly waiting for her grip to waver. She forced her hands to remain steady.

"Zeke knew. I always figured if something went wrong here, the two of you . . . Anyway, you have to go, Noa," Roy said urgently "Now. There are more of them coming."

"But Zeke—"

"I'll take care of Zeke," Roy insisted. "I won't let them hurt him. You have to trust me."

"What about Monica, and the others?"

"Monica didn't make it out of the house," Roy said, his voice thick with emotion. "I'll send along anyone else I come across. Now move!" He gave her a small push, then stepped forward and swung the rifle off the ground and up to his shoulder, aiming at the guy.

Noa hesitated, then turned and started running. She'd only gotten ten feet when the sound of a gunshot stopped her in her tracks.

She whipped around, just in time to see Roy crumple to the ground.

Standing behind him, holding Daisy by the hair with one hand and a gun in the other, was Cole.

"Hello again, sweetheart!" Cole called out, shifting the gun barrel toward her. "Miss me?"

Noa staggered back a step. She still had nightmares about Cole; he'd been the head of Project Persephone's team of goons back in Boston, a ruthless mercenary who'd pursued her through the city for days. He'd nearly recaptured her at the secret lab in Rhode Island, but Peter had saved her, nearly getting beaten to death in the process. Thankfully, at the last minute the FBI had shown up and intervened. She and Zeke had escaped in a boat, and Peter had been returned to his parents relatively unharmed.

She'd hoped that in the aftermath, Cole had been locked up. Was it too much to expect the FBI to arrest a guy who'd just murdered one of his own guards, while surrounded by teens stuffed in coolers?

Apparently so, because here he was, taunting her again. He looked exactly the same: blond hair shorn in a crew cut, a long scar running like a seam down the right side of his face. And he'd just shot Roy. Now two of the people she'd relied on for months were bleeding to death on the ground. Noa still had the gun; she'd tucked it in the back of her jeans as she started running, but she got the feeling that threatening to kill herself wouldn't work so well with him.

Cole yanked on Daisy's hair, and she yelped. The girl's eyes were wide and frantic; she looked terrified. Noa's heart sank. Had anyone gotten away?

"Come on over here and join us, Noa," Cole sneered.

Noa swallowed hard and took a small step forward. In

the distance, she could hear shouting. Superseding it was the snarl and crackle of the fire. A resounding crash as part of the house buckled and caved in. She jumped at the sound, but Cole's aim never wavered.

The wind had shifted, blowing embers and waves of smoke toward the ocean, away from them. She glanced down at the ground. Zeke was still out cold, but she could see his chest rising and falling. Roy was on his side, staring straight at her, his eyes filled with pain. A hole dotted the front of his shirt, right through the center of the Grateful Dead skull.

"It'll be okay, Daisy," Noa said, trying to sound reassuring.

Cole barked a laugh. "Yeah, it'll be swell. Long as you don't mind a little slice and dice." He tugged Daisy close, until her back was pressed to his chest. His eyes roved over her tiny tank top and boy shorts.

Daisy started sobbing harder.

"Leave her alone!" Noa snapped.

Cole trailed a finger down Daisy's side while he leered at Noa. "Not much you can do about it, sweetheart."

Daisy mewled pitiably. Noa's jaw tensed. For the first time, she wished that she was more comfortable with guns. But she couldn't risk drawing and firing it, not when he had Daisy.

Glancing down, she saw Roy groping for the rifle that had fallen a few feet away. She jerked her eyes back up, but too late—Cole had noticed. He clucked his tongue and said, "Sorry, old man. Can't let you play with that," then kicked it away.

Roy's hand dropped back down and his eyes squeezed shut. His whole body sagged. Seeing him reduced to this made Noa want to scream.

Cole squinted down at him, then barked a laugh. "Well, I'll be damned. If it ain't Ray Forbes. How the hell are you, Ray? This your place?"

"His name's Roy, not Ray," Noa snapped, the words popping out before she could stop herself.

Cole was shaking his head. "Nope, it's definitely Ray. We go way back, don't we, Ray?"

"You're lying," Noa snarled, but a small seed of doubt had sprouted in her mind.

"What, you think PEMA came out of nowhere? Hell, Ray and his old lady invented it. Made a killing off it, too."

Noa shifted her gaze back to Roy, hoping he'd deny it. Tears streamed down his face as he gazed back at her, looking stricken. He silently mouthed, "I'm sorry."

"Gotta say, though, they were pretty clever." Cole shook his head with admiration. "Cashed out when the stock was at its peak, and left before things got ugly. Nice little place they retired to here."

"It's not true," Noa protested weakly. "Roy and Monica wouldn't have done that."

"No?" Cole grinned at her. "Tell me something, sweetheart. They do any tests, maybe draw some blood while they were 'helping' you?"

Her face must have betrayed her, because Cole laughed unpleasantly again. "Right. Bet they promised to cure you. Meanwhile, they were just cutting out the middle man, so they could keep the profits for themselves next time. Smart."

"Not . . . true," Roy gasped from the ground.

Cole tapped him with his boot. "Still lying to the girl, Ray? That's cold, man. Even I wouldn't do that."

"Noa . . ." Roy wheezed. His mouth was working hard as he choked out, "Don't . . . believe . . ."

"Good chat, Ray," Cole said. "Nice seeing you again. Oh, and by the way: This time, your termination is permanent."

Another shot, and Roy went limp. Daisy started screaming uncontrollably. Noa froze, unable to tear her eyes away. A tumult of emotions coursed through her. Roy—*Ray*, she corrected herself—had been more than just a friend, he'd become a father figure. But Cole's claims had shaken her to the core. Had Roy and Monica really just been using her all along?

And where did Zeke fit in? Her gaze shifted back to him. He was lying still, not even reacting to the gunshot. Noa couldn't tell if he was still breathing. He might be gone, too.

Which left her and Daisy.

"Enough of this crap," Cole said, sounding bored. He pointed the gun back at Noa. "You're going to walk ahead of us and do exactly what I say, when I say it. Any messing around, I put a bullet in this one's skull" —he jerked his head toward Daisy—"and shoot you in the foot, so you can hop the rest of the way there. They said I had to bring you in alive, they didn't say anything about walking."

He gestured with the gun for Noa to move toward the driveway.

Noa took a deep breath. Her hands felt tingly; she kept them loose at her sides. All she needed was a single distraction to give her a chance to go for the gun. And for Daisy to not be in the way when she fired it. All her earlier qualms about firearms seemed silly now that she was possessed by murderous rage. She wanted to wipe that smirk off Cole's face, to stand over him and empty the magazine, channeling all her frustration into the bullets that would rip him apart.

One chance. Noa repeated it in her mind, her whole body

tensed and ready. She didn't care anymore what happened to her. As long as she killed Cole, the rest of it seemed superfluous.

She walked through the trees, heading in the direction of the highway and whatever waited for her there.

Twenty feet into the trees, as if guessing what she was thinking, Cole called out, "Nice and easy, now. No more games."

Noa didn't respond. The hem of her shirt covered the gun, and between the mist and shadows Cole hadn't noticed it. She wondered how long it would take to draw it, and where she should aim. She was pretty sure you were supposed to try to hit the chest, since that was the biggest target. But Cole was probably wearing a bulletproof vest, so maybe she should aim for his head instead. . . .

She was interrupted by Cole spewing a tirade of curses.

Swiveling, Noa saw that Daisy had somehow escaped and was running back the way they'd come, toward the burning house. Unfortunately, that meant she was framed perfectly, silhouetted against the wall of flame. Cole raised his rifle and stabilized it with both hands.

"No!" Noa shouted, fumbling to free her own gun.

But she was too late. The *crack* of a shot split the air. "Daisy!" Noa shrieked, struggling to dig the gun from her waistband.

But Daisy was still running. And Cole had been flung back, as if he'd been punched in the chest. He landed on his back, hard.

Teo emerged from the trees, halfway between them and Daisy. Holding one of the commando's rifles, he walked tentatively toward Cole.

"Teo, stop!" Noa called out. "He's wearing a vest!"

Too late, Teo started backpedaling. With mounting horror, Noa watched Cole snatch his gun off the ground and stagger to his feet.

He was too good a shot, and they weren't far enough away. He was going to kill them. And she couldn't let any more of her people die tonight. She just couldn't.

Without allowing herself time to think about it, Noa lifted the gun, gripped it hard in both hands, and fired.

Cole dropped again, falling forward this time. Cautiously, she approached him.

He wasn't moving. Drawing a deep breath, she pushed hard on his side until he rolled all the way over.

His eyes gazed blankly at the sky. Cole was dead.

Everything went still for a moment, and Noa started shaking. She'd never killed anyone before. Horrified, her fingers trembled so badly she nearly dropped the gun.

A shout to her left got her attention—someone else was coming. She could see Teo and Daisy at the edge of the woods, near the house. They'd stopped, and were waving at her frantically.

Noa drew a deep, shuddery breath. She was the only one who knew the way out. She had to get the two of them to safety.

Breaking into a run, she tore after them.

Peter crawled up the side of the server, willing his legs to function. They felt floppy and helpless, like he'd suddenly turned into a scarecrow. Mason had nearly reached the door. Wisps of gas were still seeping in, wrapping around him in an embrace.

Peter's vision had narrowed to pinpoints, and with every movement bile rose up his throat. The closer he got to the door, the worse it grew. But he focused on moving forward, setting one foot in front of the other. Everything Mason had just said spun through his mind. Mason had to be lying—he had to know where Amanda was. A flare of rage powered Peter's limbs forward, and he lunged into the corridor.

Mason was rounding the bend in the hall.

The gas appeared to have dissipated, although Peter felt increasingly dizzy and disoriented. It was difficult to focus, and even harder to move. He gritted his teeth and lurched along the hall, rebounding off the walls on either side as he staggered along. He made it to the corner, feeling like he'd run a marathon. He leaned heavily against the wall, on the verge of collapse.

The sight of Mason heading toward the exit provided a renewed burst of stamina.

Peter stumbled forward. His brain fought him every step of the way, a small voice in his head murmuring for him to give up and lie down. His eyelids were sliding closed— through the slits, he watched Mason push open the door.

Peter could never have explained what gave him the strength to make it those last fifteen feet. He tripped and nearly went sprawling over the unconscious guard. His feet twisted over each other; it was more of a slow, sustained fall than anything else. But somehow, he made it to the end.

Mason had taken no notice of him; either the gas mask had restricted his sight and hearing to such an extent that he was unaware of Peter's ragged pursuit, or he didn't consider him enough of a threat to care.

When Peter launched into him from behind, Mason's head snapped around and his eyes widened with surprise. His arms flung out for balance, but too late—Peter's forward momentum sent them both tumbling down the stairs.

They landed in a pile at the bottom.

The gas had numbed his nerves to the point where Peter barely registered the collisions with hard concrete. Mason wasn't so lucky. He landed on his side, with Peter on top of him.

Using his last ounce of energy, Peter tore the mask from Mason's head.

Mason struggled to extricate himself. With a leap, he regained his feet, one hand cocked back in a fist.

Peter lay on the ground panting. The adrenaline was dissipating, his will to fight leaving along with it. He braced himself for the blow.

It never came.

Mason suddenly went completely rigid. His eyes sprung wide, the pupils dilating as his mouth opened in a silent scream.

Then he collapsed in a pile on the floor next to Peter.

A kid was standing behind him. A scarf covered his mouth, and he held a Taser in both hands.

He eyed Peter, then said, "Good to see you again, Vallas."

Peter managed a weak nod. It had been a long time since anyone had called him by his handle.

"You, too," Peter gasped. The darkness was overwhelming him. Luke swayed and flickered like a mirage. Before it swept him away entirely, he muttered, "Took you long enough."

CHAPTER TWENTY-THREE

oa raced through the trees toward the wreckage of the house. The fire didn't show any signs of stopping, but thanks to the thick layer of moisture in the air, at least it hadn't spread to the surrounding forest.

Within seconds she'd reached the house. Teo was hunched down next to Zeke. Daisy stood beside them, her face buried in her hands. Teo looked up at Noa, his eyes steady and surprisingly calm. He looked like he'd aged a decade in the past hour.

"Roy's gone," he said bluntly. "But Zeke's still breathing. Together, we should be able to carry him."

Noa's heart gave a thud at the news. There was still a chance to save him. "We have to hurry," she said, bending down and tucking her arm under his shoulder. Teo followed suit on the other side. "Do you know where the beach is?"

"Yeah," Teo said. "Daisy showed me earlier."

"Okay. There are kayaks stowed at the south end. We'll take them to Steamer Lane. There's a truck in the lot by the pier—"

Noa paused, suddenly concerned. Roy had given her this plan, and she was no longer certain he could be trusted. Would the kayaks and truck be waiting for them?

If not, she'd come up with something else. There was no alternative. The beach was their last chance. "Let's go . . . now!"

They made it to the stairs that led down to the beach without incident. The sound of sirens in the distance: Someone had finally alerted the fire department. Too late to save the house, but hopefully the firefighters would drive off their pursuers. Project Persephone strike teams usually vanished when the authorities showed up.

She and Teo struggled to bear Zeke between them. At the top of the stairs, they carefully lowered him to the ground and peered dubiously down the steep, rickety wooden staircase.

"Do you see anyone down there?" Noa hissed.

"No one." Teo shook his head. "No lights, either."

"It's pretty dark," Daisy said doubtfully. "Do you really think we can carry him?"

Noa hesitated. Could these two scrawny kids haul Zeke down a hundred feet of stairs? She'd help, but someone had to watch their backs. And she didn't want to saddle them with the responsibility of shooting anyone, not even the bastards who were after them.

"It's okay, Noa," Teo said, reading her expression. "We can handle it."

He and Daisy carefully lifted Zeke up, cradling him in their arms. As they started down the stairs, Noa stayed low, keeping an eye on the tree line. Occasionally she thought she discerned darting shapes, and each time her heart clenched; but no one approached.

When Daisy and Teo were nearly at the bottom, she eased onto the stairs. In the dark, it was hard to make out where one step ended and the next began. Mist draped from the cliff in folds like a dense gray curtain, which didn't help visibility. It seemed to take an eternity to reach the bottom.

Teo and Daisy had lowered Zeke to the ground and were standing over him uncertainly. "Find the kayaks and get them in the water," Noa said, kneeling on the sand beside him. "I'm going to try to stop the bleeding."

Daisy broke into a run, headed for the far end of the beach. Teo ran a few steps, then stopped and turned back. "This isn't your fault," he said.

Noa looked up at him. "What?"

"You're everything I thought you'd be," he said. "Just thought you should know that, just in case."

He turned and bolted after Daisy.

Noa was already pulling off her scarf. She drew Zeke onto her lap and started to carefully wrap the makeshift bandage around his waist. There was so much blood everywhere, soaking his shirt, his pants. His face was so pale, it practically glowed. Noa ran a hand over his forehead. It was still warm to the touch, which was reassuring.

"Where'd they go?" a voice suddenly yelled from the top of the cliff.

"Dunno. Didn't see them by the house."

"Spread out and keep looking, we gotta roll in five. Fire

department won't hold off forever."

Zeke's eyes blinked open. "Noa?" he said groggily.

"Shh," she warned. A red laser light flicked across the sand like a rogue firefly. Carefully, she dragged Zeke closer to the base of the stairs, where a rocky outcropping hid them from view. "We're almost out of here."

Zeke tried to sit up, then winced and fell back. "My . . . side . . ."

"Easy," Noa said, gently pressing on his shoulder to settle him. "You have to stay still."

The pungent, coppery smell of blood saturated the air. Noa did some mental calculations: a mile south in the kayaks to the parking lot—that could take up to an hour, depending on the current. Once on the road she could stop at a pharmacy and get basic first-aid supplies, or maybe Roy had had the foresight to leave a medical kit in the truck. . . .

"It hurts," he gasped through clenched teeth. "God, Noa, it hurts so much."

The terror and pain in his voice almost unhinged her. Noa struggled to sound reassuring as she stroked his hair. "You're going to be okay, I promise. Roy stashed some kayaks, we're going to get out of here."

Just saying Roy's name made her feel sick. Zeke had no idea how badly they'd been betrayed. And in the state he was in, she couldn't bear to tell him.

"The others?" he asked in the same strained voice.

"Teo and Daisy are here," Noa said, hesitating before she continued, "I'm not sure about the rest."

Zeke reached for her hand and squeezed it. "You have to go."

"*We* have to go," she insisted. "I'm not leaving without you."

More yelling above. Any minute now, they'd find the stairs. She had to get them out of here before that happened.

Her heart sank. It was impossible. She could barely make out the dim forms of Daisy and Teo, digging frantically in the sand at the other end of the beach.

"Noa," he wheezed. "Go."

"No," she said fiercely. "I'm not leaving you."

"You have to." Zeke's voice hardened as he continued, "I need to know that you're safe."

"We're all making it out of here," she protested desperately, battling pinpricks of tears. Noa realized she was squeezing his shoulder hard, and forced herself to ease her grip.

"Please, Noa," he said softly. "I won't make it anyway."

Noa shook her head, refusing to acknowledge what he was saying.

"Do you still have the gun?" he asked.

She nodded, not trusting herself to speak.

"Give it to me. I'll make sure they don't follow you." He held out a shaky hand.

Noa could feel his blood, hot and wet, seeping across her legs as she held him in her lap. She searched her mind desperately for an alternative, but couldn't come up with one. He was right. There was no way he'd make it all the way to Steamer Lane, not after losing so much blood. The strange wheeze in his chest was becoming more pronounced with every breath.

With trembling hands, she passed the gun to him.

Zeke's fingers closed around it, and he sighed. Half-smiled, then said, "You really don't remember me from The Center, huh?"

It took Noa a minute to understand, but then she shook her head. When they'd first met, he'd told her that they'd overlapped in Boston's foster care facility years earlier. But she hadn't recognized him.

"I remember you," he continued softly. "You walked in wearing black jeans and a T-shirt. Your hair was longer then." He reached out a cold hand and carefully swept it back from her face. "I swear I stopped breathing. You were the prettiest thing I'd ever seen in my whole life. I watched you grab a glass of milk and go to a table by yourself. I wanted so badly to go over and sit next to you, but I was scared."

Noa had a hard time speaking past the lump in her throat. "Why are you telling me this?"

"Because I should have said it a long time ago," Zeke said. "I fell for you the minute I saw you. It was like you were something I'd lost that I never even knew was missing, until right at that moment. But I was too much of a coward. I figured I'd see you again, but the next day, you were gone. Probably got placed somewhere. And I hated myself for letting you go without even finding out your name."

"But you did find me," Noa said, her voice quavering. "You never told me how you found me."

"I never stopped looking." Zeke closed his eyes. "I'm sorry for what they did to you. I wish I could've gotten there sooner."

"Noa!" a voice hissed.

Noa looked up. There were two shadowy figures by the surf line, each bracing a rocking, narrow ocean kayak.

"Go," Zeke said softly. "They need you."

"But they'll take you again," she choked.

Zeke shook his head slightly, then winced, as if even that small movement hurt. "I won't let them," he said. "Don't worry."

The ramifications of what he was saying sank in, and more tears coursed down her cheeks.

"Hey," he said gently. "It'll be okay."

"No," she sobbed. "It won't. I can't do this without you."

"You can." Zeke dug a hand into her hair and pulled her face down. This time, Noa let herself sink into the kiss. His lips were dry but soft. He pressed his mouth gently to hers, and breathed out her name.

His eyes twinkled as she pulled away. "Man," he said. "You sure do make a guy regret dying."

Noa was crying too hard to answer. Zeke trailed the back of his hand against her cheek, then said, "I love you. Now go."

Noa stumbled to her feet. Somehow she made it to the kayaks, even though she could barely see through the tears. She was dimly aware of the paddle Teo thrust in her hands, and of nearly capsizing as Teo tried to maneuver them past the breakers.

The next ten minutes were a blur of biting water and crashing waves and gunshots that receded in the distance as they rounded the point. There were four shots in tight succession, answered by a much louder barrage.

Noa flinched as one final shot rang out, followed by silence. She slumped in her seat, letting the paddle drop into her lap as she bowed her head and let the tears flow freely.

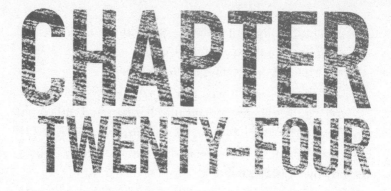

CHAPTER
TWENTY-FOUR

Peter sat beside Amanda's hospital bed, head perched on his fists. She was asleep, probably sedated. Her hair spread across the pillow like a fan. She looked angelic, almost like she wasn't ill.

He'd torn off the paper mask as soon as the nurse closed the curtains. He'd spent months in a PEMA ward with his dying brother without getting sick. If he was willing to risk it then, he could certainly do the same for Amanda. Part of him almost hoped he'd catch the disease—it would help assuage his guilt.

It still wasn't clear why her name hadn't registered when he'd searched the hospitals; the nurse claimed it must have been an oversight, some sort of computer glitch. He knew better. Either Mason had been lying—which was likely—or Charles Pike had taken an interest in Amanda, too. Either way, when he'd regained consciousness, there had been a text message from Diem explaining that Amanda was a patient at Boston Medical. And that it didn't look like she'd be released anytime soon.

Gently, he took her hand. It was limp in his, and disconcertingly cold. "I'm so sorry this happened to you," he whispered.

Amanda didn't respond. She hadn't moved the entire time he'd been here. Peter had arrived a few minutes before visiting hours ended, waiting until her parents had left before slipping inside. He didn't have long. And there was a chance that after tonight, he'd never see her again.

Thank God he'd sent that Mayday, asking Luke's unit to keep an eye out while he went into Mason's apartment. They'd tailed him and Mason to the warehouses, hanging around outside until it was clear that something had gone wrong. The nerve gas had slowed them down, but they'd come through in the end. They'd left Mason tied to the bottom of the banister, a present for Charles Pike. Peter hoped he appreciated it. And that he made sure the smarmy bastard never saw the light of day again.

Luke had initially tried to enlist him, abashedly admitting that he was having a hard time keeping the group in line, especially since they hadn't had a real operation in a while. But the Northeast unit was based too close to home, and Peter wanted out. Boston only held bad memories for him now. So Luke offered to help get him where he needed to go. He hawked the Prius to a chop shop and gave Peter the cash, and set him up with a Taser, radio, and other things they employed during raids. Peter had no idea if he'd ever use any of it, but decided it couldn't hurt to have just in case. He ditched his laptop and cell phone—better to start fresh, just to be on the safe side. Where he was going, he needed to be absolutely certain no one followed.

Peter brushed his fingers over Amanda's forehead, pushing back the stray strands of hair plastered there. "I'll be back," he said softly. "But I have to go do something first. Don't—"

His voice broke, and it took a minute to regain his composure. "I'll see you again," he said, more firmly this time. "I'm coming back with a cure. Wait for me."

Peter nervously shifted the backpack, the weight of the hard drives heavy against his lower back. It was freezing outside the bus terminal, an icy wind buffeting him as he sat on a bench, waiting.

He'd spent the past few days on buses, frequently backtracking, meandering across the country in an unpredictable pattern designed to throw off any pursuers. So far, at least, it appeared to have worked. He'd studied the faces of every fellow passenger from Boston to St. Louis, Memphis to Columbus; none had been familiar. They all looked as tired and worn as he felt, resigned to rattling across the uneven topography of America's back roads and highways in rickety Greyhounds.

The miles had given him time to think, his mind running over the same tracks over and over like the groove in a record. He wondered how Charles Pike had reacted to finding Mason locked up in his building, and all his medical research gone. He wondered if Amanda had regained consciousness yet. He wondered what his parents thought of the note he'd left, explaining that he was leaving and never coming back. Had they sent anyone after him? Did they even want him found?

It didn't matter anymore. Because he'd finally arrived.

Peter wished the terminal was still open so that he could at least grab a warm drink from a vending machine. It was almost three a.m., and the few passengers who had disembarked with him had already vanished into the night. This was a desolate stretch of land on the outskirts of Omaha, a rickety depot with only a few slots for buses to park and offload passengers. Most of the spaces were occupied by silent, still metal behemoths whose tinted windows seemed to be glaring at him. The single bulb overhead barely penetrated the shadows. It was spooky as hell. He had to fight the sense that he was the last person left alive after some terrible apocalyptic event.

Headlights approaching. Peter jumped to his feet, relieved. If they hadn't shown up, he didn't know what he would have done. This was as far as he'd planned.

The lights swung into the parking lot, bouncing up and down as they navigated through a pothole. An ancient SUV stopped a few feet away, its engine idling.

The rear passenger door opened, and Noa got out. They stood there for a minute staring at each other, then Peter nodded and said, "Hey."

"Hey." She looked thinner than he remembered, and paler. Older, too, like the past few months had aged her in some incalculable way.

But then, he probably looked much the same. "It's good to see you."

"You, too," she said, smiling thinly. It was hard to tell if she meant it, though. Her voice sounded weary, defeated. This wasn't the same girl who had left him four months ago, determined to wage war against a massive conspiracy.

"Is Zeke in the car?"

Her face fell. "No. Zeke . . . He didn't make it."

"Oh. God, Noa. I'm sorry." Peter wanted to take her into his arms and offer some comfort, but she actually took a step back and went rigid.

"Amanda's sick," he said, hands dangling uselessly by his sides. "PEMA."

"Bastards," she spat.

"Yeah. But I've got new data. I think that maybe this time, there's something there."

Noa just shrugged, which worried him. He wasn't expecting her to jump up and down with elation, especially not at this hour, but some sort of positive reaction would've been nice.

"So where are we going?" he asked.

Noa's shoulders slumped even farther. "I have no idea," she said, looking utterly bereft. "It's all gone. They're all gone."

"Hey." He reached out and rubbed her arm awkwardly. "It's okay. We'll figure it out together, all right?"

She raised her head to look at him. They stared at each other for a long moment. Finally, a flicker of a smile flitted across her mouth. "I could really use some of your eggs."

He laughed, feeling inexplicably relieved. "Yeah? Well, this time I'll try not to burn them."

They smiled at each other for another beat, then she gestured to the backseat and said, "We should get off the streets."

"Definitely," Peter answered firmly. "Let's get out of here."

You probably heard that we're beaten, that we've been taken out. That Project Persephone managed to crush us.

Well, it's not true. We're still here—in smaller numbers, but those of us who are left are stronger than ever. And we're coming for them.

We still need help. The people we're facing are ruthless and cruel, and they'll stop at nothing to get what they want. There is a cure for PEMA, and they have it.

We're going to get it from them.

Even if it kills us.

Stay strong. Protect each other. And know that this fight is far from over.

Posted by PER5EF0NE on February 22nd
/ALLIANCE/ /NEKRO/ /#PERSEF_ARMY/
<<<<>>>

Acknowledgments

It's funny that while writing a trilogy about hackers, I've ended up dealing with more computer gremlins that at any other point in my career; the PERSEF0NE curse, maybe? This time around, human error was involved when 30,000 feet above Bakersfield, a flight attendant accidentally spilled an entire glass of liquid onto my laptop. Fortunately, the stars at Hard Drive 911 were able to salvage my nascent draft of *Don't Look Now*, and all was not lost. But suffice it to say that now I'm officially the queen of backing up data. I like to think that would make Noa and Peter proud. (And thanks to Southwest Airlines for covering all the costs. Despite this mishap, they remain my favorite airline.)

Because of my hard-drive issues the last time around, I made an egregious oversight in the acknowledgments of *Don't Turn Around*. Rocket Science Consulting is a real company that specializes in IT services, web design, and truly epic Friday happy hours at their San Francisco office. CEO Matt McGraw was kind enough to allow me use of the company name to serve as Noa's fictitious employer for freelance work, and I, inexcusably, forgot to thank him. So as promised, there's a muffin basket en route, along with my sincerest apologies. On the bright side, my frequent computer headaches promise them much future business. They're also located in New York, Los Angeles, and Portland, and I highly recommend them for anything computer related. (Consider that an extra thanks, Matt.)

Diem Ha was my roommate at Wesleyan University

junior and senior year. She's a fantastic person to live with, and if I ever got carted off in an ambulance, she would insist on climbing in to escort me to the hospital (unlike her namesake in the book).

Kelly Essoe kindly provided me with post-op surgical forms, which helped enormously with research. I'm also indebted to Colin Dangel, who responded quickly to any and all Beantown-related queries.

And once again, tech guru Bruce Davis not only wrote the informative "Top Ten Techniques a Hacker May Have Already Tried on You" (still available on Pitch Dark!), he also painstakingly combed through a draft of the manuscript to make sure that I didn't confuse KiBs with MiBs. I owe him a huge debt.

Beta readers Noah Wang and Marissa Gaylin helped ensure that this was the cleanest, most accurate manuscript possible—and as teenagers, they would know. Any remaining errors belong to me and me alone.

I really can't say enough good things about the amazing folks at HarperTeen—working with them has been an absolute pleasure.

Karen Chaplin is the best editor I've ever worked with, period. She's also extremely generous with deadline extensions, a novelty that I've deeply appreciated.

Olivia deLeon is my dream publicist—this series couldn't have a better champion. And Barbara Lalicki has been a great person to have in my corner.

My crack copyediting team—Brenna Franzitta and Aaron Murray—never cease to amaze me with their ability to unearth mistakes in what I had believed was a perfect manuscript. In fact, it's a safe bet that they caught some errors in the previous sentence and corrected them before this went to print.

I'm graced with the best agent on the planet, Stephanie Kip Rostan. Not only is Steph an astute editor and agent, her market savvy and taste in dining establishments can't be beat. I'm exceedingly fortunate to have her and the rest of the team at Levine Greenberg representing my work.

The plight of the foster kids in this trilogy, while it has been fictionalized, is sadly all too real. Nearly 40 percent of former foster children end up living on the streets after they turn eighteen. Fortunately, a fantastic nonprofit has been formed to help. Every donation goes directly to a foster kid who is aging out of the system, supporting their educational and life needs through crowdfunding. And any amount of money helps. Please visit www.rising-tides.org for more information.

Thanks, as always, to my family, for tolerating "working vacations" and not minding when I vanish into my writing cave for extended periods. I promise to always come back out.

Finally, years ago I met the perfect man, but at the time I was too young and foolish to realize it. Luckily, nearly two decades later, we got a second chance. So it seemed appropriate to dedicate the second book of this trilogy to Kirk, my first and last reader. There's no one I'd rather eat eggs with, burnt or otherwise.